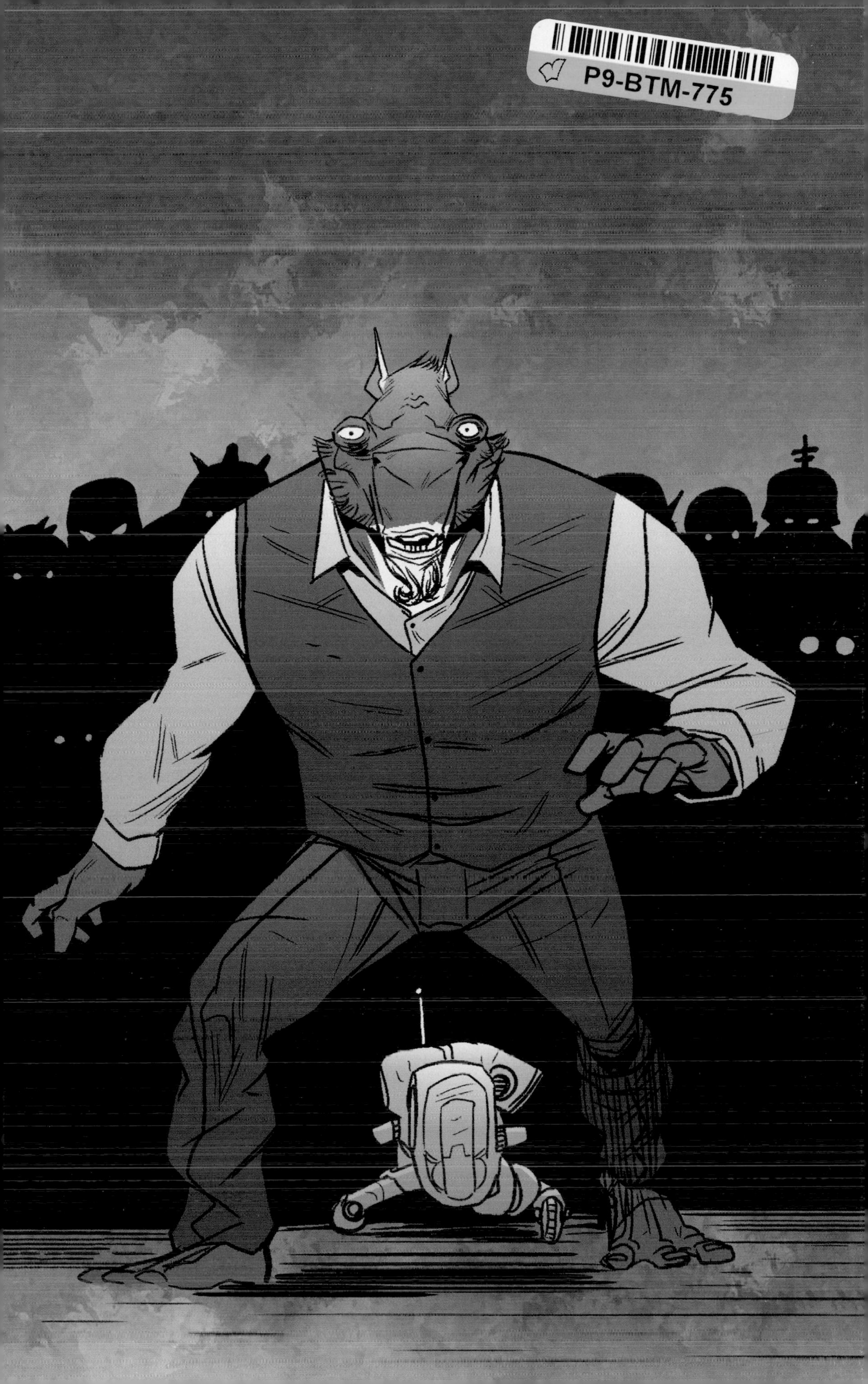

IMAGE COMICS, INC.

Robert Kirkman—Chief Operating Officer
Erik Larsen—Chief Financial Officer
Todd McFarlane—President
Marc Silvestri—Chief Executive Officer
Jim Valentino—Vice President
Eric Stephenson—Publisher / Chief Creative Officer
Corey Hart—Director of Sales
Jeff Boison—Director of Publishing Planning
& Book Trade Sales
Chris Ross—Director of Digital Sales
Jeff Stang—Director of Specialty Sales
Kat Salazar—Director of PR & Marketing
Drew Gill—Art Director
Heather Doornink—Production Director
Nicole Lapalme—Controller

www.imagecomics.com

COPPERHEAD, VOL. 4
ISBN: 978-1-53430-499-4
First Printing. April 2018.

COPPERHEAD

Volume 4

writer
JAY FAERBER
artist
DREW MOSS
colorist
RON RILEY
letterer & designer
THOMAS MAUER
cover artist
SCOTT GODLEWSKI

created by
JAY FAERBER & SCOTT GODLEWSKI

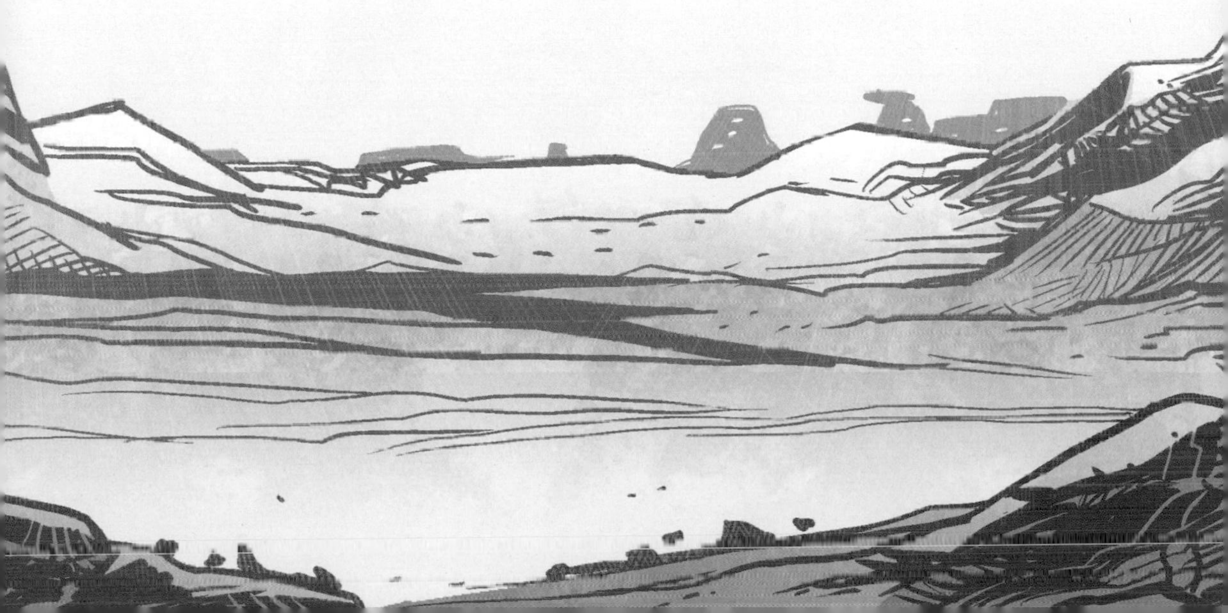

CHAPTER I

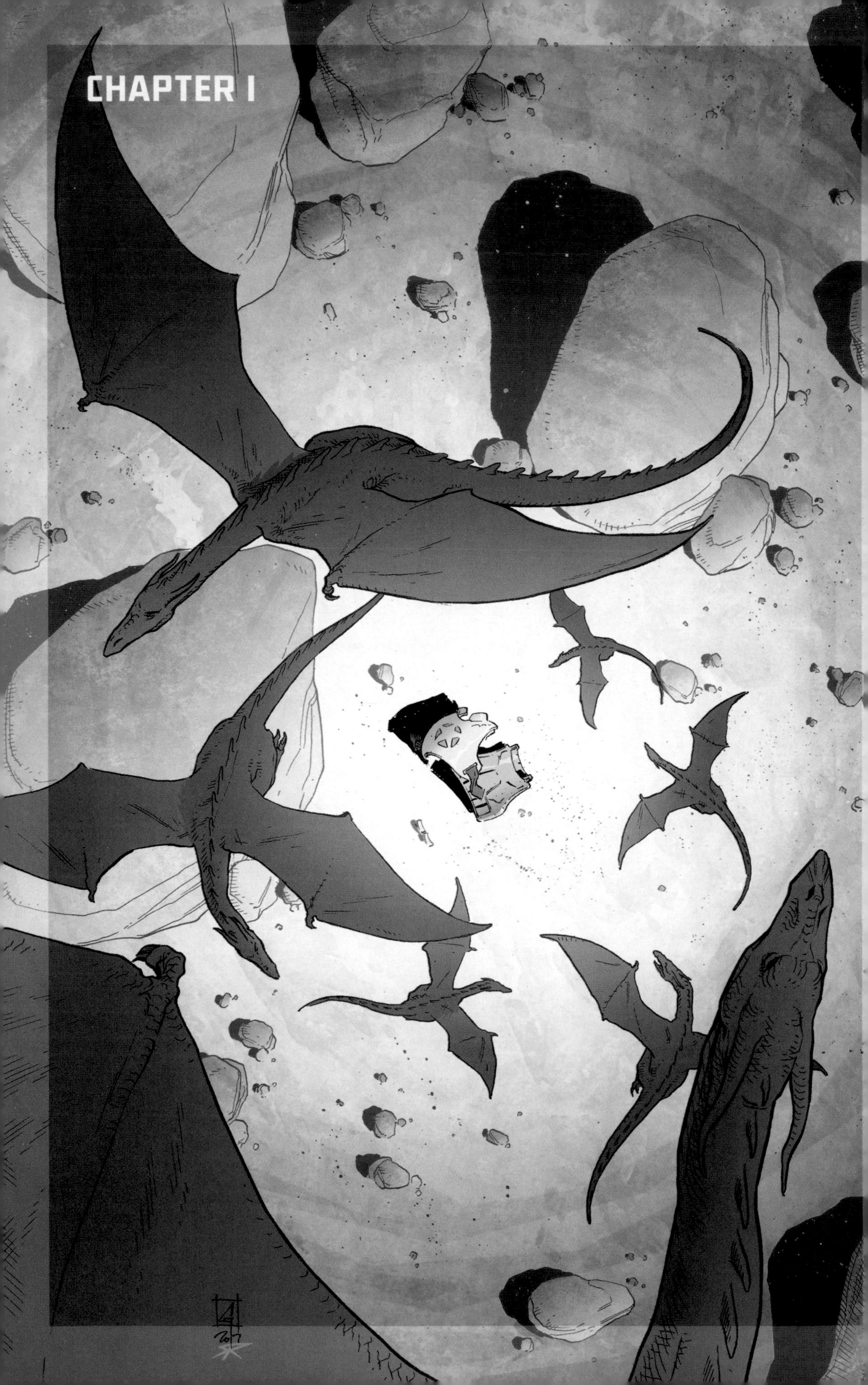

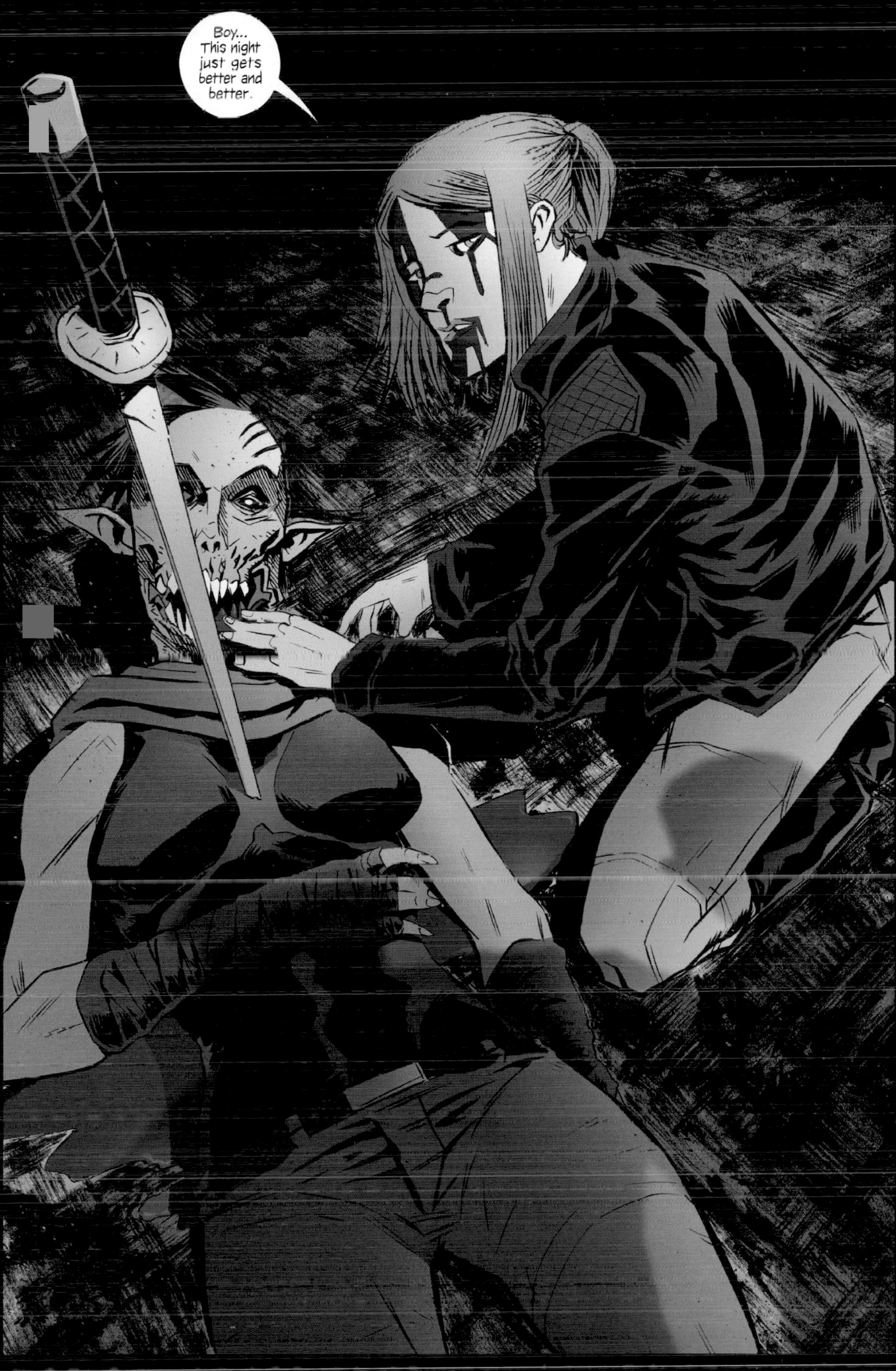
Boy... This night just gets better and better.

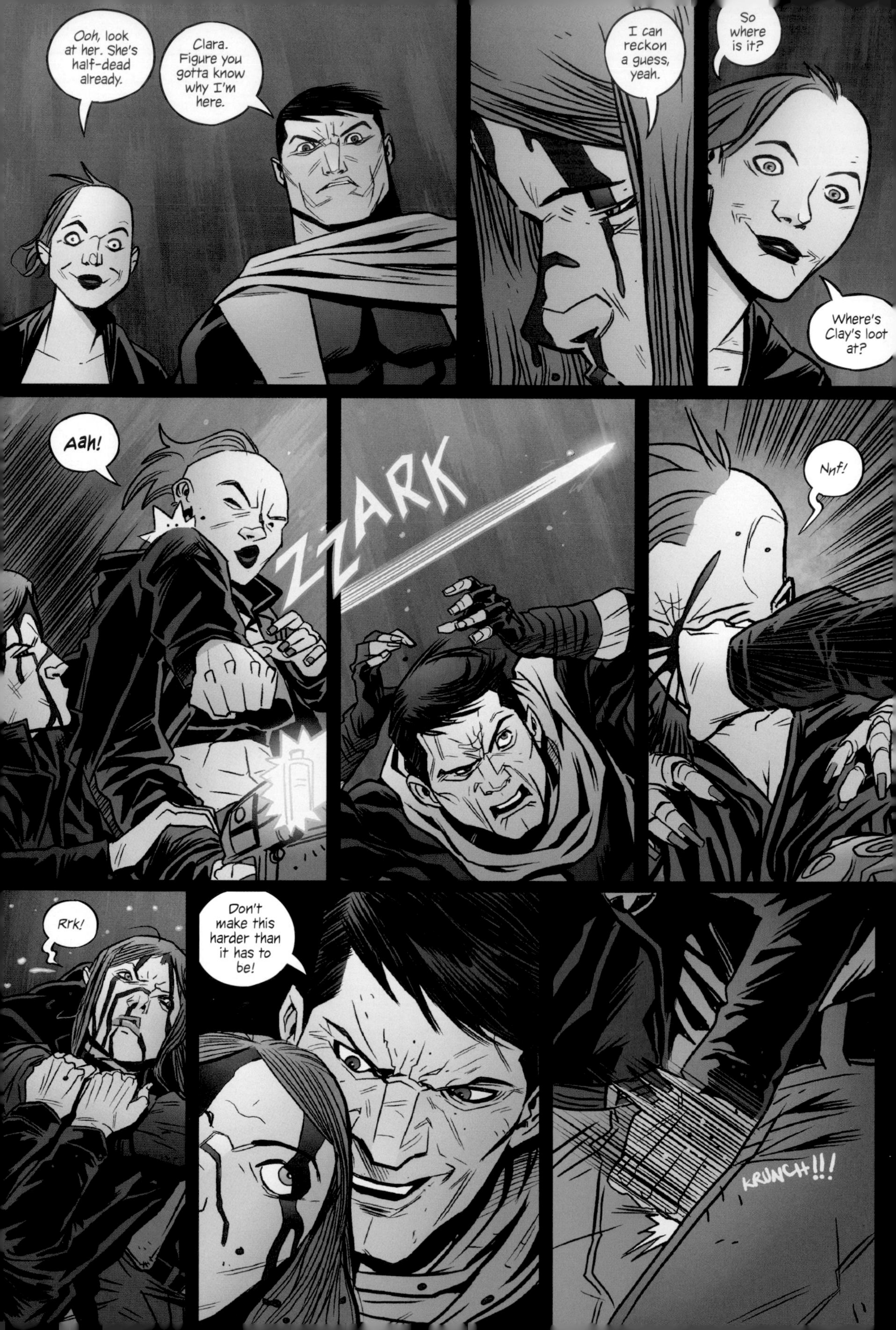
Ooh, look at her. She's half-dead already.
Clara. Figure you gotta know why I'm here.
I can reckon a guess, yeah.
So where is it?
Where's Clay's loot at?
Aah!
ZZARK
Nnf!
Rrk!
Don't make this harder than it has to be!
KRUNCH!!!

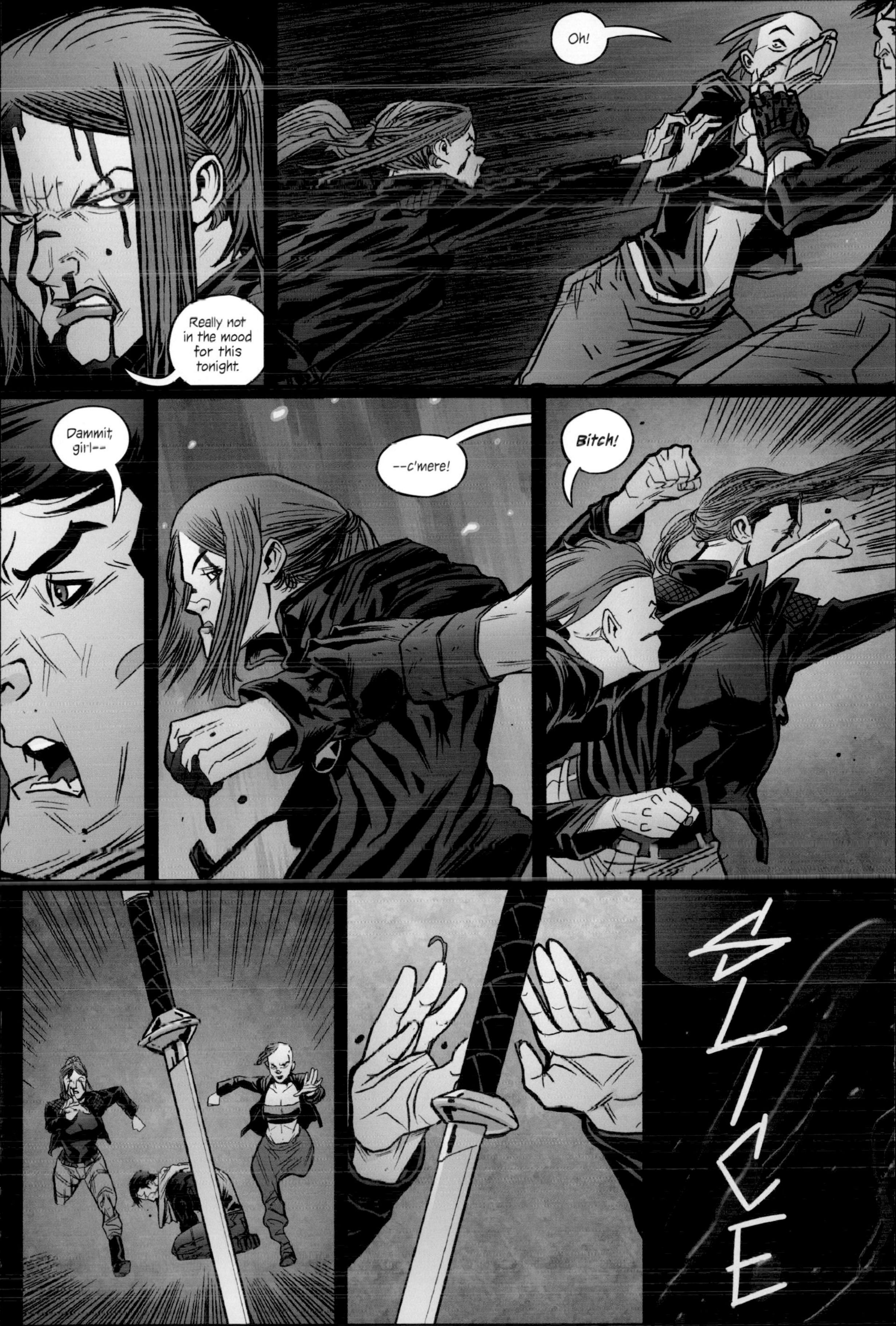
Really not in the mood for this tonight.
Oh!
Dammit, girl--
--c'mere!
Bitch!
SLICE

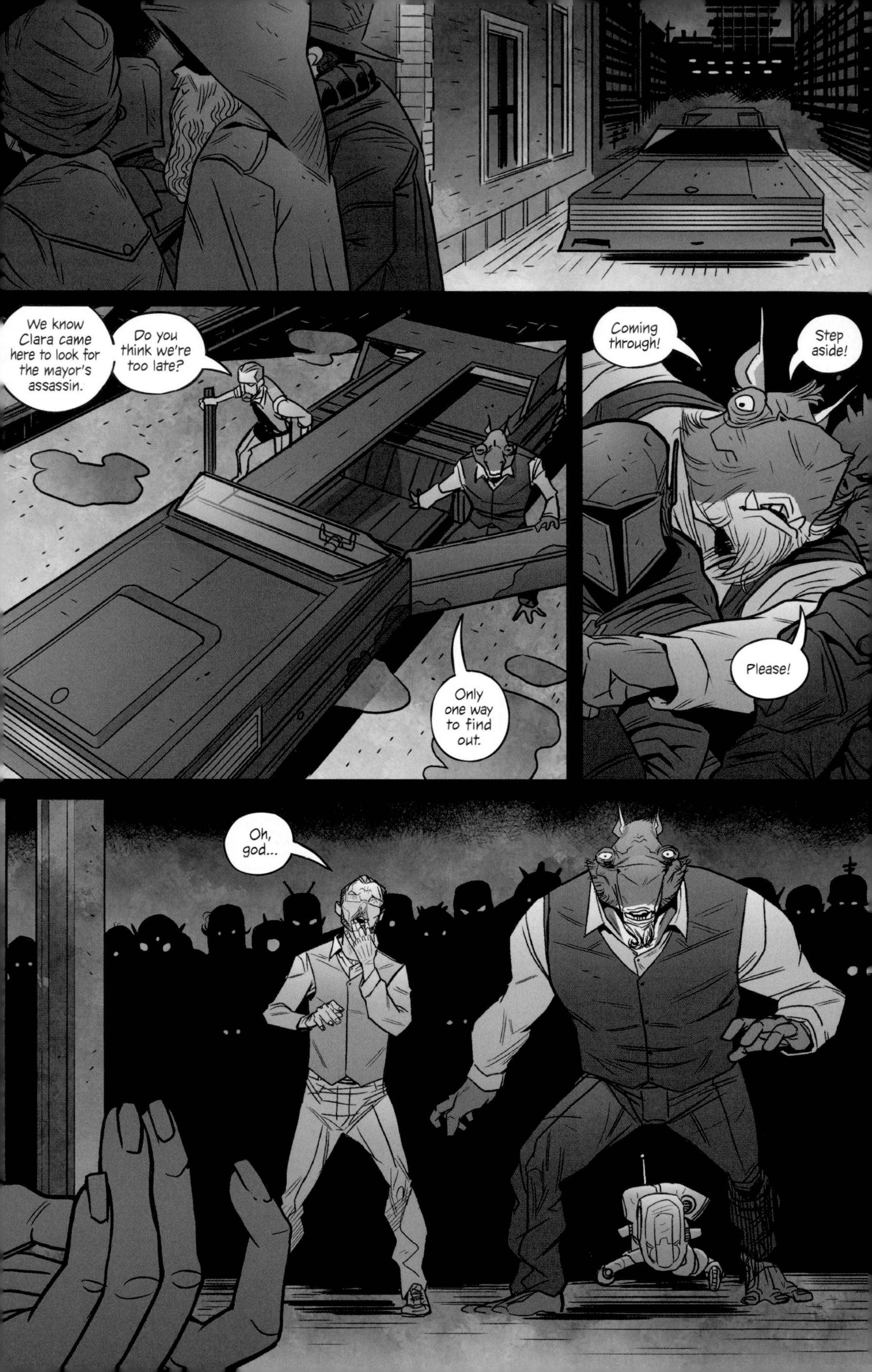
We know Clara came here to look for the mayor's assassin.
Do you think we're too late?
Only one way to find out.
Coming through!
Step aside!
Please!
Oh, god...

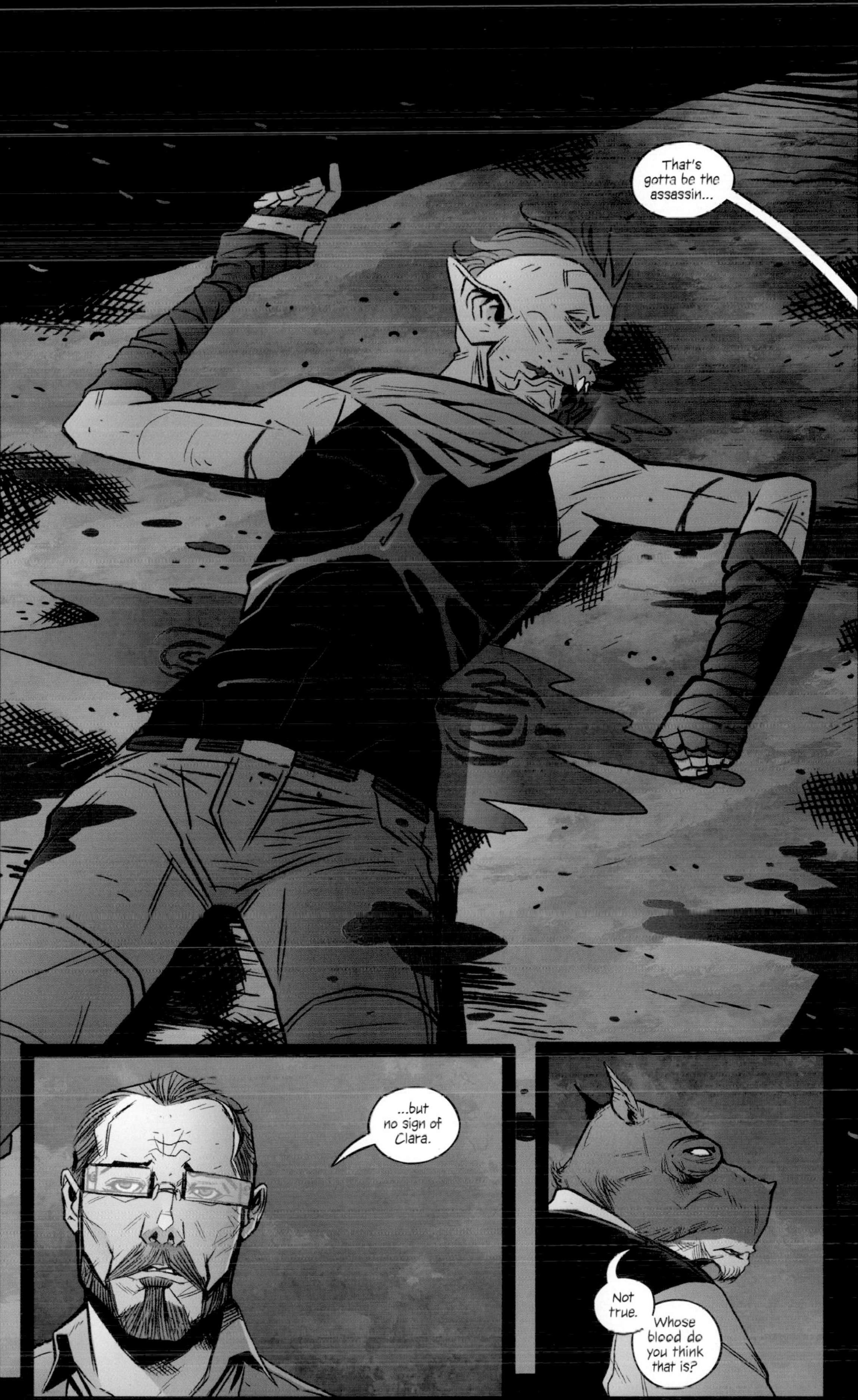

That's gotta be the assassin...
...but no sign of Clara.
Not true.
Whose blood do you think that is?

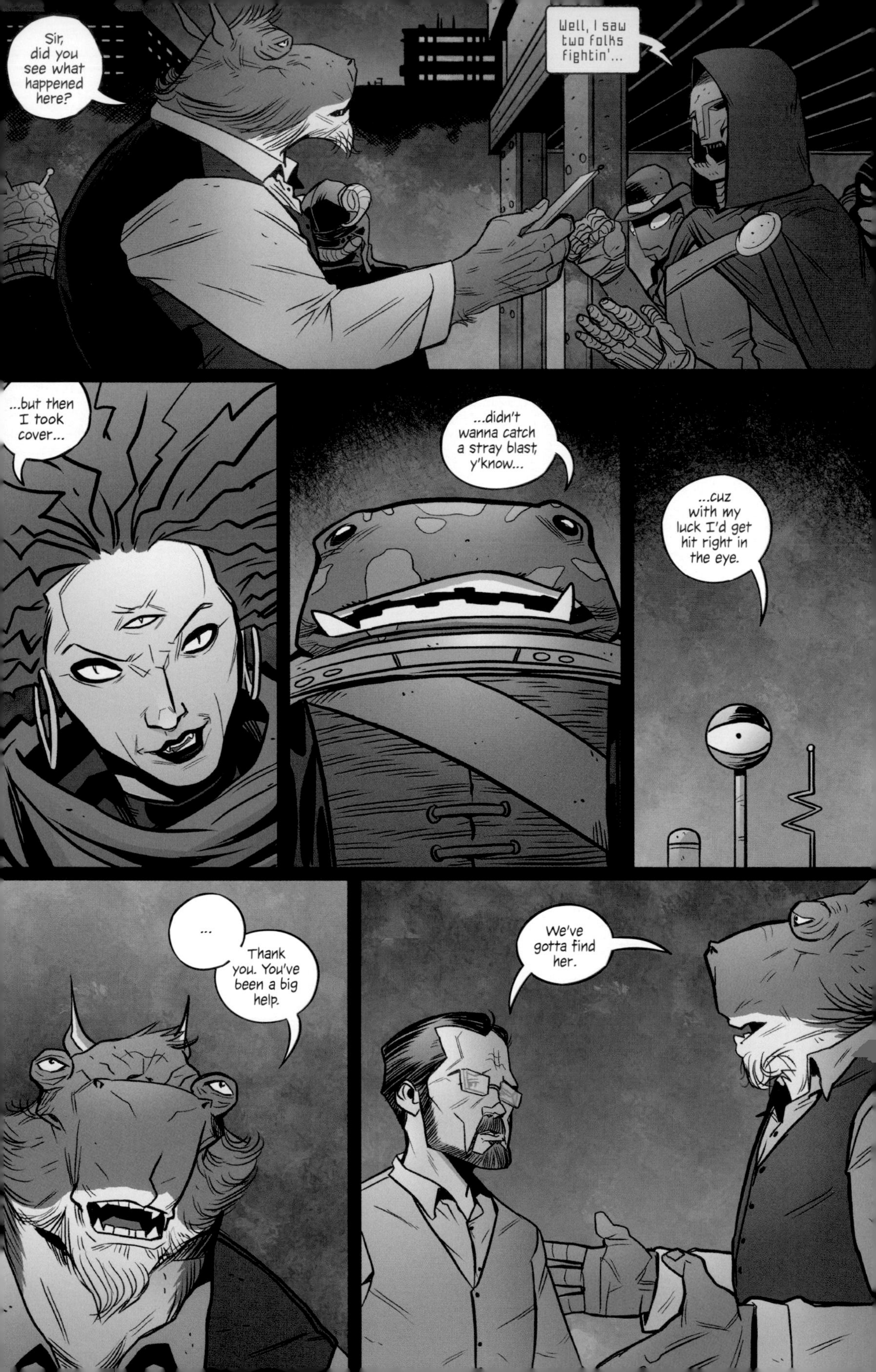
Sir, did you see what happened here?
Well, I saw two folks fightin'...
...but then I took cover...
...didn't wanna catch a stray blast, y'know...
...cuz with my luck I'd get hit right in the eye.
...
Thank you. You've been a big help.
We've gotta find her.

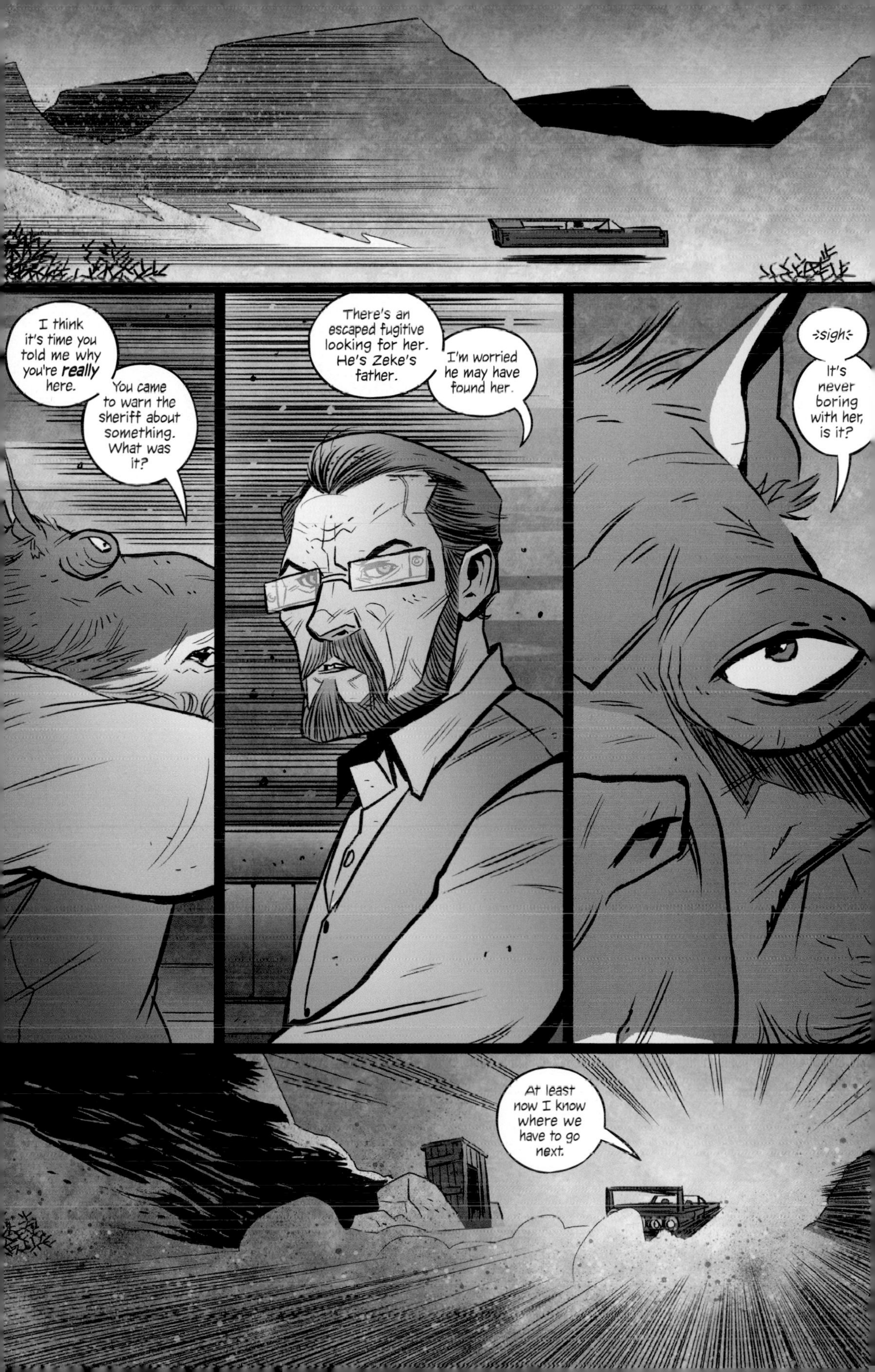

I think it's time you told me why you're ***really*** here.
You came to warn the sheriff about something. What was it?
There's an escaped fugitive looking for her. He's Zeke's father.
I'm worried he may have found her.
sigh
It's never boring with her, is it?
At least now I know where we have to go next.

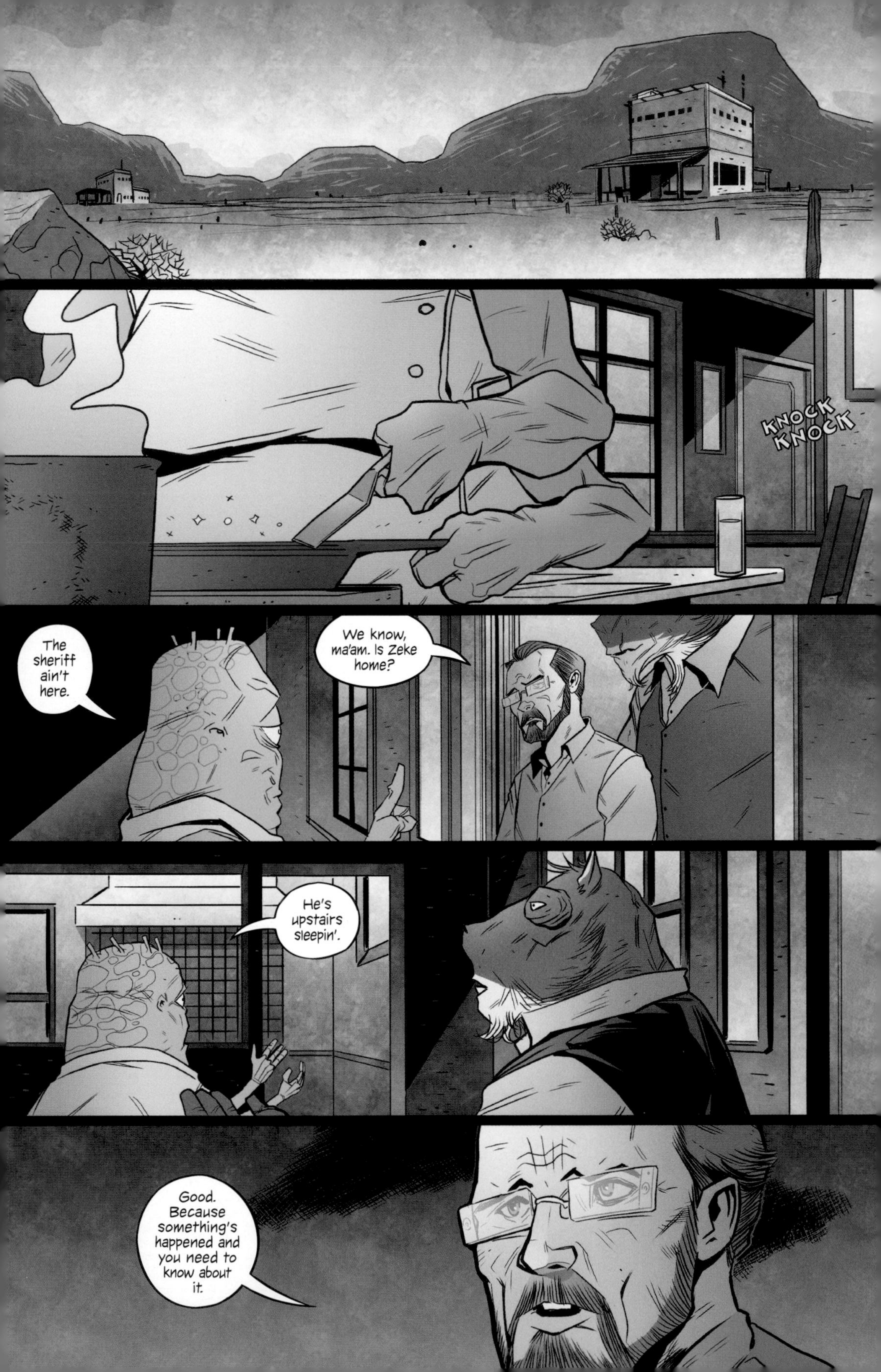
KNOCK KNOCK
The sheriff ain't here.
We know, ma'am. Is Zeke home?
He's upstairs sleepin'.
Good. Because something's happened and you need to know about it.

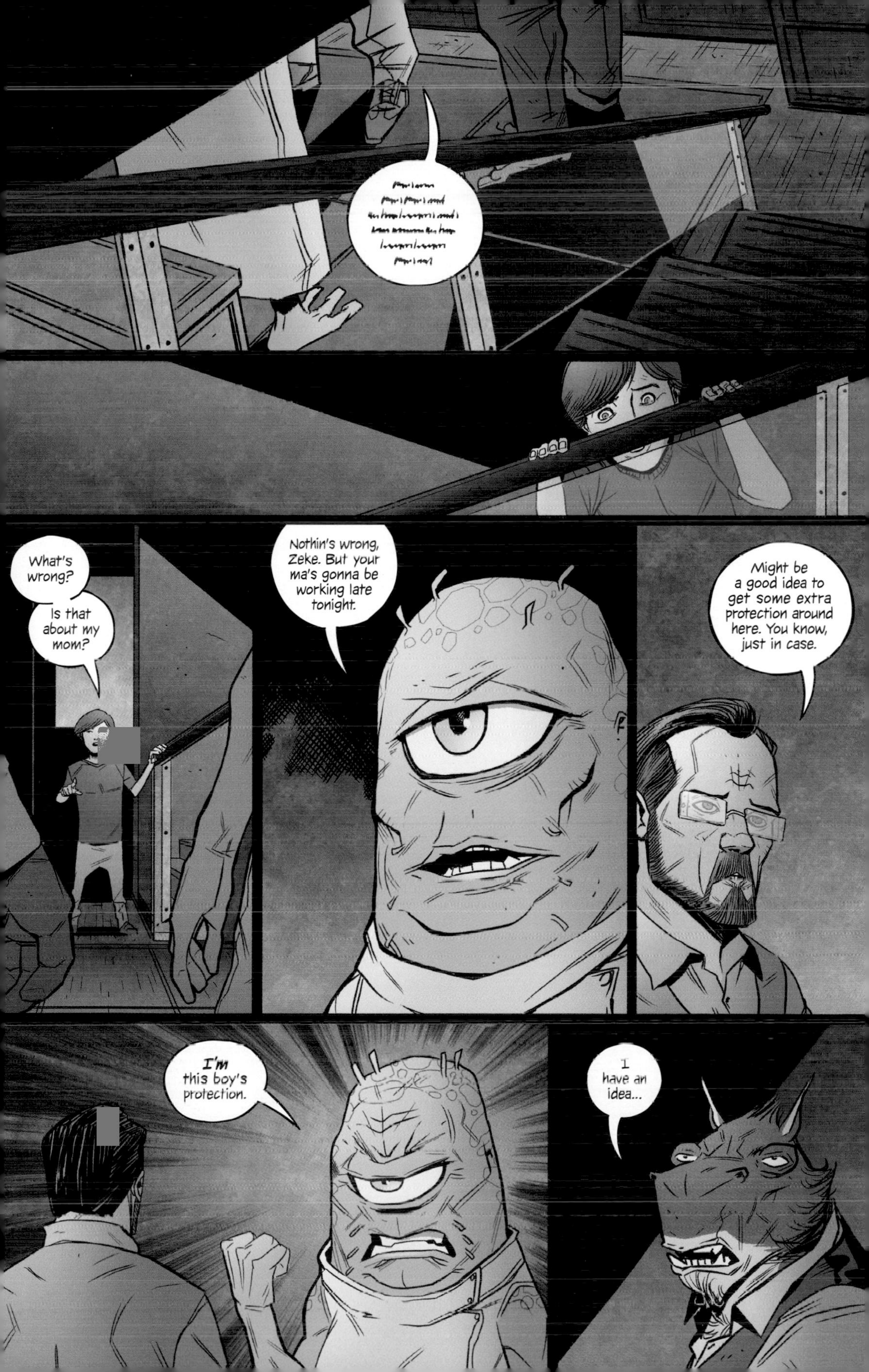
What's wrong?
Is that about my mom?
Nothin's wrong, Zeke. But your ma's gonna be working late tonight.
Might be a good idea to get some extra protection around here. You know, just in case.
I'm this boy's protection.
I have an idea...

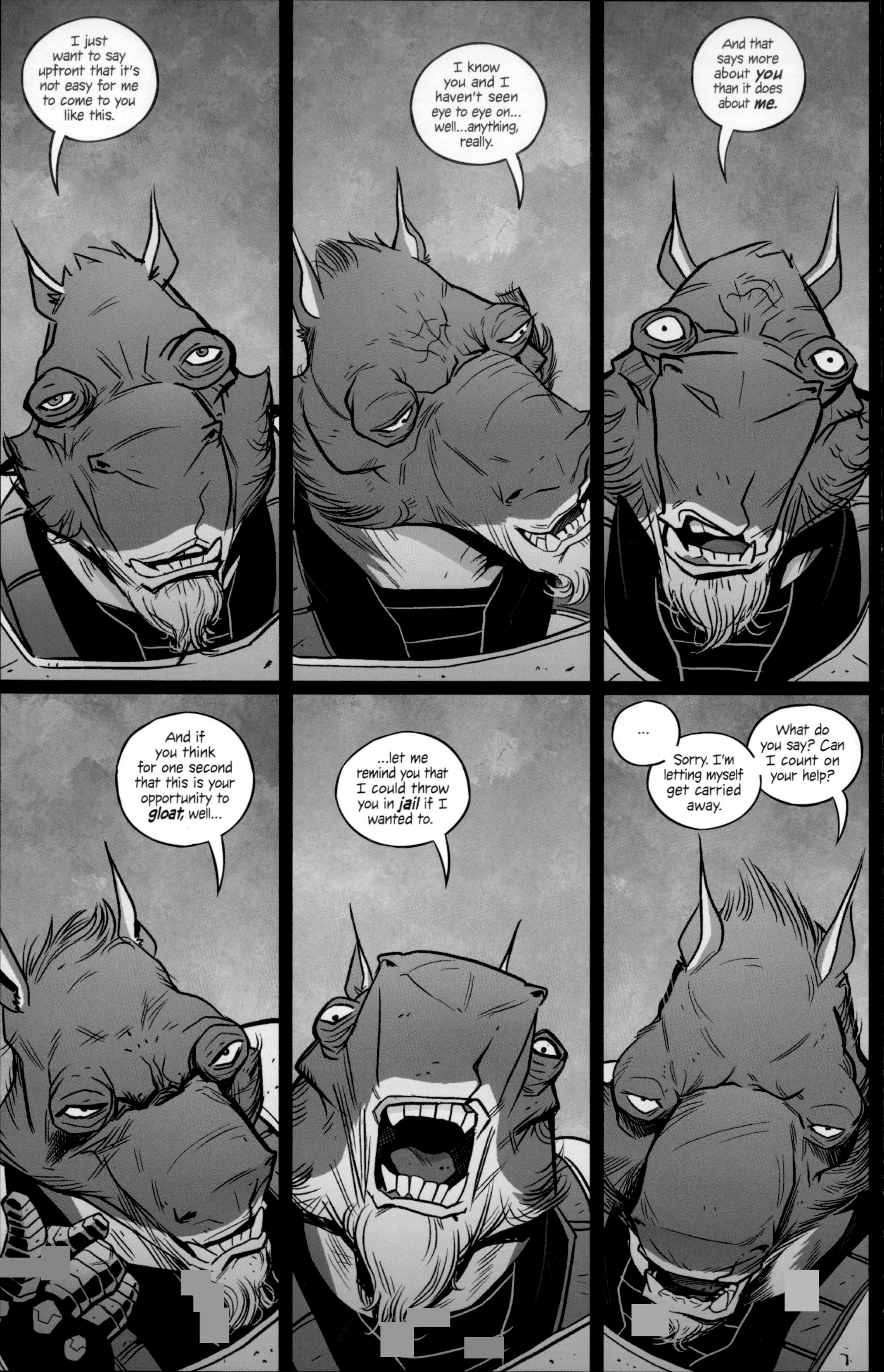
I just want to say upfront that it's not easy for me to come to you like this.
I know you and I haven't seen eye to eye on... well...anything, really.
And that says more about ***you*** than it does about ***me.***
And if you think for one second that this is your opportunity to ***gloat,*** well...
...let me remind you that I could throw you in ***jail*** if I wanted to.
...
Sorry. I'm letting myself get carried away.
What do you say? Can I count on your help?

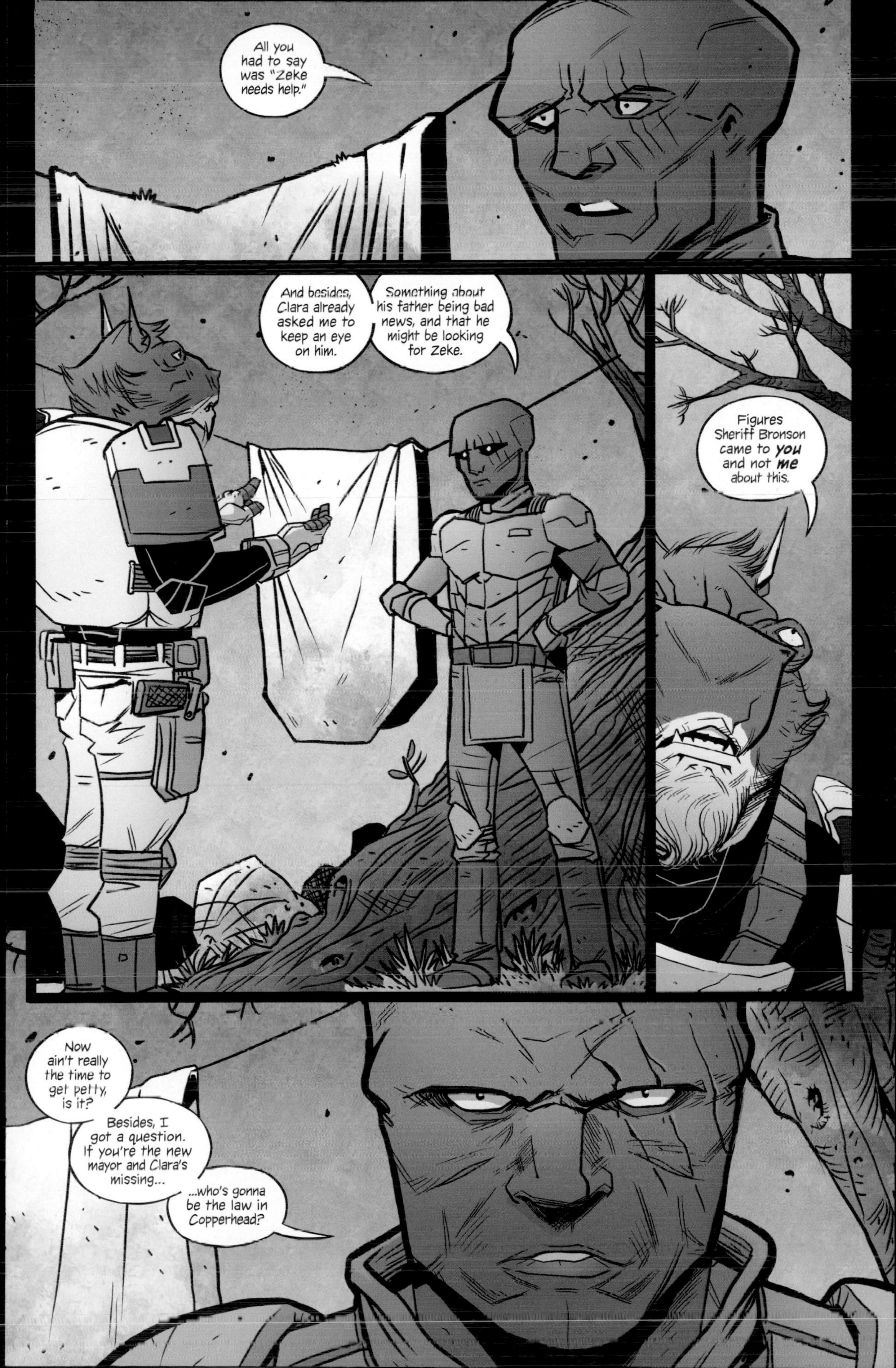
All you had to say was "Zeke needs help."
And besides, Clara already asked me to keep an eye on him.
Something about his father being bad news, and that he might be looking for Zeke.
Figures Sheriff Bronson came to **you** and not **me** about this.
Now ain't really the time to get petty, is it?
Besides, I got a question. If you're the new mayor and Clara's missing...
...who's gonna be the law in Copperhead?

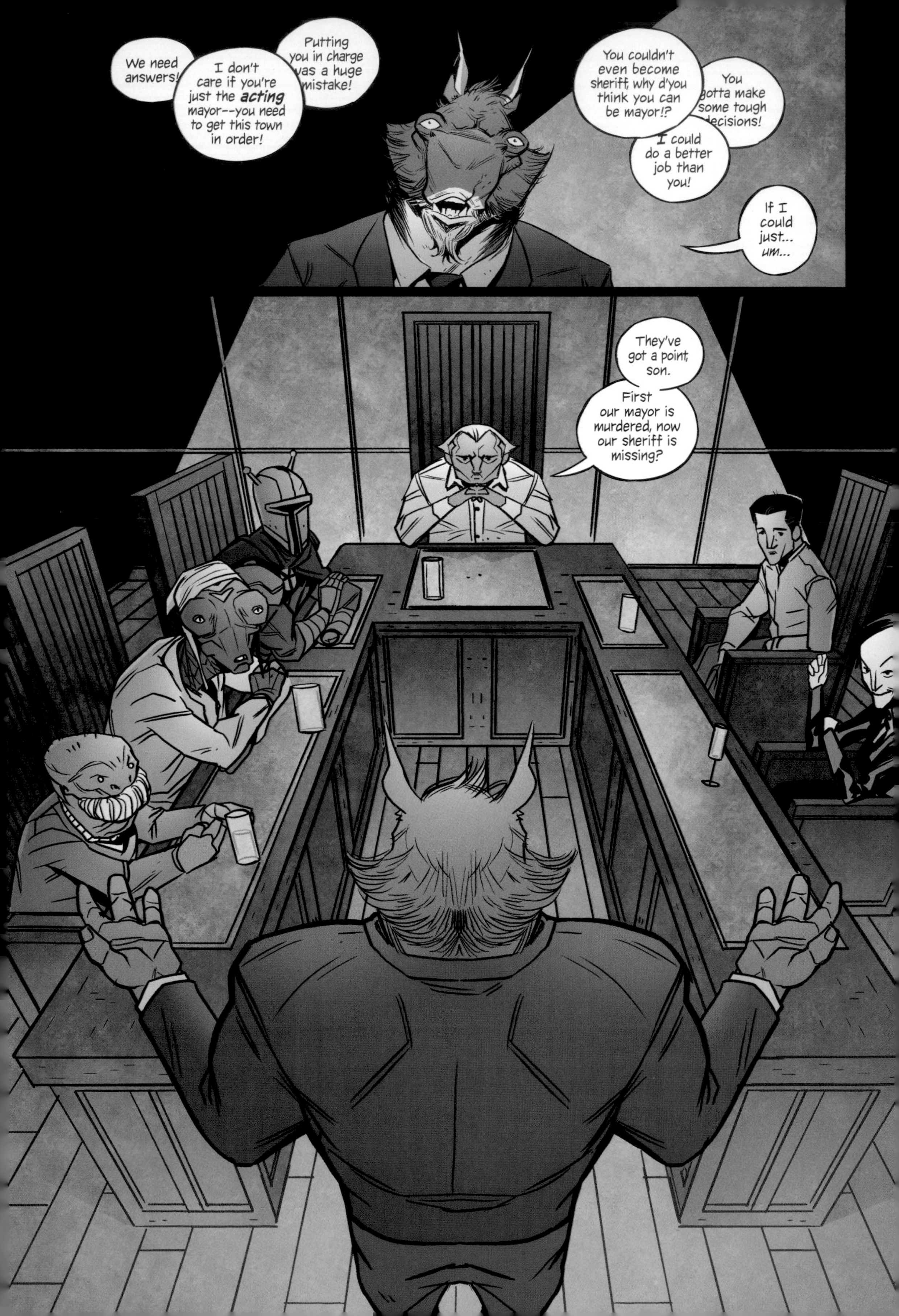
We need answers!
I don't care if you're just the *acting* mayor--you need to get this town in order!
Putting you in charge was a huge mistake!
You couldn't even become sheriff, why d'you think you can be mayor!?
You gotta make some tough decisions!
I could do a better job than you!
If I could just... um...
They've got a point, son.
First our mayor is murdered, now our sheriff is missing?

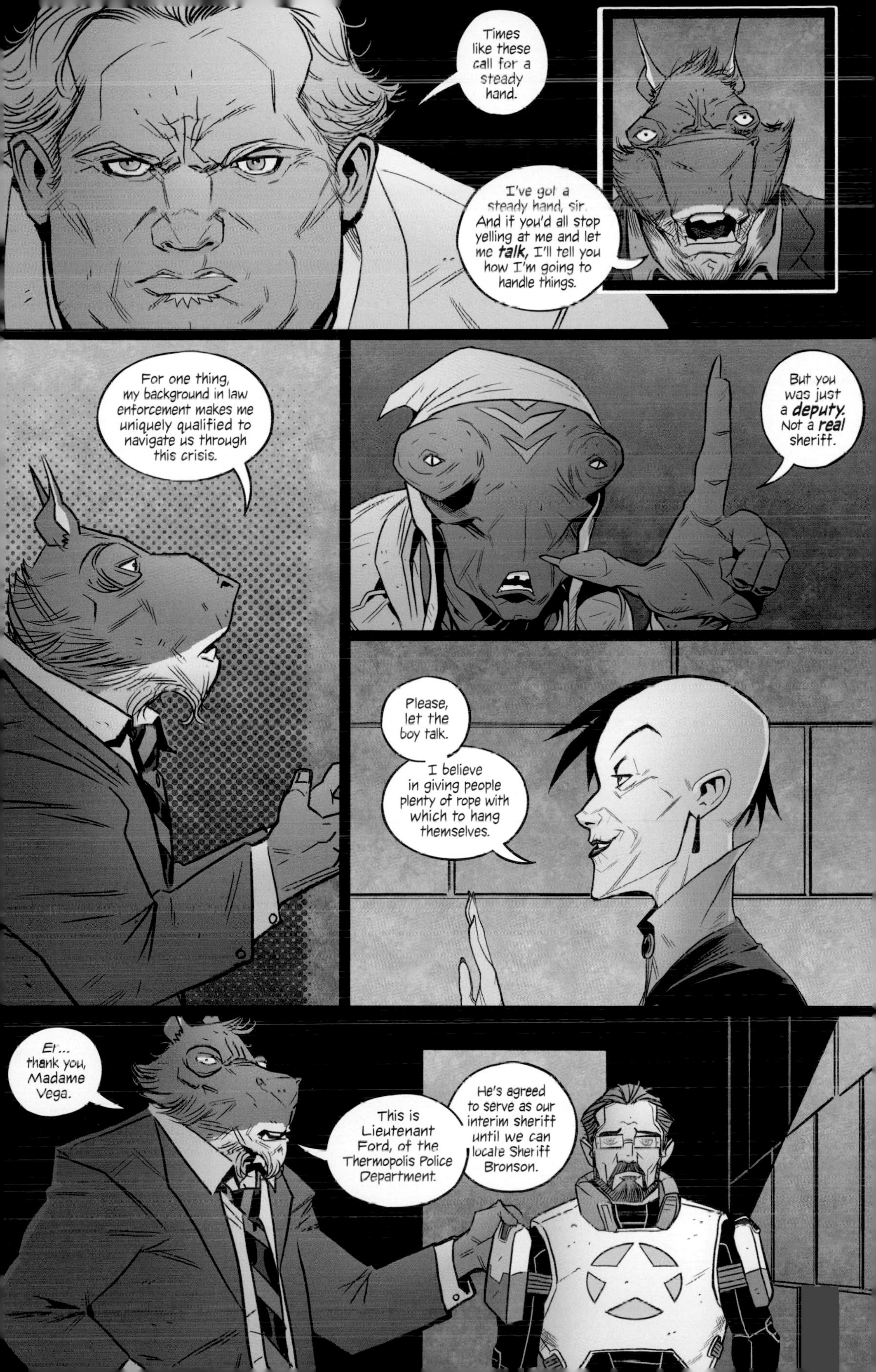
Times like these call for a steady hand.
I've got a steady hand, sir. And if you'd all stop yelling at me and let me talk, I'll tell you how I'm going to handle things.
For one thing, my background in law enforcement makes me uniquely qualified to navigate us through this crisis.
But you was just a deputy. Not a real sheriff.
Please, let the boy talk.
I believe in giving people plenty of rope with which to hang themselves.
Er... thank you, Madame Vega.
This is Lieutenant Ford, of the Thermopolis Police Department.
He's agreed to serve as our interim sheriff until we can locate Sheriff Bronson.

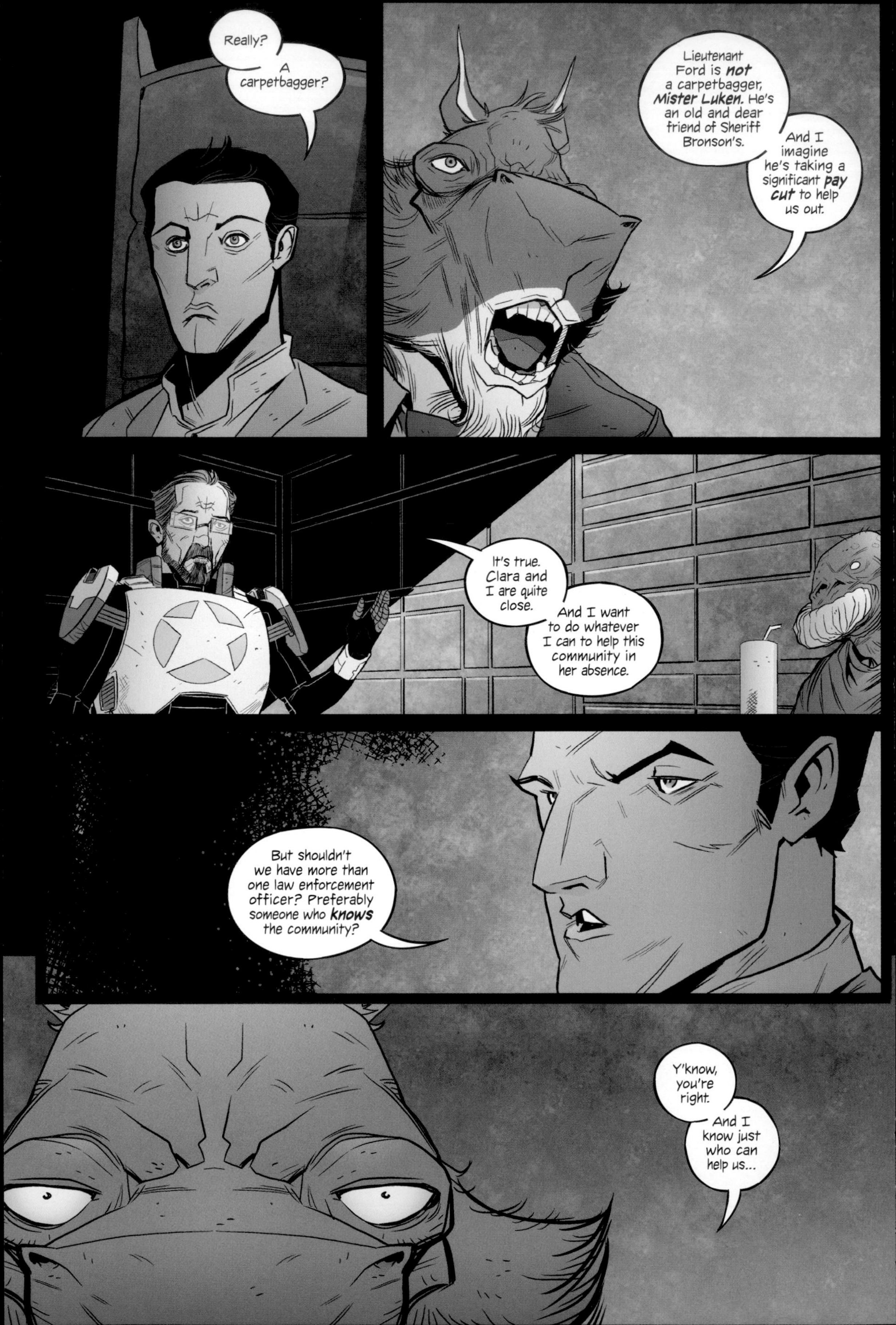
Really? A carpetbagger?
Lieutenant Ford is **not** a carpetbagger, **Mister Luken.** He's an old and dear friend of Sheriff Bronson's.
And I imagine he's taking a significant **pay cut** to help us out.
It's true. Clara and I are quite close.
And I want to do whatever I can to help this community in her absence.
But shouldn't we have more than one law enforcement officer? Preferably someone who **knows** the community?
Y'know, you're right.
And I know just who can help us...

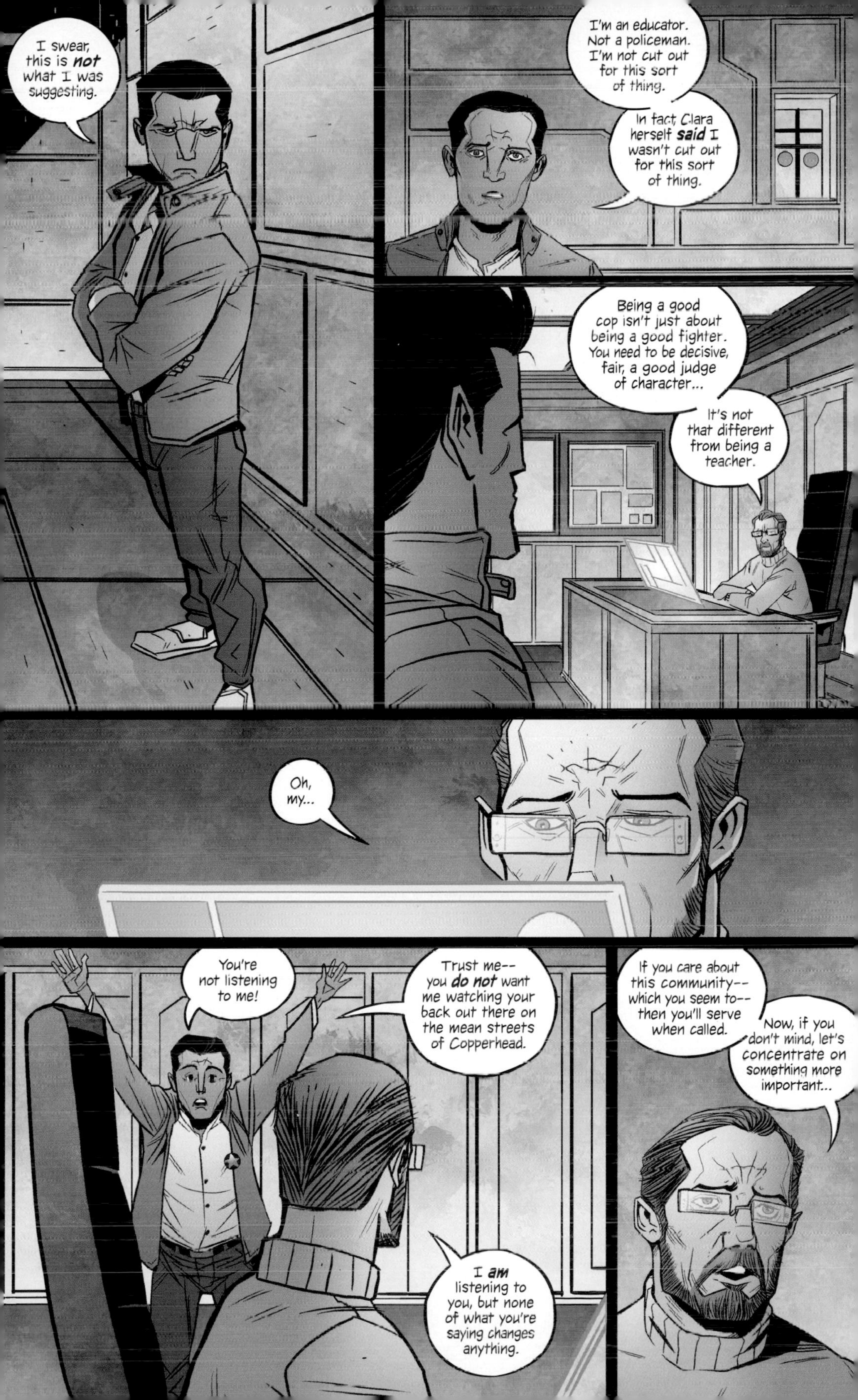
I swear, this is **not** what I was suggesting.
I'm an educator. Not a policeman. I'm not cut out for this sort of thing.
In fact, Clara herself **said** I wasn't cut out for this sort of thing.
Being a good cop isn't just about being a good fighter. You need to be decisive, fair, a good judge of character...
It's not that different from being a teacher.
Oh, my...
You're not listening to me!
Trust me-- you **do not** want me watching your back out there on the mean streets of Copperhead.
I **am** listening to you, but none of what you're saying changes anything.
If you care about this community-- which you seem to-- then you'll serve when called.
Now, if you don't mind, let's concentrate on something more important...

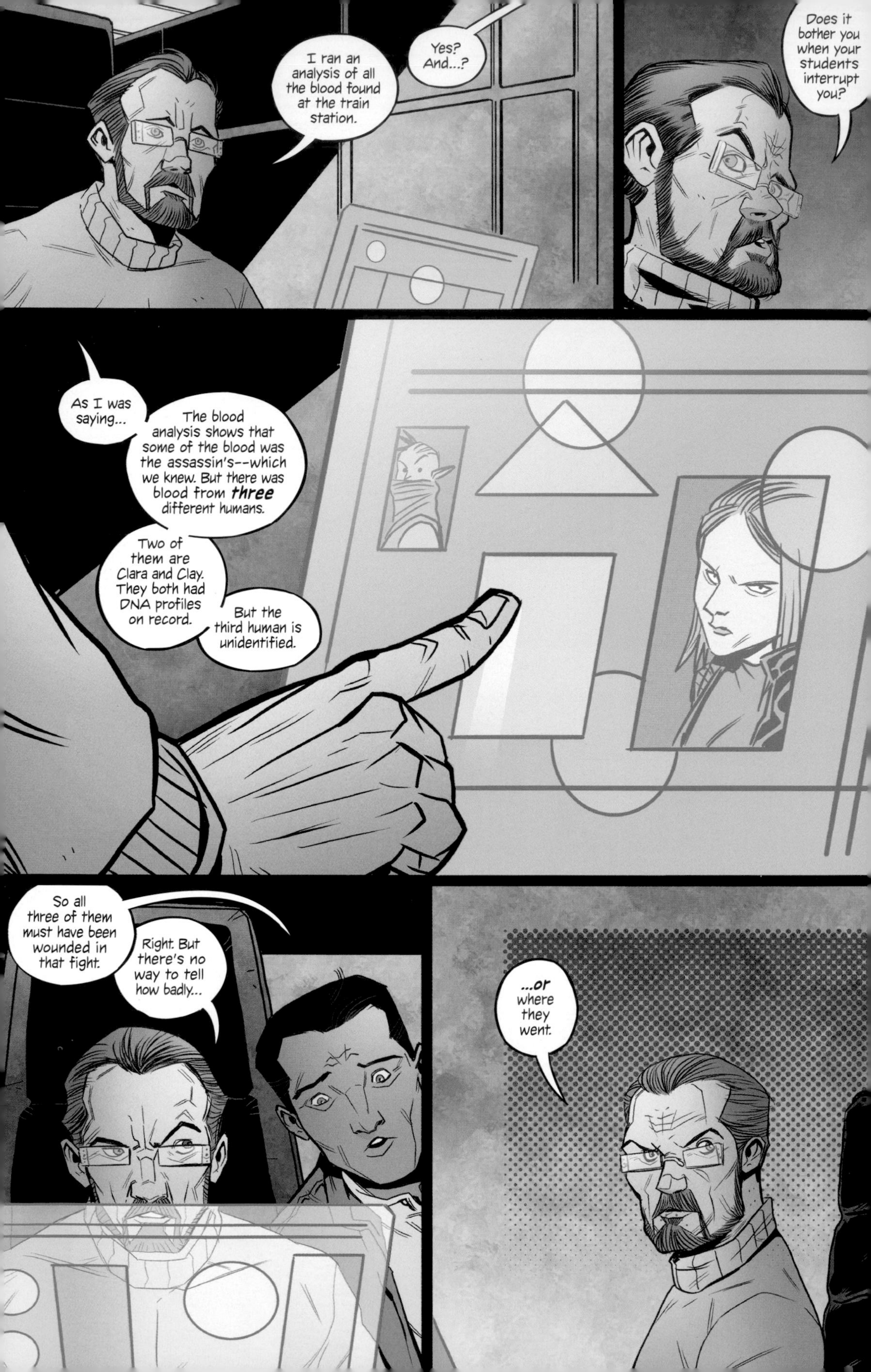
I ran an analysis of all the blood found at the train station.
Yes? And...?
Does it bother you when your students interrupt you?
As I was saying...
The blood analysis shows that some of the blood was the assassin's--which we knew. But there was blood from ***three*** different humans.
Two of them are Clara and Clay. They both had DNA profiles on record.
But the third human is unidentified.
So all three of them must have been wounded in that fight.
Right. But there's no way to tell how badly...
...or where they went.

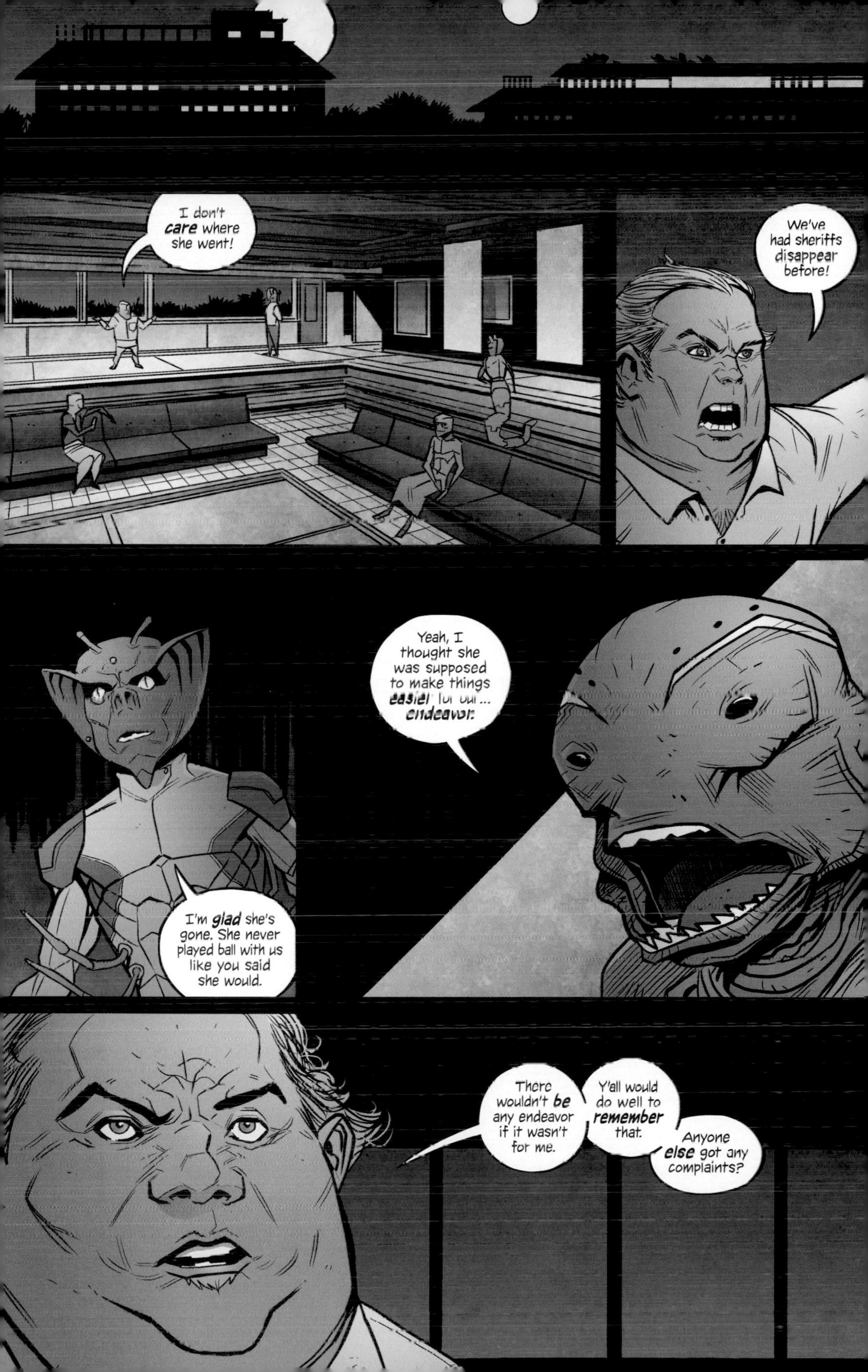
I don't *care* where she went!
We've had sheriffs disappear before!
I'm *glad* she's gone. She never played ball with us like you said she would.
Yeah, I thought she was supposed to make things *easier* for our... *endeavor.*
There wouldn't *be* any endeavor if it wasn't for me.
Y'all would do well to *remember* that.
Anyone *else* got any complaints?

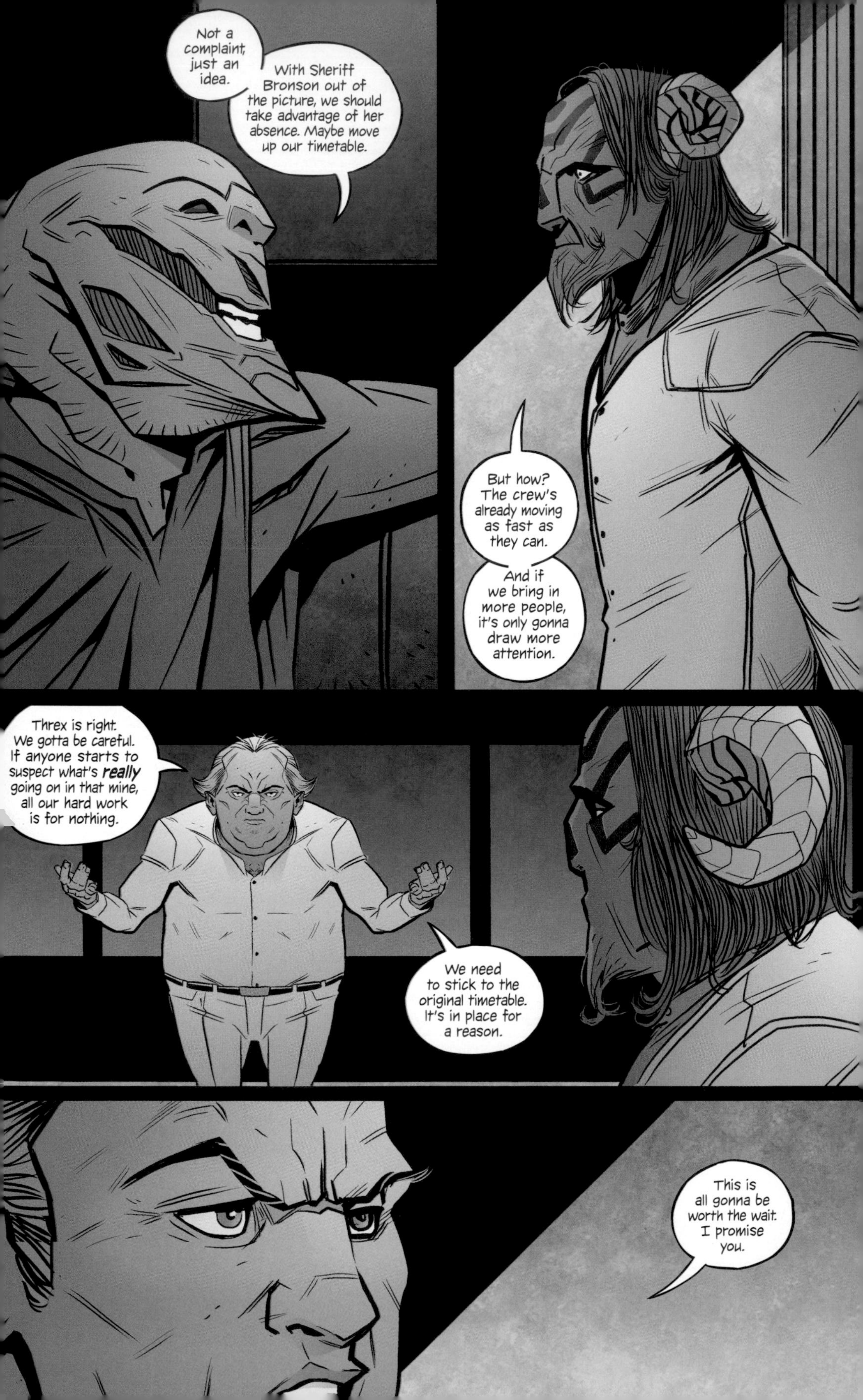
Not a complaint, just an idea.
With Sheriff Bronson out of the picture, we should take advantage of her absence. Maybe move up our timetable.
But how? The crew's already moving as fast as they can.
And if we bring in more people, it's only gonna draw more attention.
Threx is right. We gotta be careful. If anyone starts to suspect what's really going on in that mine, all our hard work is for nothing.
We need to stick to the original timetable. It's in place for a reason.
This is all gonna be worth the wait. I promise you.

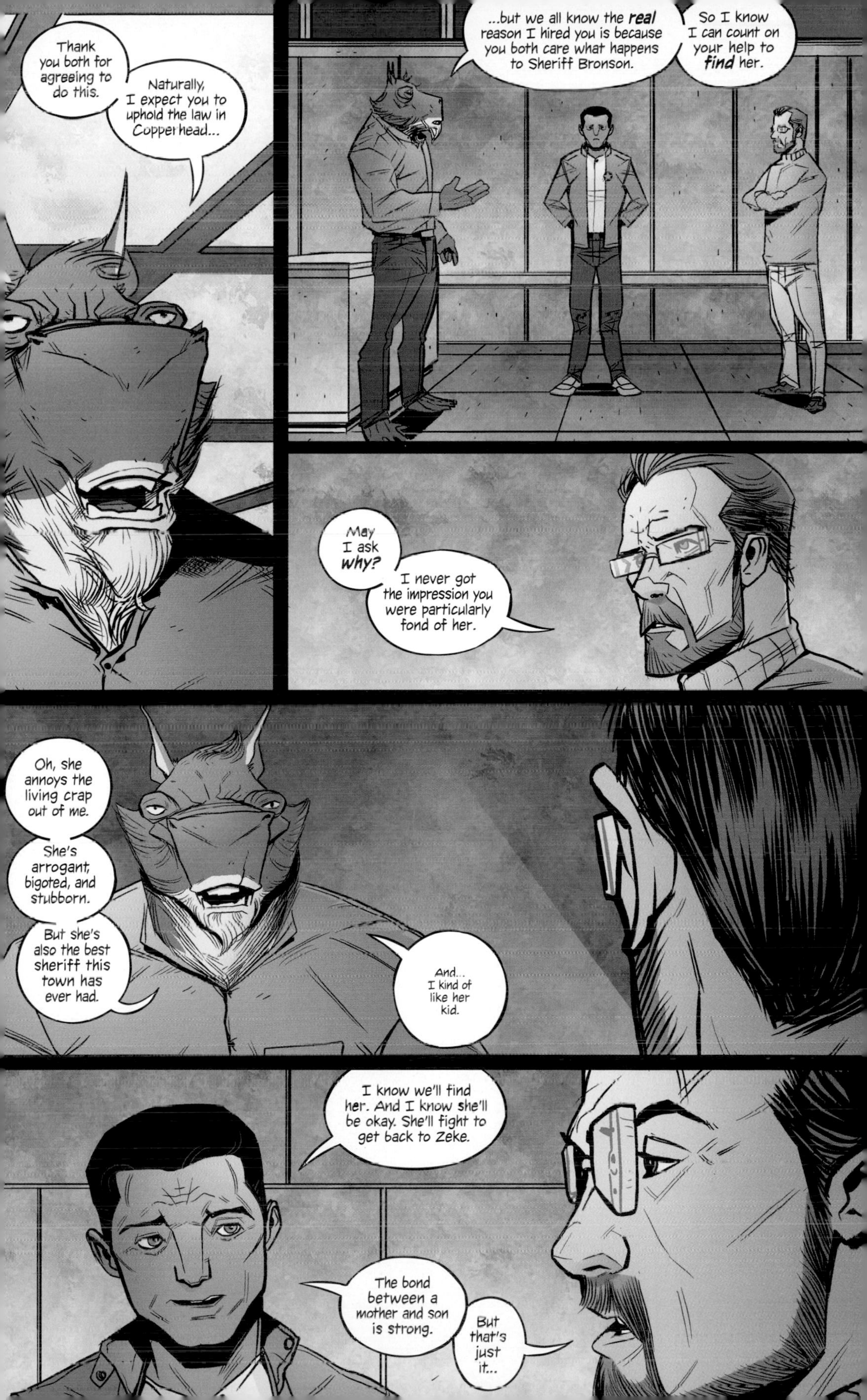
Thank you both for agreeing to do this.
Naturally, I expect you to uphold the law in Copperhead...
...but we all know the **real** reason I hired you is because you both care what happens to Sheriff Bronson.
So I know I can count on your help to **find** her.
May I ask **why?**
I never got the impression you were particularly fond of her.
Oh, she annoys the living crap out of me.
She's arrogant, bigoted, and stubborn.
But she's also the best sheriff this town has ever had.
And... I kind of like her kid.
I know we'll find her. And I know she'll be okay. She'll fight to get back to Zeke.
The bond between a mother and son is strong.
But that's just it...

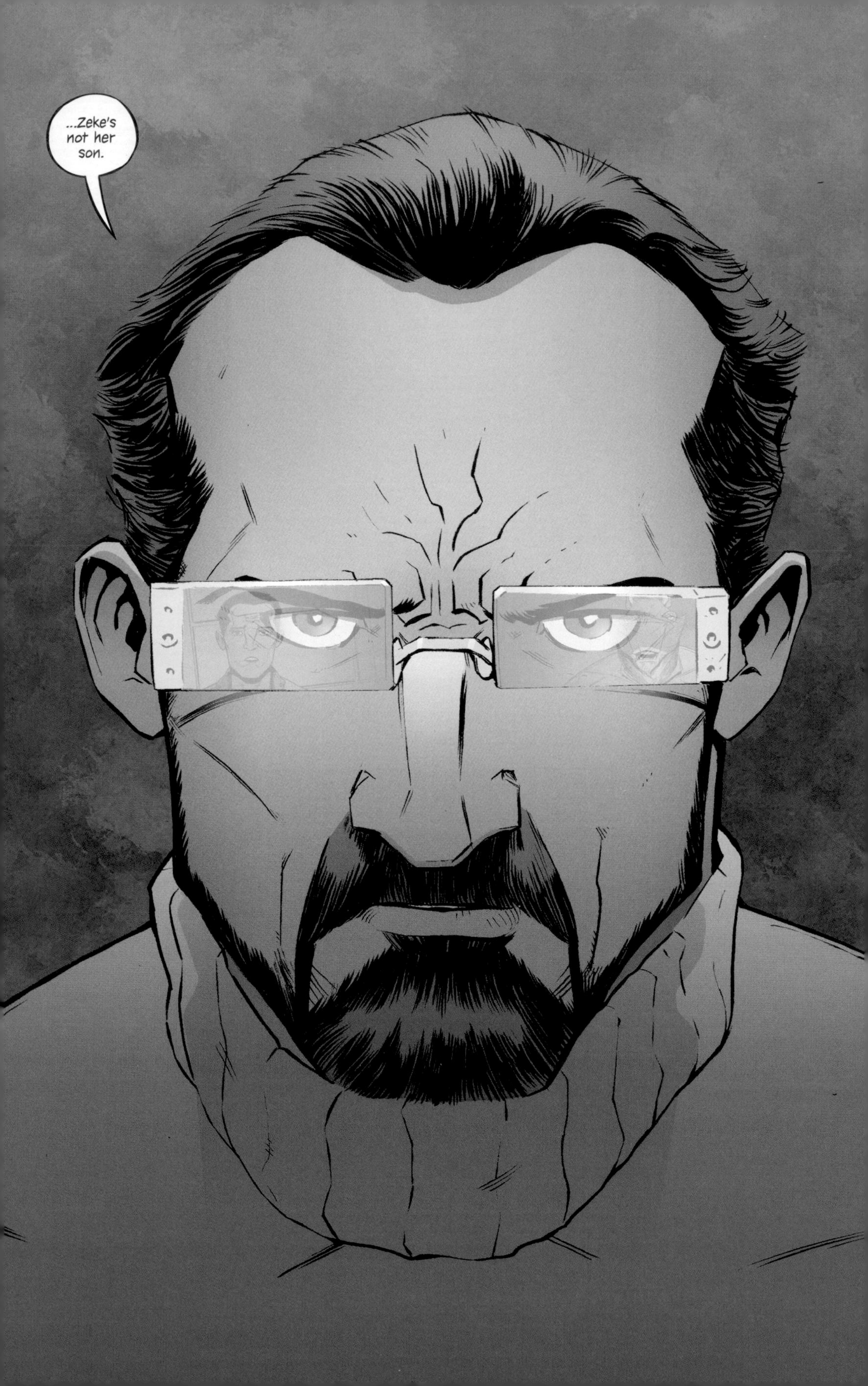
...Zeke's not her son.

CHAPTER II

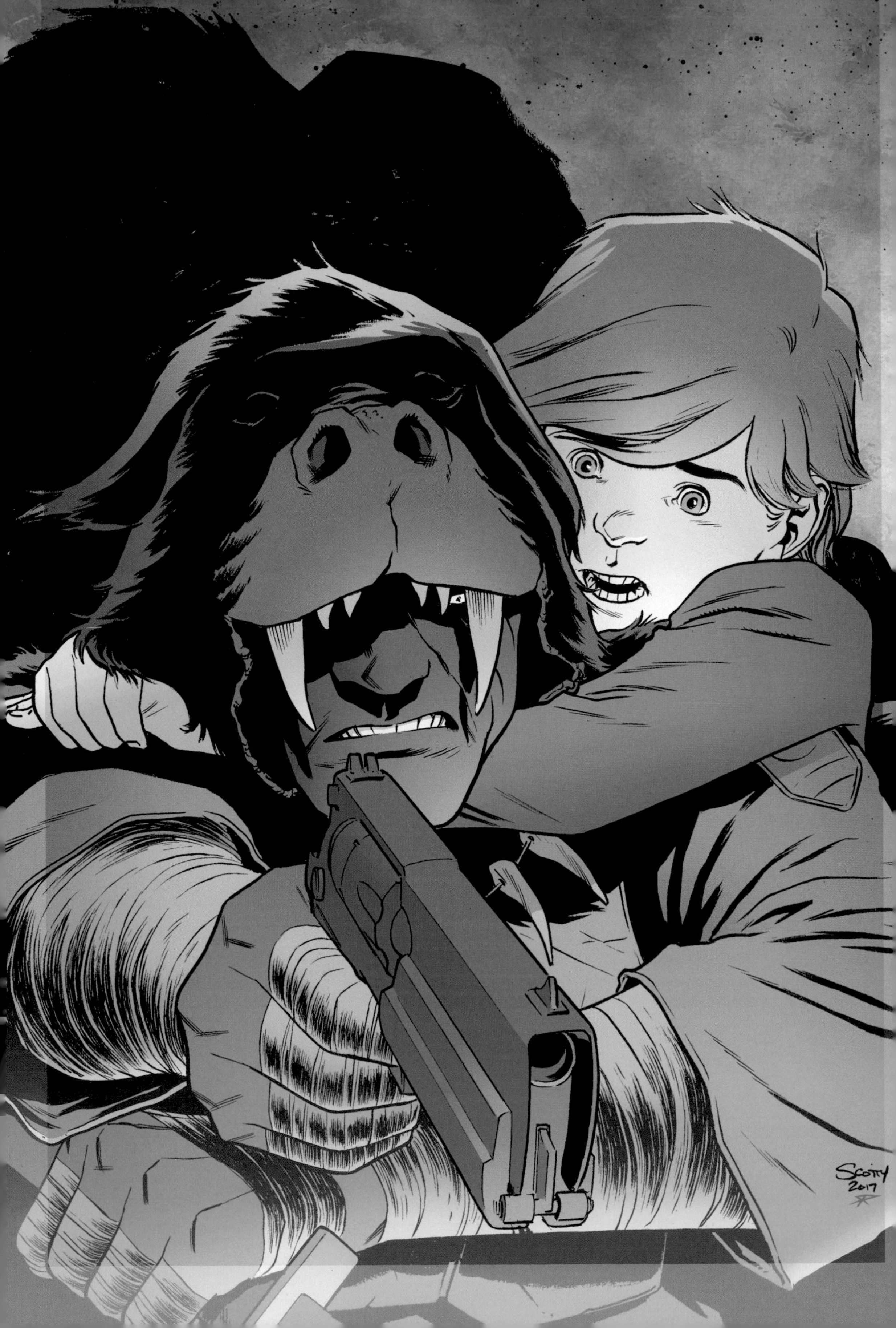
SCOTTY 2017

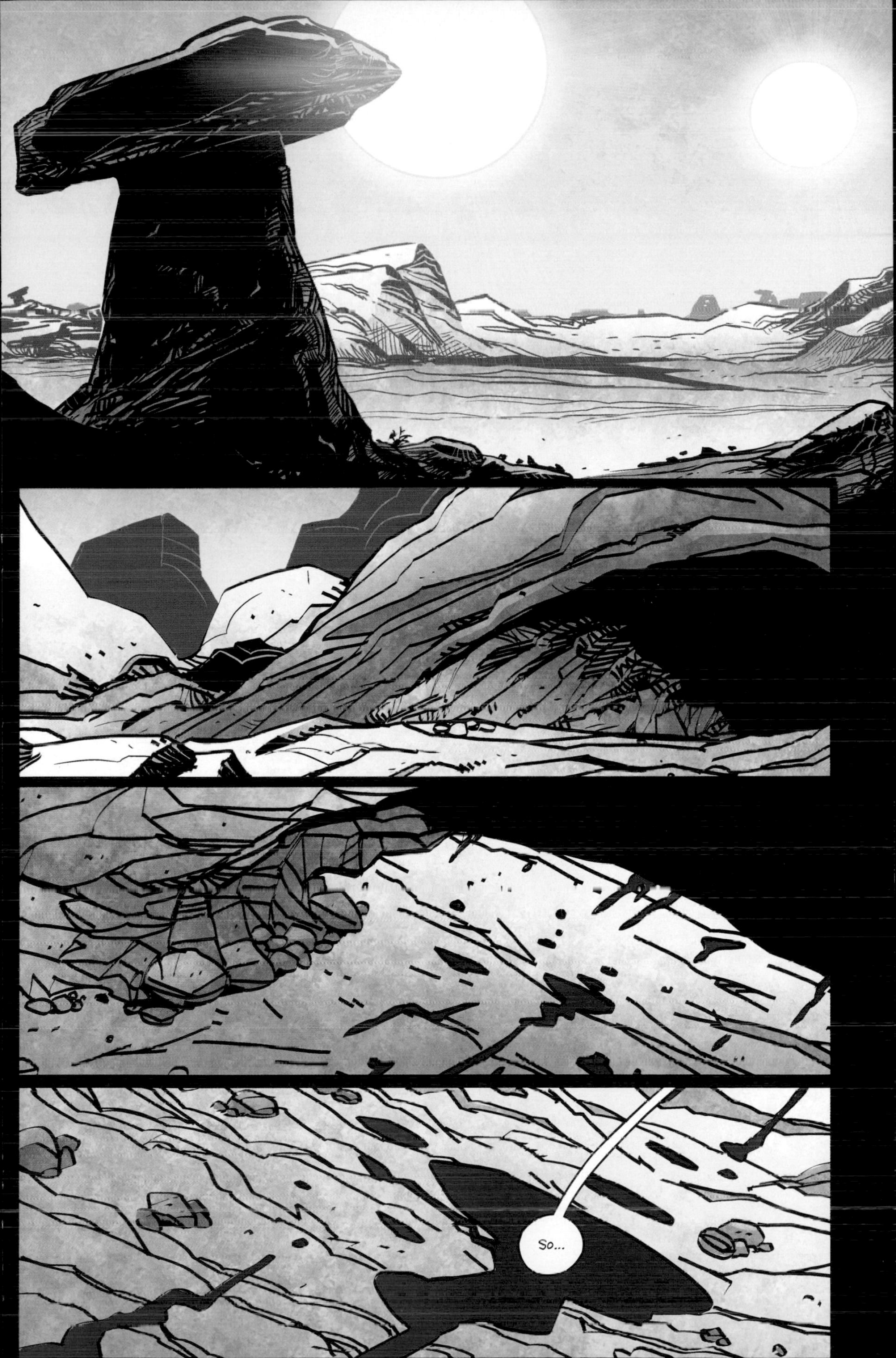
SO...

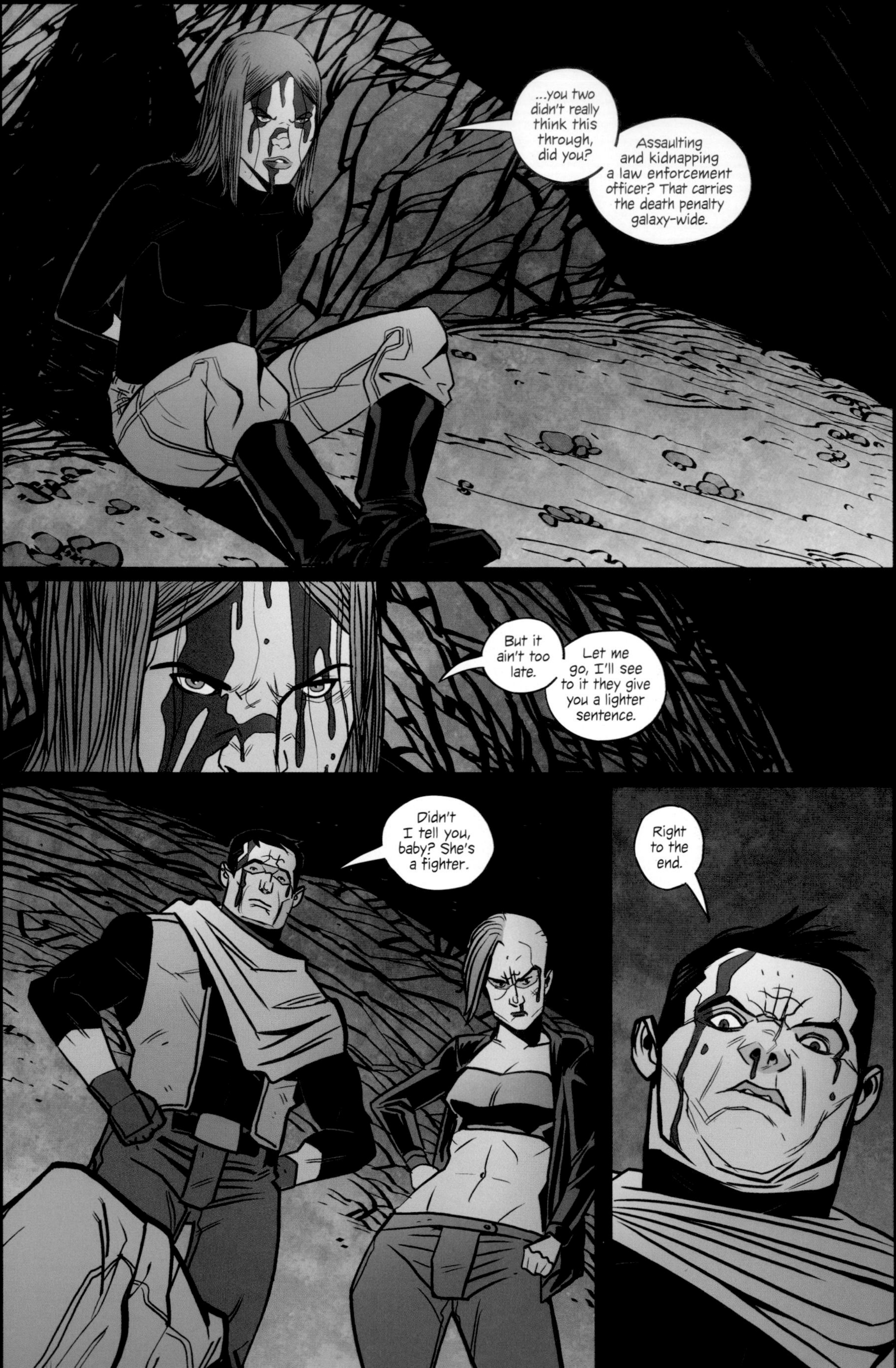
...you two didn't really think this through, did you?
Assaulting and kidnapping a law enforcement officer? That carries the death penalty galaxy-wide.
But it ain't too late.
Let me go, I'll see to it they give you a lighter sentence.
Didn't I tell you, baby? She's a fighter.
Right to the end.

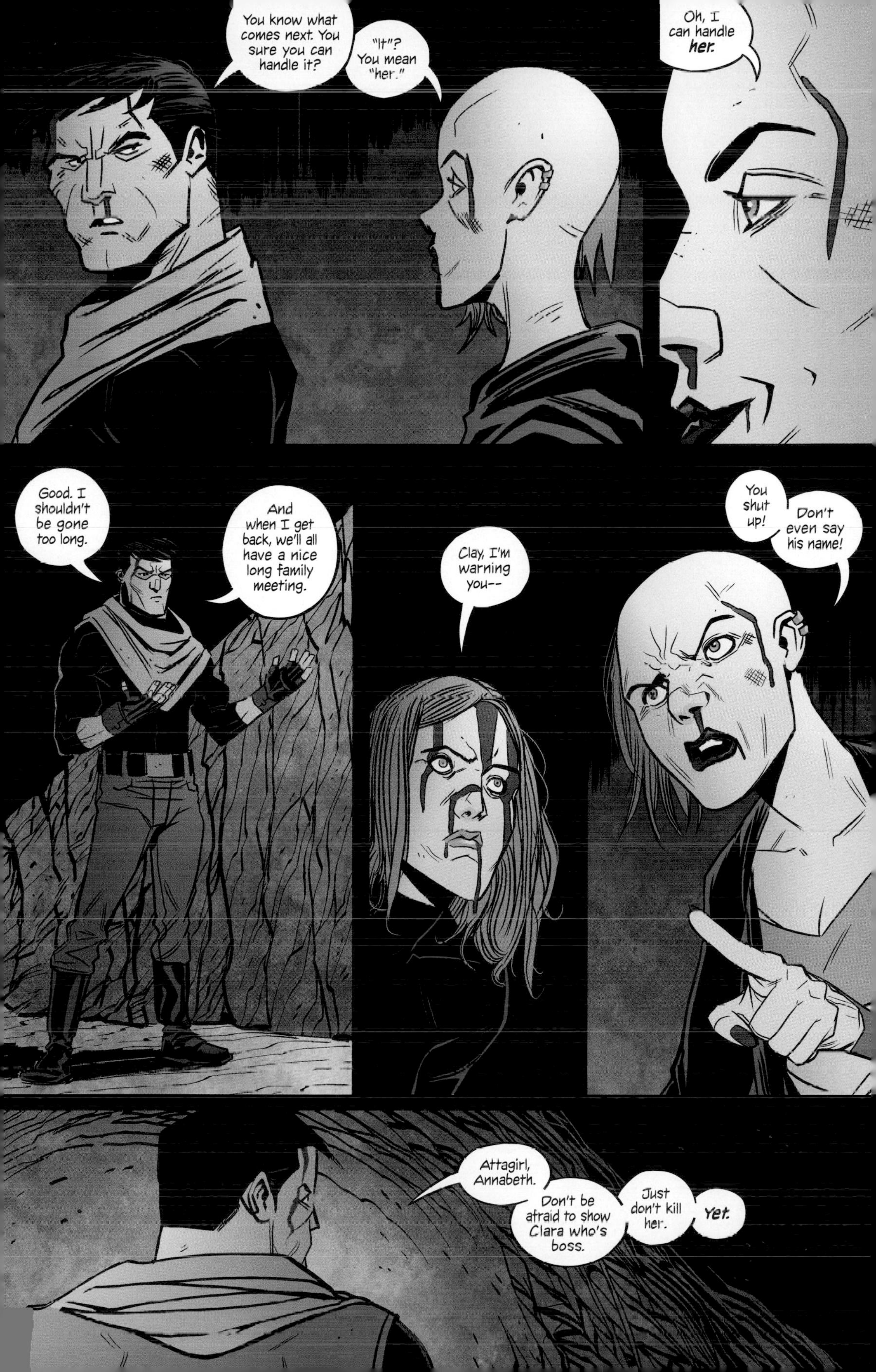
You know what comes next. You sure you can handle it?
"It"? You mean "her."
Oh, I can handle **her.**
Good. I shouldn't be gone too long.
And when I get back, we'll all have a nice long family meeting.
Clay, I'm warning you--
You shut up!
Don't even say his name!
Attagirl, Annabeth.
Don't be afraid to show Clara who's boss.
Just don't kill her.
Yet.

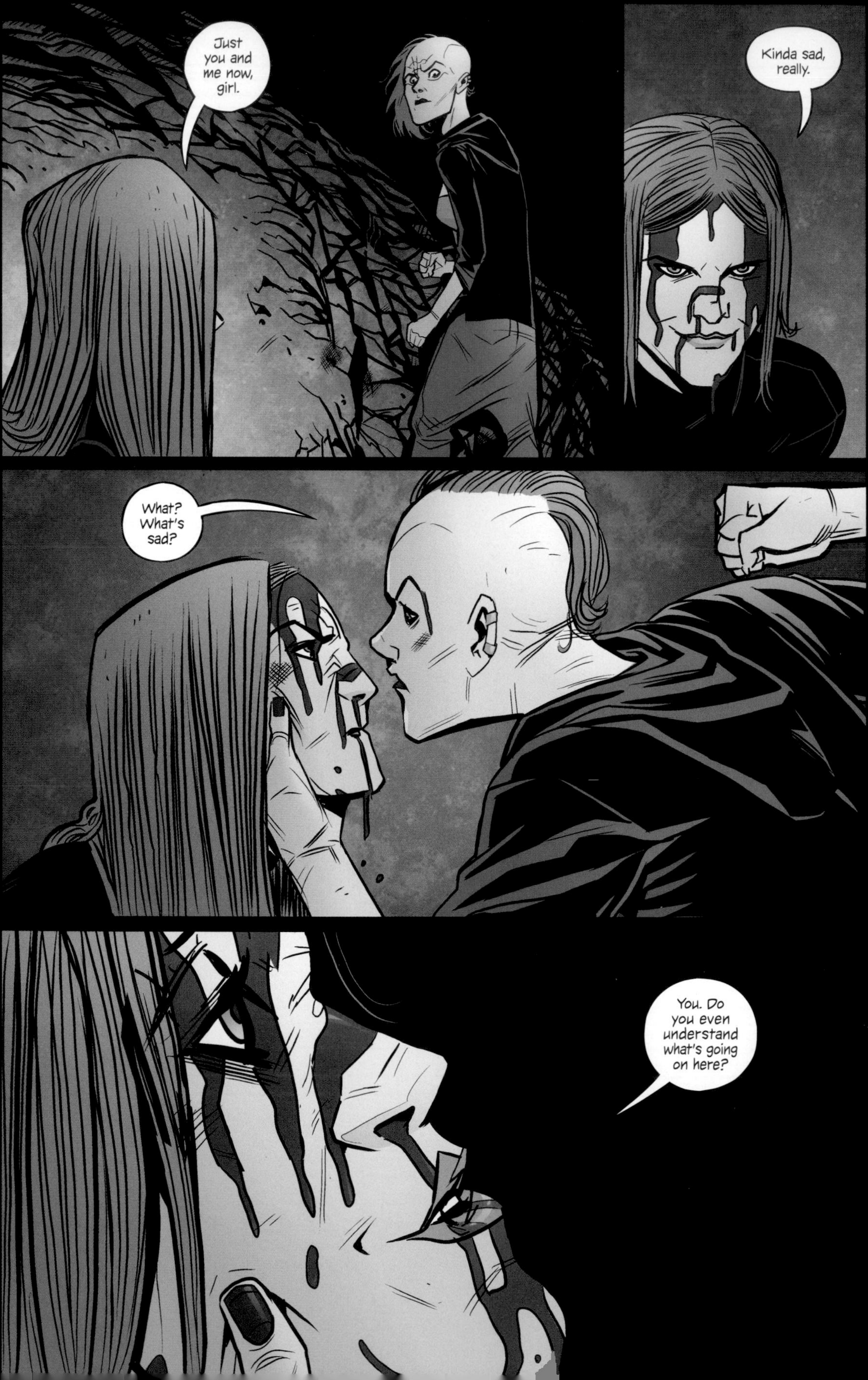
Just you and me now, girl.
Kinda sad, really.
What? What's sad?
You. Do you even understand what's going on here?

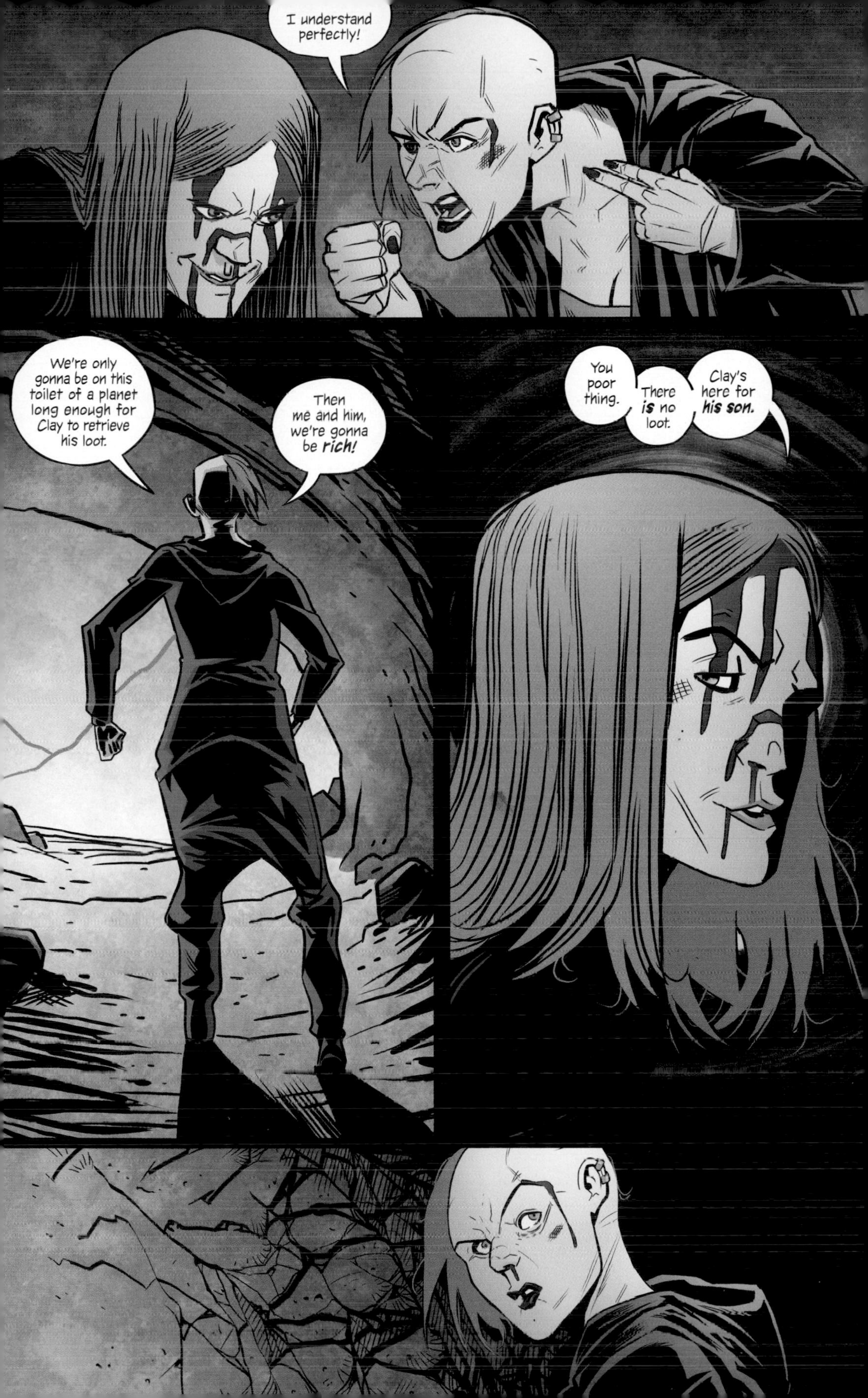
I understand perfectly!
We're only gonna be on this toilet of a planet long enough for Clay to retrieve his loot.
Then me and him, we're gonna be **rich!**
You poor thing.
There **is** no loot.
Clay's here for **his son.**

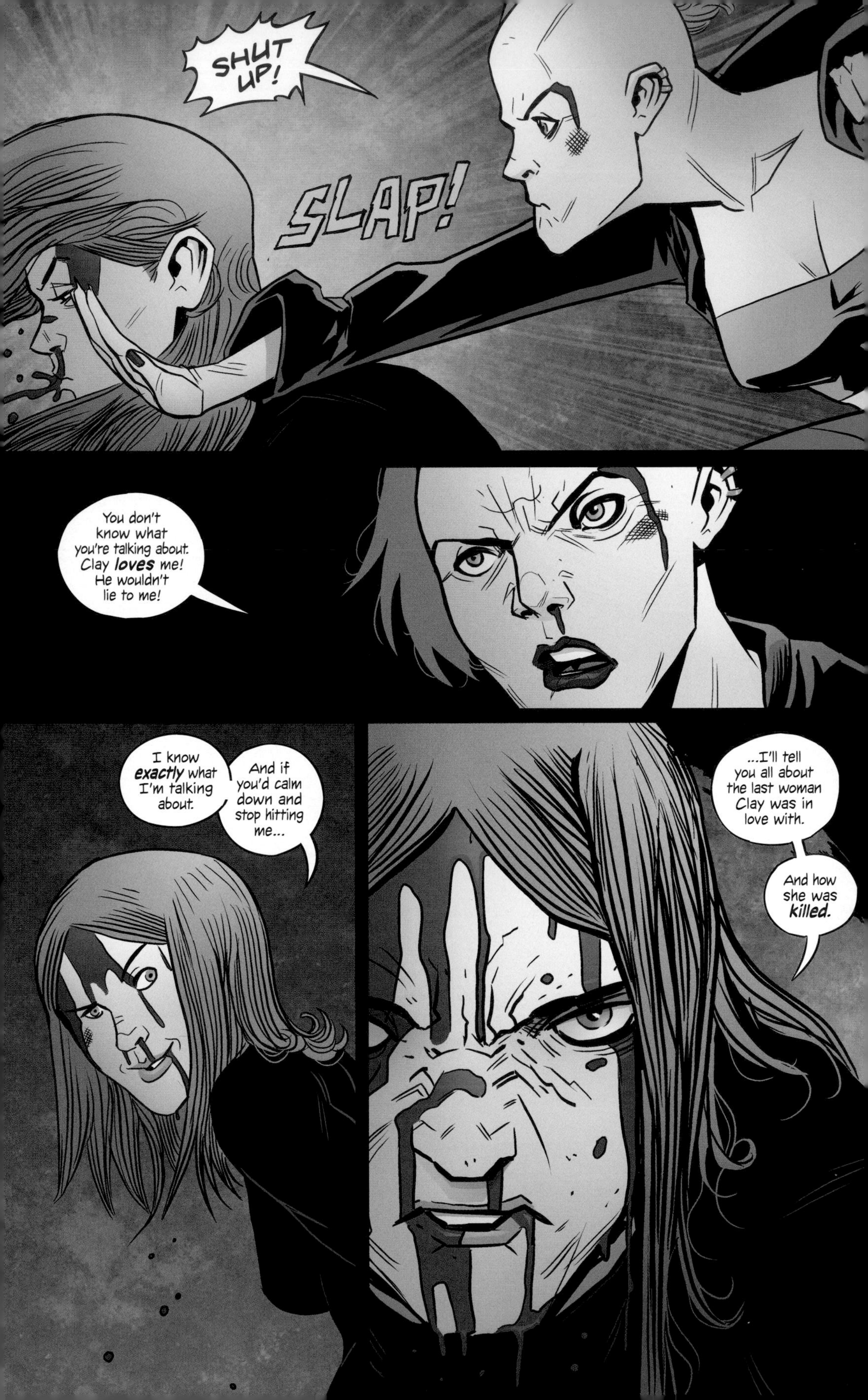
SHUT UP!
SLAP!
You don't know what you're talking about. Clay loves me! He wouldn't lie to me!
I know exactly what I'm talking about.
And if you'd calm down and stop hitting me...
...I'll tell you all about the last woman Clay was in love with.
And how she was killed.

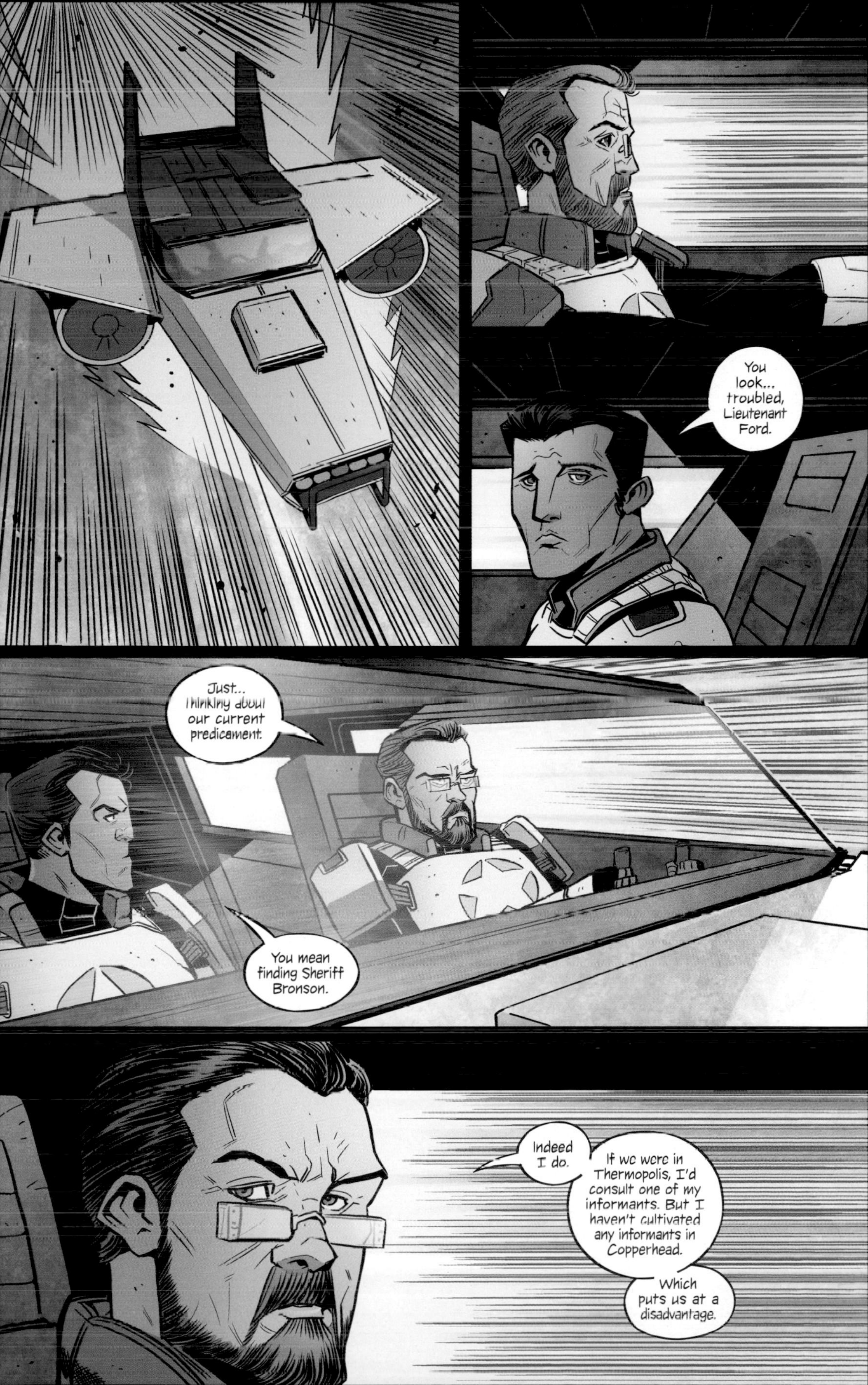
You look... troubled, Lieutenant Ford.
Just... thinking about our current predicament.
You mean finding Sheriff Bronson.
Indeed I do.
If we were in Thermopolis, I'd consult one of my informants. But I haven't cultivated any informants in Copperhead.
Which puts us at a disadvantage.

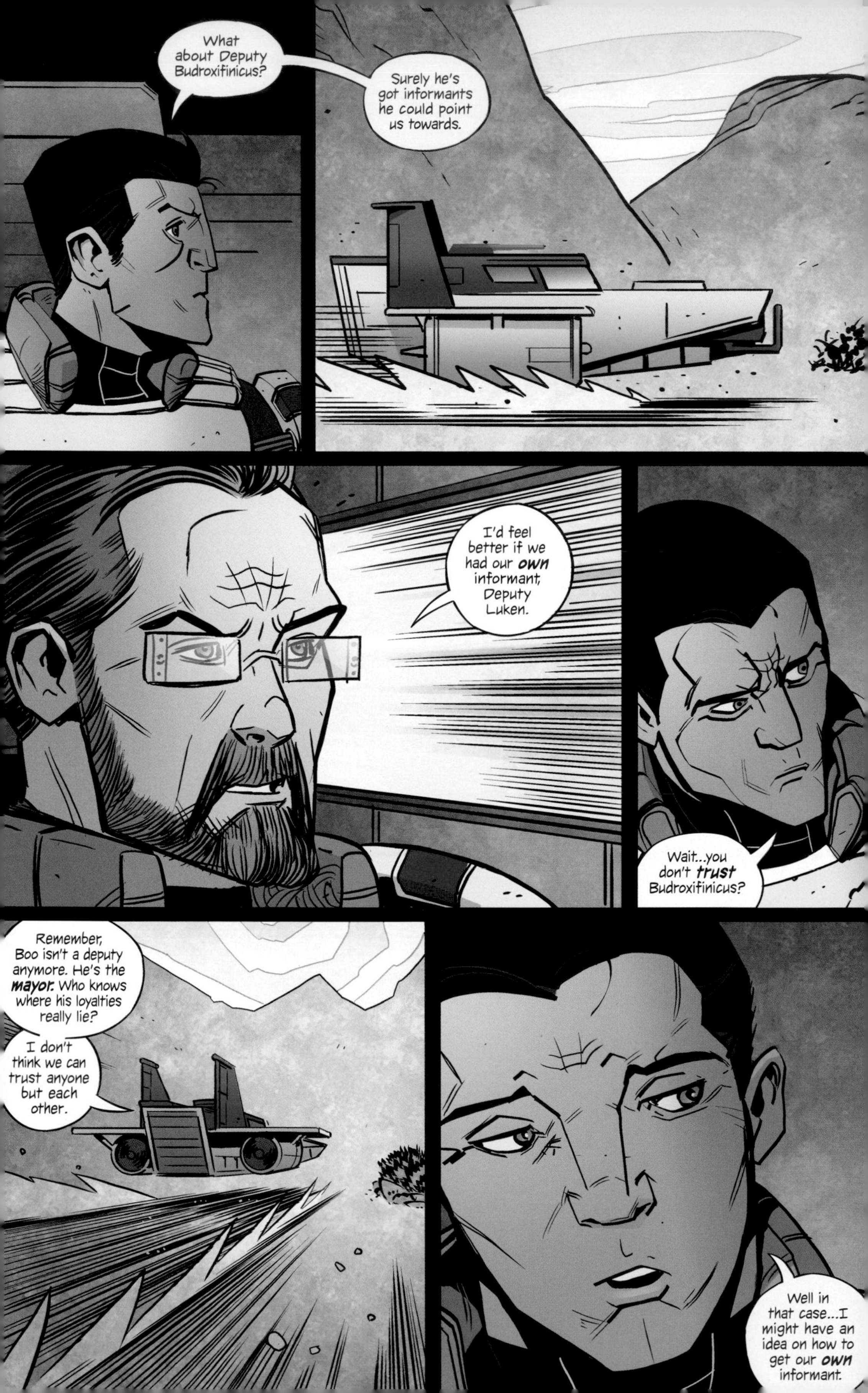
What about Deputy Budroxifinicus?
Surely he's got informants he could point us towards.
I'd feel better if we had our ***own*** informant, Deputy Luken.
Wait...you don't ***trust*** Budroxifinicus?
Remember, Boo isn't a deputy anymore. He's the ***mayor.*** Who knows where his loyalties really lie?
I don't think we can trust anyone but each other.
Well in that case...I might have an idea on how to get our ***own*** informant.

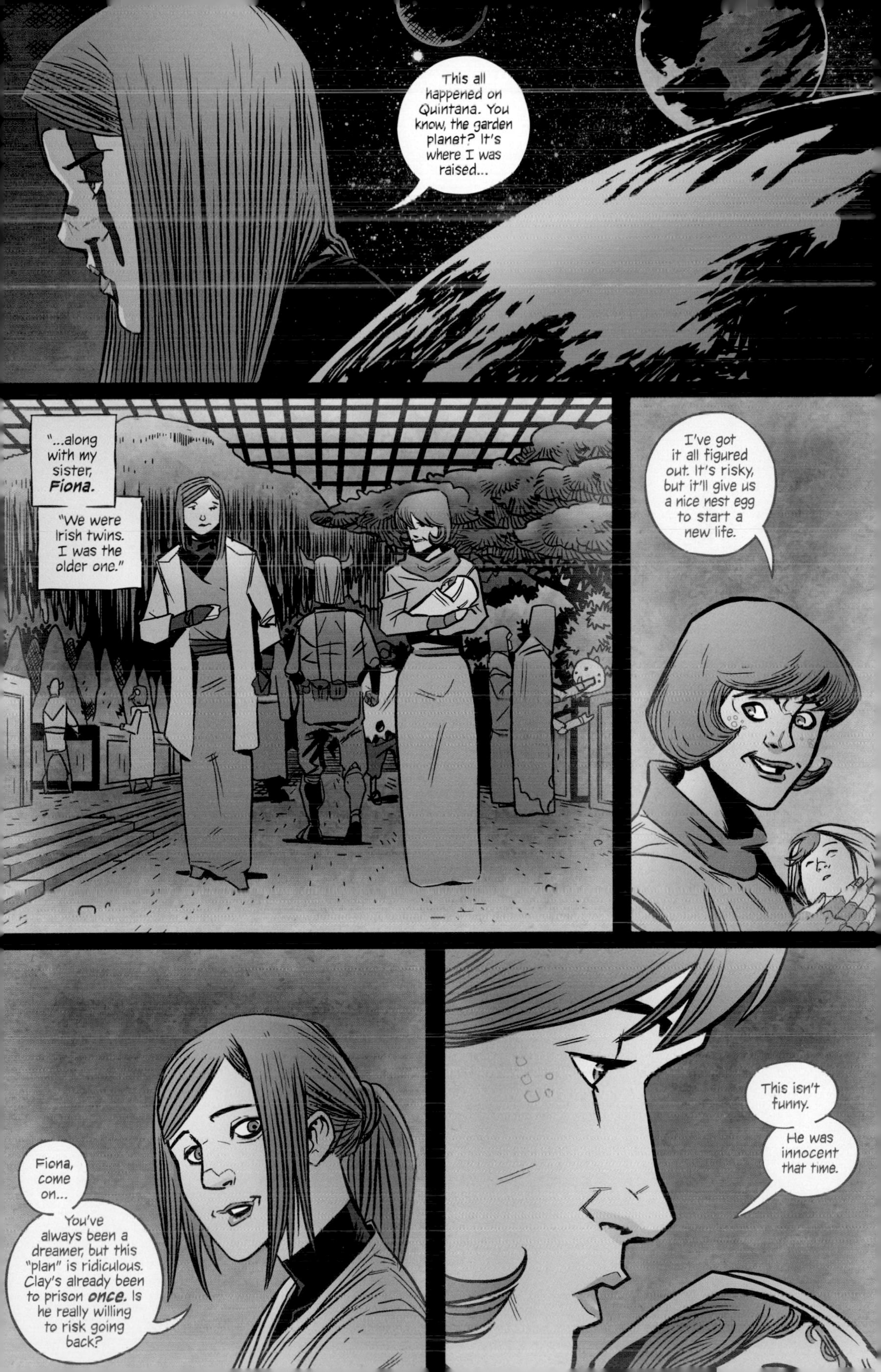
This all happened on Quintana. You know, the garden planet? It's where I was raised...
"...along with my sister, **Fiona.**
"We were Irish twins. I was the older one."
I've got it all figured out. It's risky, but it'll give us a nice nest egg to start a new life.
Fiona, come on...
You've always been a dreamer, but this "plan" is ridiculous. Clay's already been to prison **once.** Is he really willing to risk going back?
This isn't funny.
He was innocent that time.

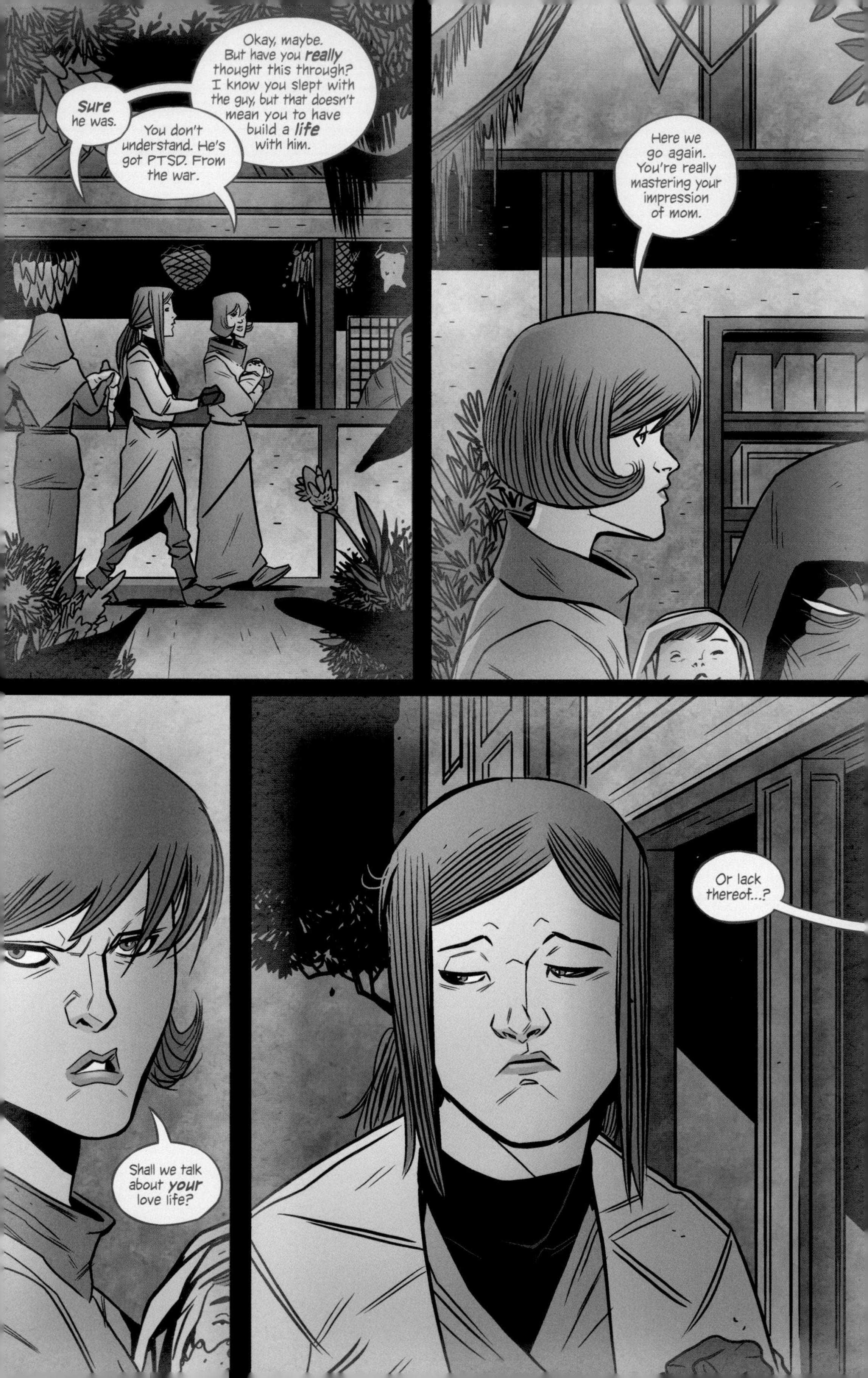
Okay, maybe. But have you **really** thought this through? I know you slept with the guy, but that doesn't mean you to have build a **life** with him.
Sure he was.
You don't understand. He's got PTSD. From the war.
Here we go again. You're really mastering your impression of mom.
Shall we talk about **your** love life?
Or lack thereof...?

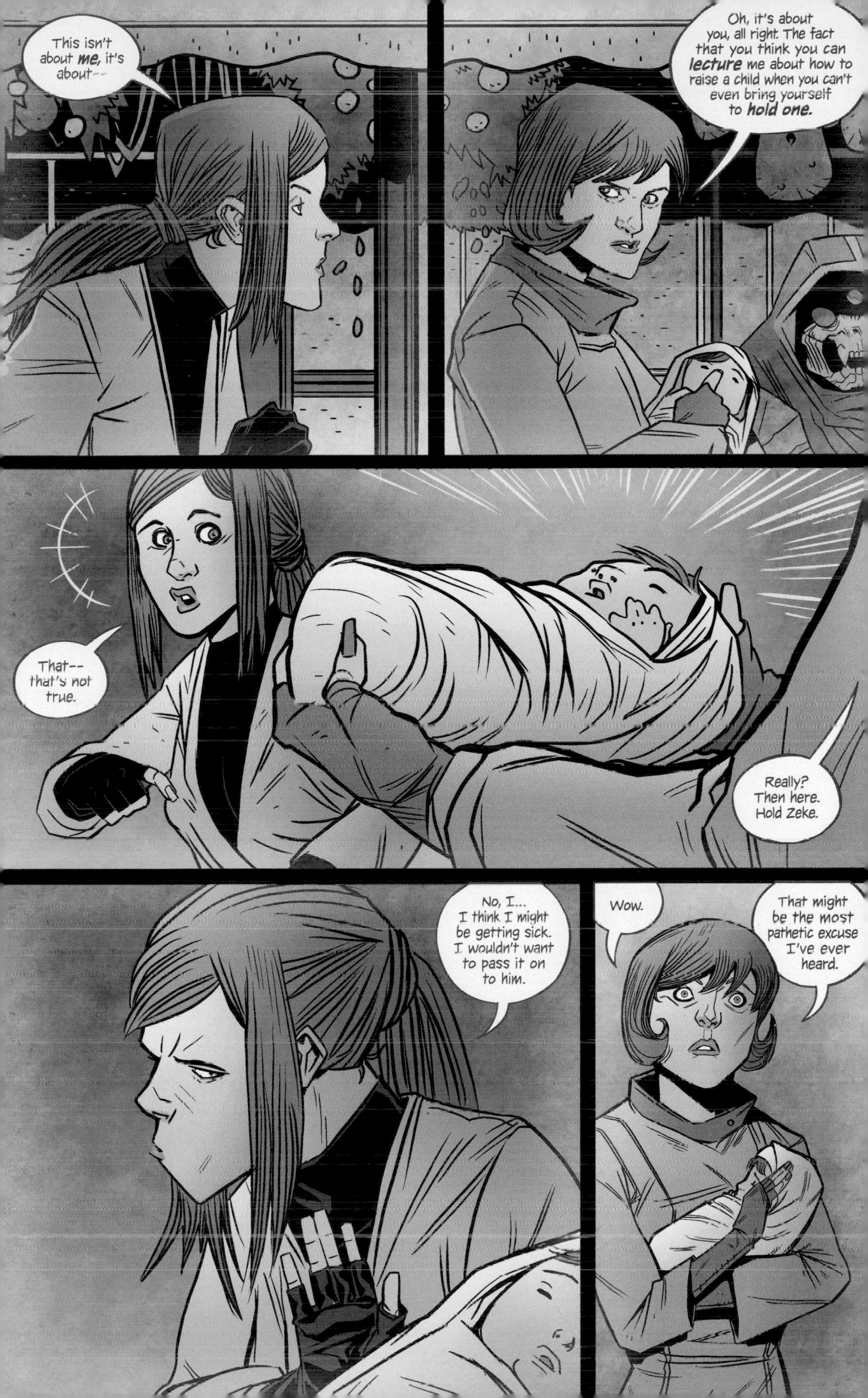
This isn't about **me,** it's about--
Oh, it's about you, all right. The fact that you think you can **lecture** me about how to raise a child when you can't even bring yourself to **hold one.**
That-- that's not true.
Really? Then here. Hold Zeke.
No, I... I think I might be getting sick. I wouldn't want to pass it on to him.
Wow.
That might be the most pathetic excuse I've ever heard.

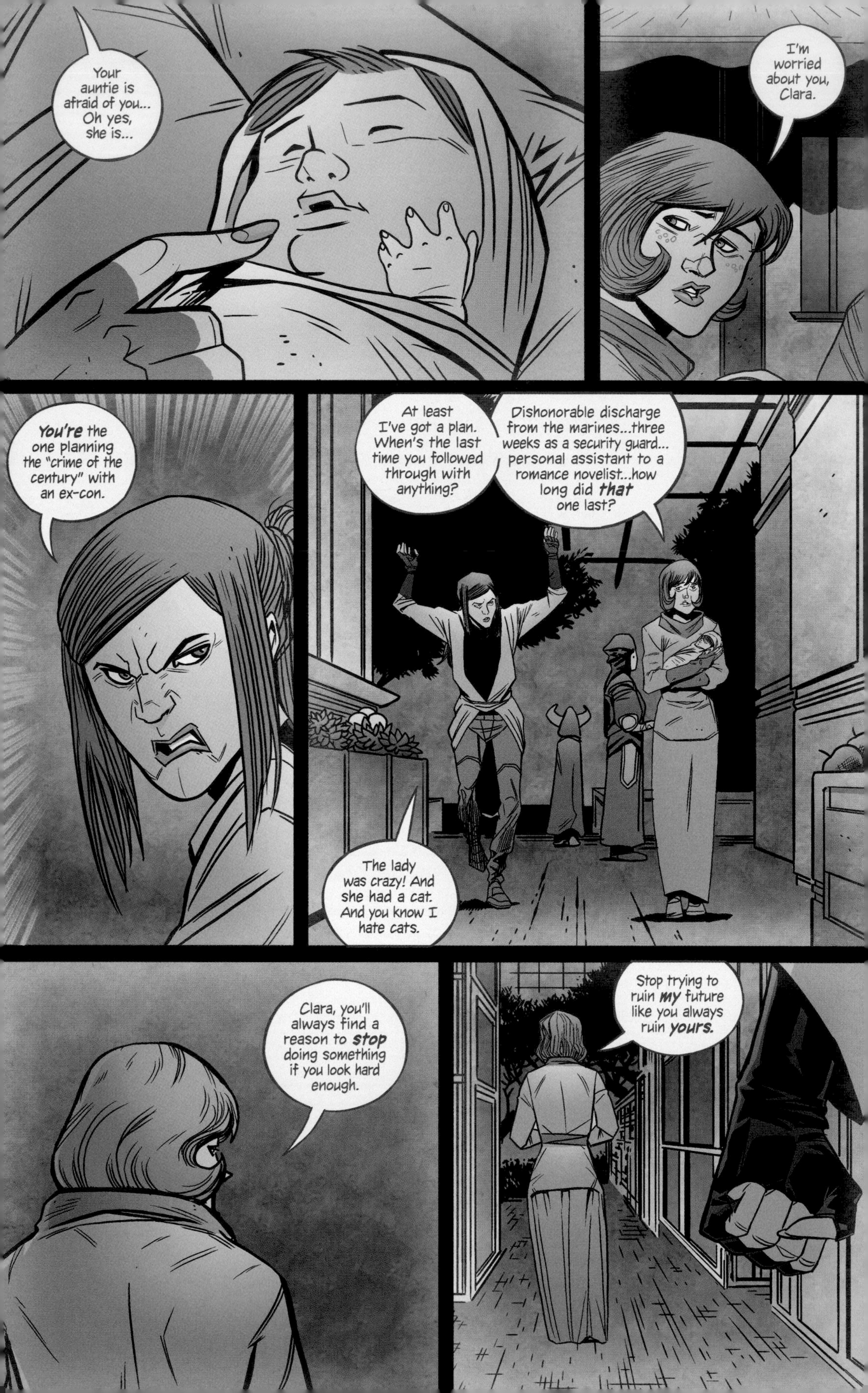
Your auntie is afraid of you... Oh yes, she is...
I'm worried about you, Clara.
You're the one planning the "crime of the century" with an ex-con.
At least I've got a plan. When's the last time you followed through with anything?
Dishonorable discharge from the marines...three weeks as a security guard... personal assistant to a romance novelist...how long did that one last?
The lady was crazy! And she had a cat. And you know I hate cats.
Clara, you'll always find a reason to stop doing something if you look hard enough.
Stop trying to ruin my future like you always ruin yours.

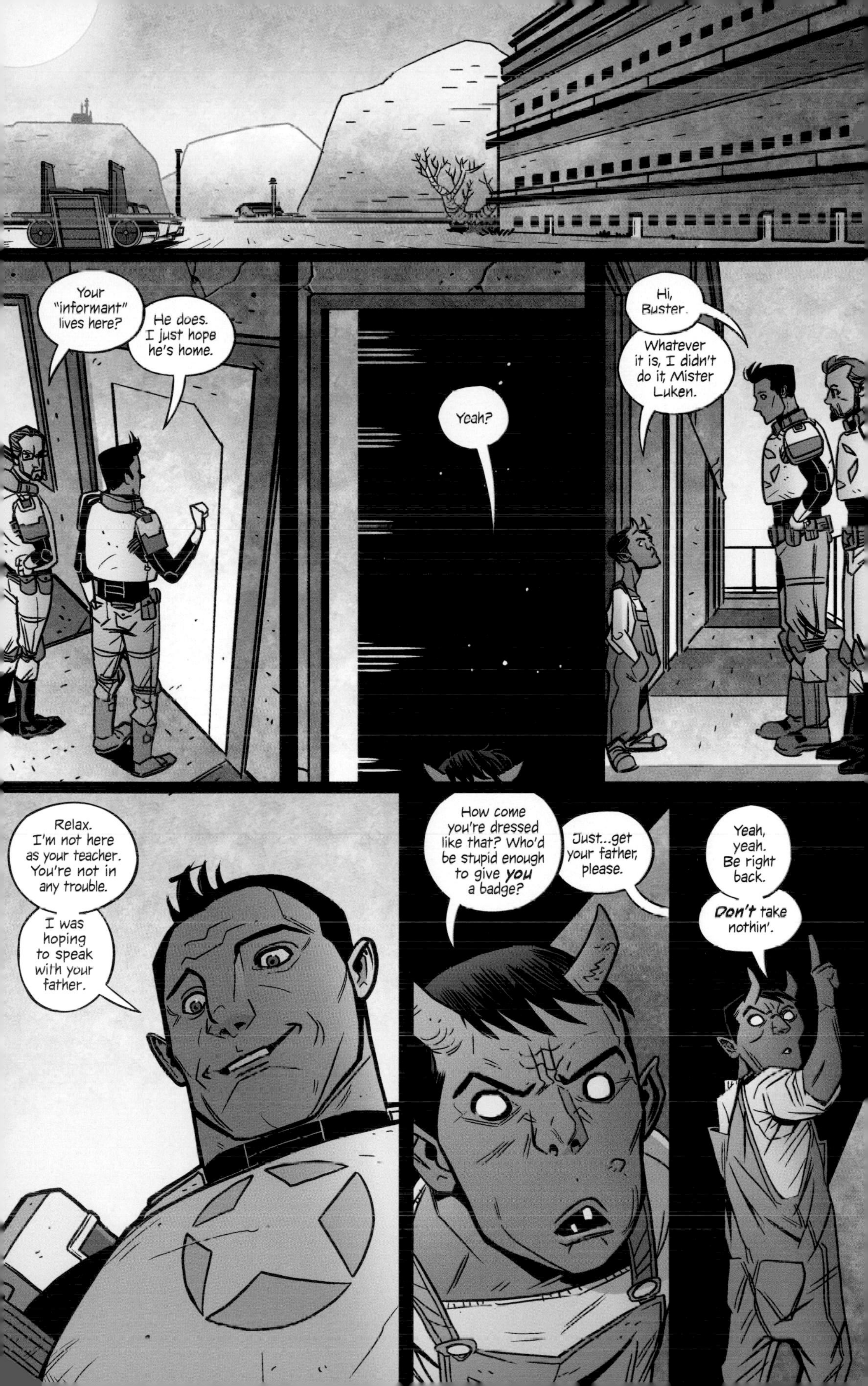
Your "informant" lives here?
He does. I just hope he's home.
Yeah?
Hi, Buster.
Whatever it is, I didn't do it, Mister Luken.
Relax. I'm not here as your teacher. You're not in any trouble.
I was hoping to speak with your father.
How come you're dressed like that? Who'd be stupid enough to give *you* a badge?
Just...get your father, please.
Yeah, yeah. Be right back.
Don't take nothin'.

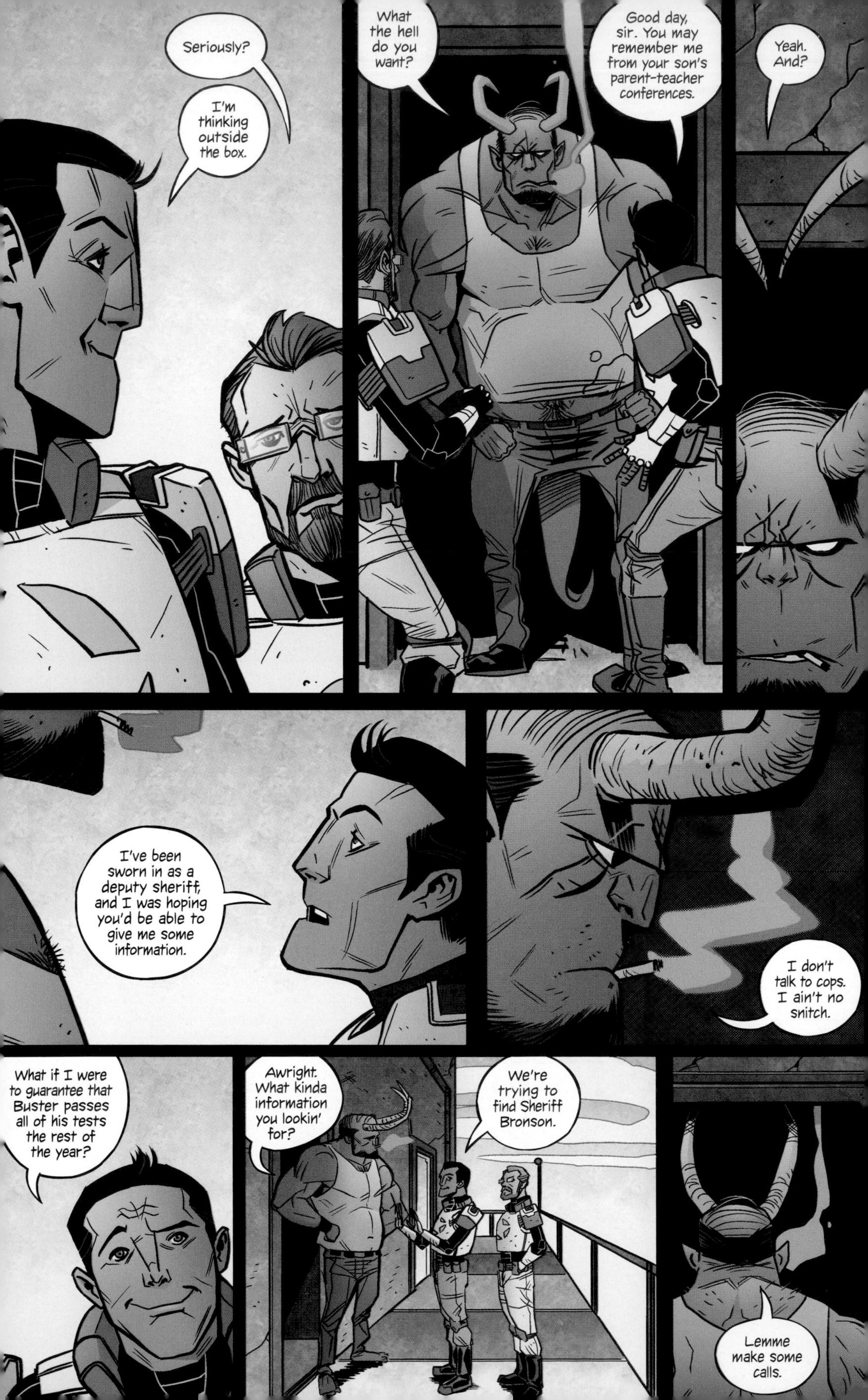
Seriously?
I'm thinking outside the box.
What the hell do you want?
Good day, sir. You may remember me from your son's parent-teacher conferences.
Yeah. And?
I've been sworn in as a deputy sheriff, and I was hoping you'd be able to give me some information.
I don't talk to cops. I ain't no snitch.
What if I were to guarantee that Buster passes all of his tests the rest of the year?
Awright. What kinda information you lookin' for?
We're trying to find Sheriff Bronson.
Lemme make some calls.

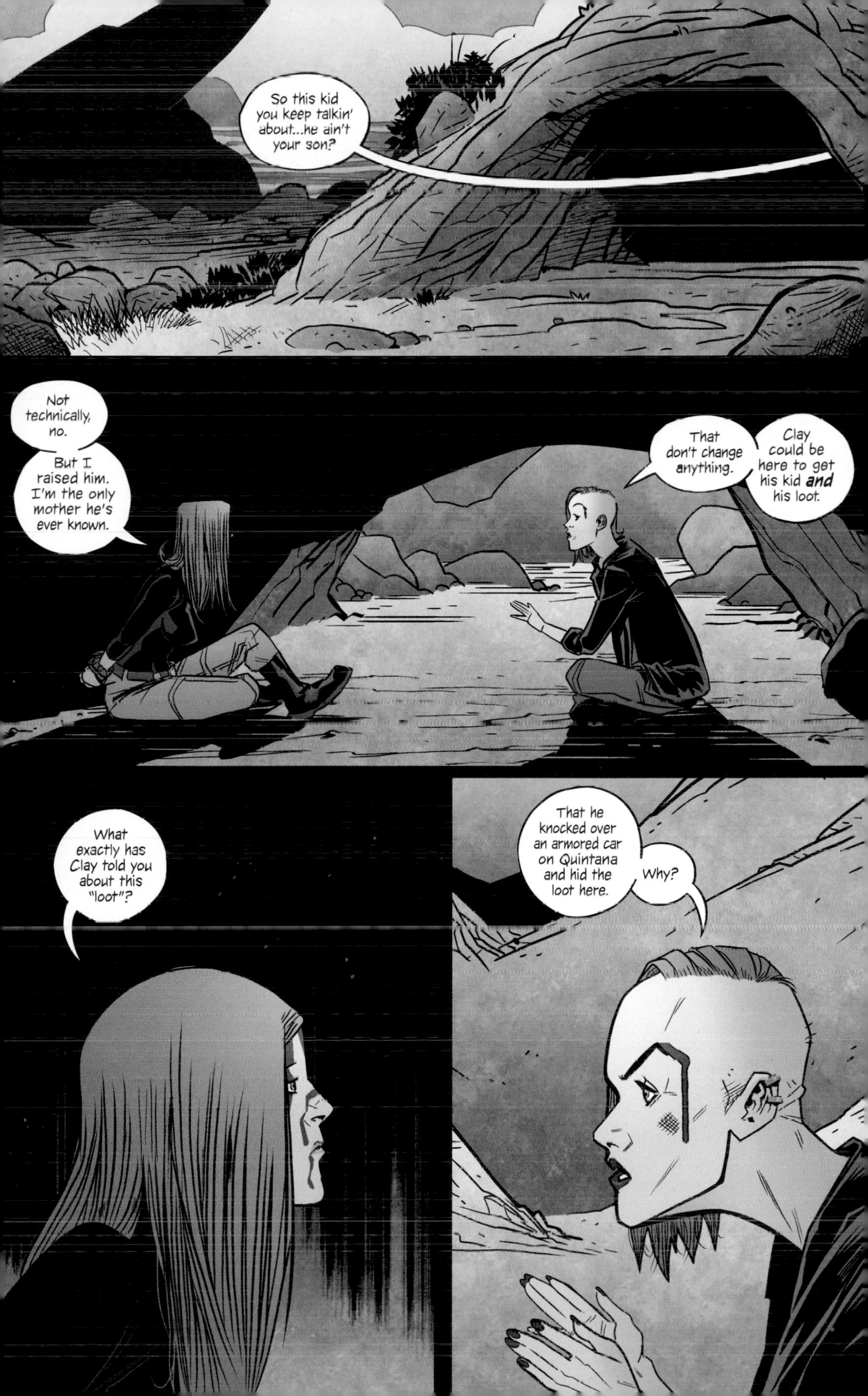
So this kid you keep talkin' about...he ain't your son?
Not technically, no.
But I raised him. I'm the only mother he's ever known.
That don't change anything.
Clay could be here to get his kid **and** his loot.
What exactly has Clay told you about this "loot"?
That he knocked over an armored car on Quintana and hid the loot here.
Why?

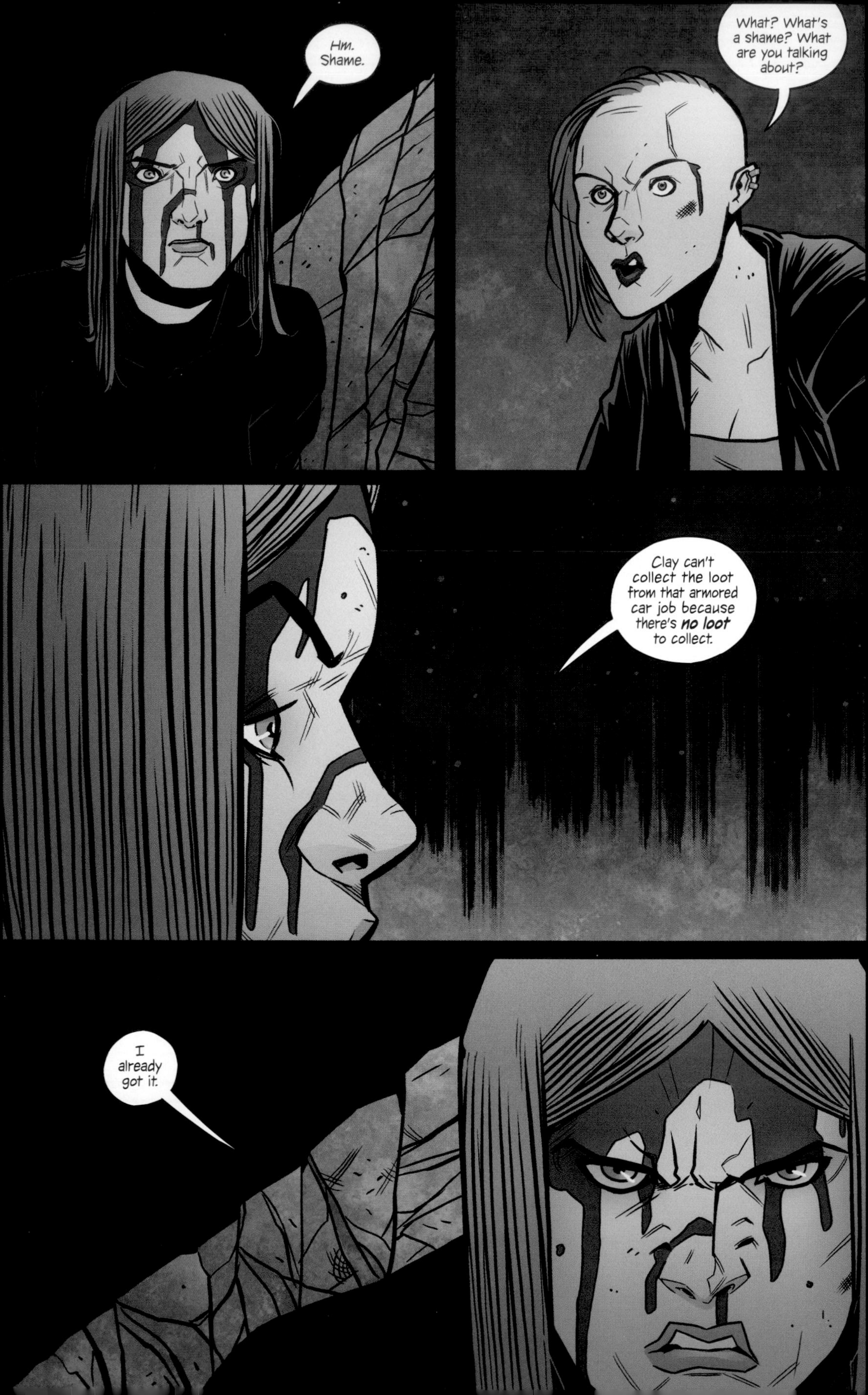
Hm. Shame.
What? What's a shame? What are you talking about?
Clay can't collect the loot from that armored car job because there's **no loot** to collect.
I already got it.

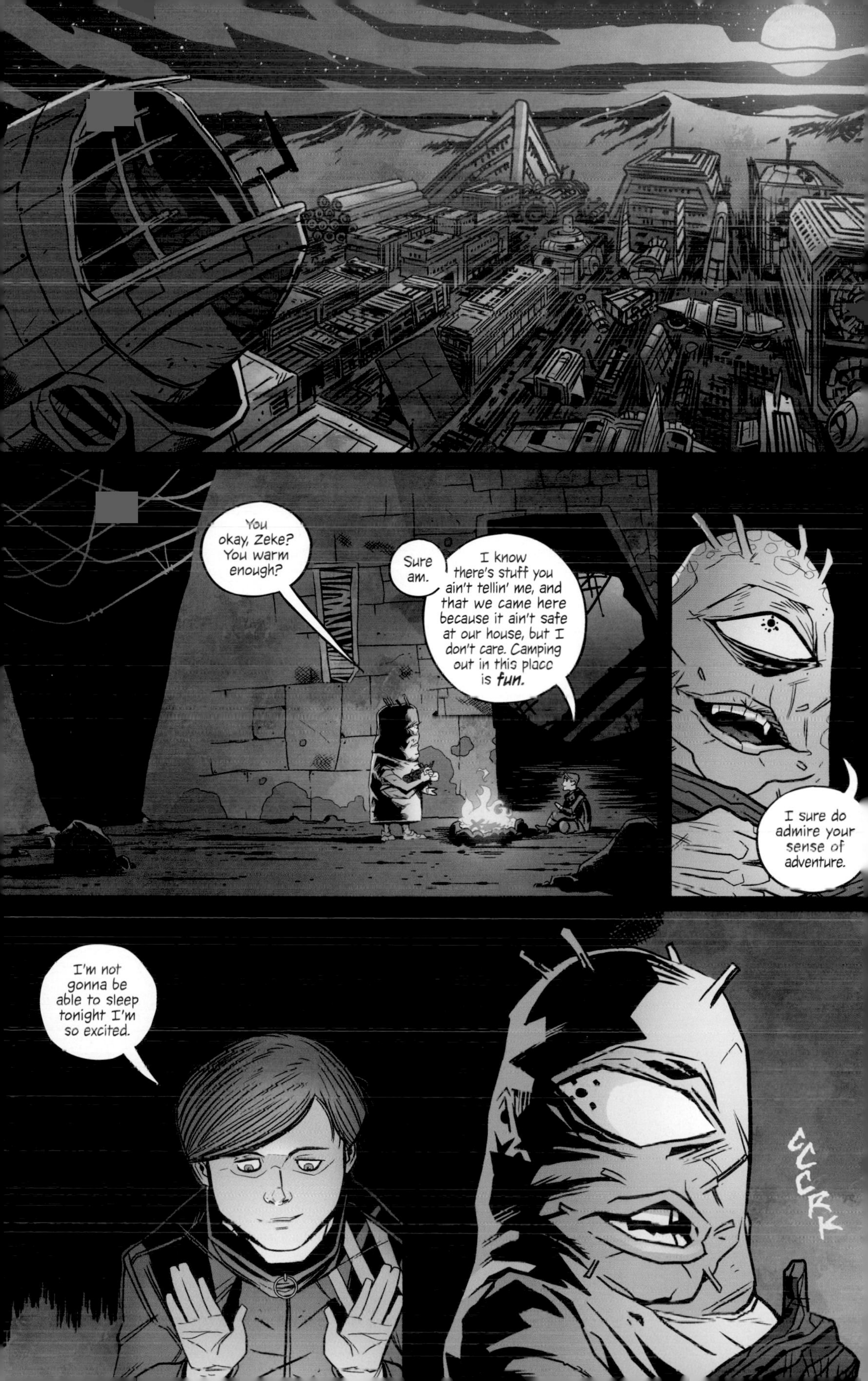
You okay, Zeke? You warm enough?
Sure am.
I know there's stuff you ain't tellin' me, and that we came here because it ain't safe at our house, but I don't care. Camping out in this place is fun.
I sure do admire your sense of adventure.
I'm not gonna be able to sleep tonight I'm so excited.
GCCRK

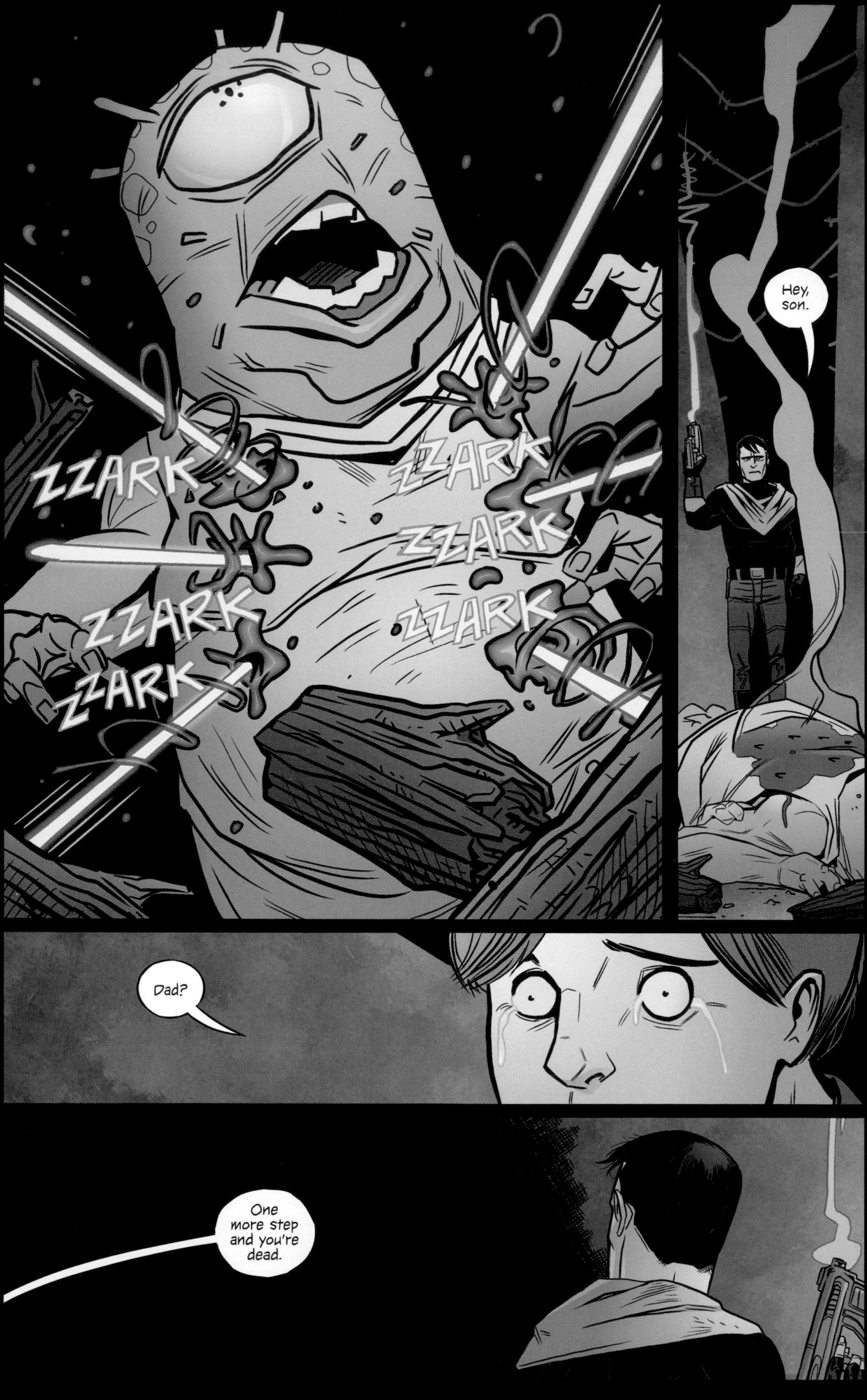
ZZARK
ZZARK
ZZARK
ZZARK
ZZARK
ZZARK
Hey, son.
Dad?
One more step and you're dead.

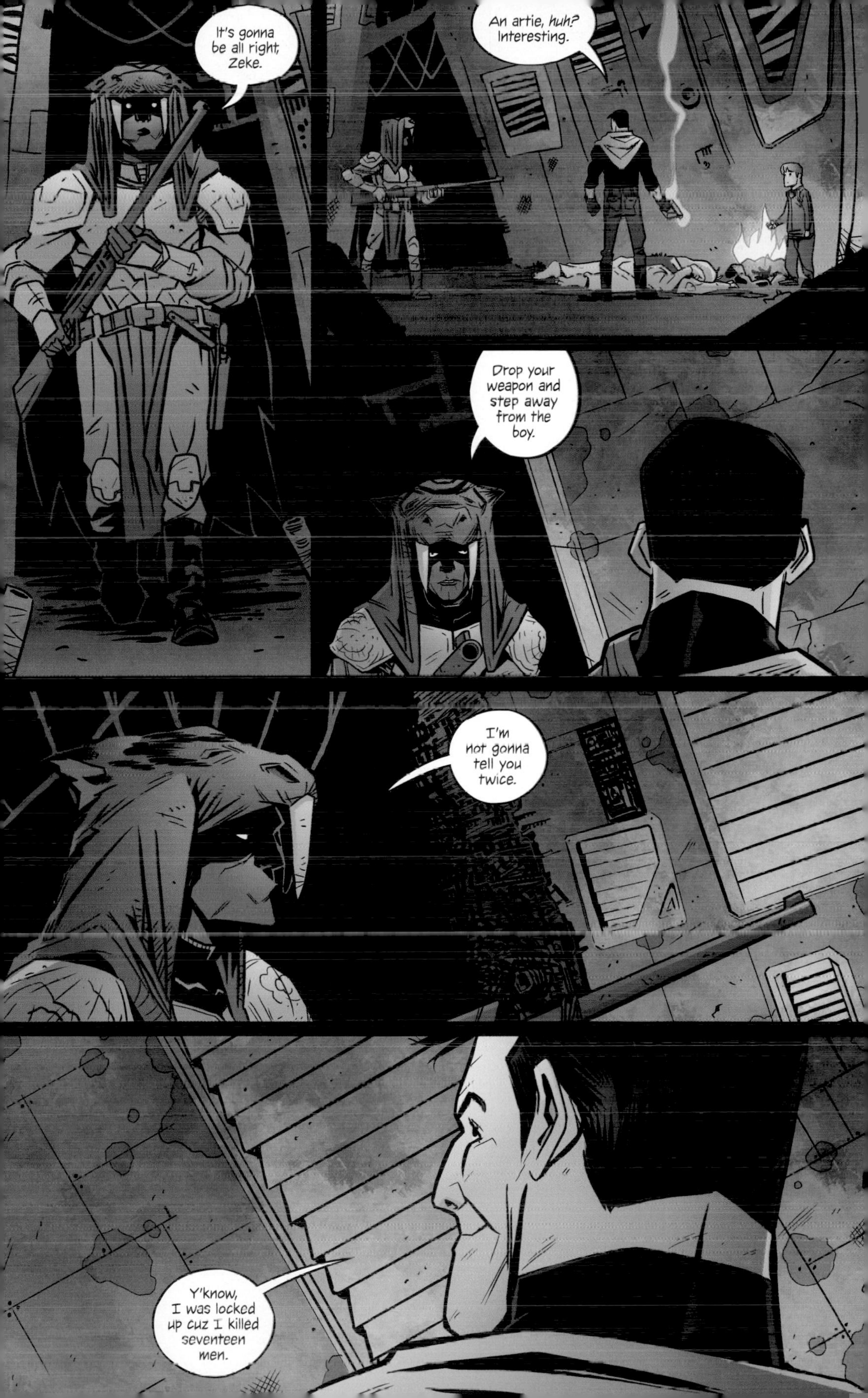
It's gonna be all right, Zeke.
An artie, *huh?* Interesting.
Drop your weapon and step away from the boy.
I'm not gonna tell you twice.
Y'know, I was locked up cuz I killed seventeen men.

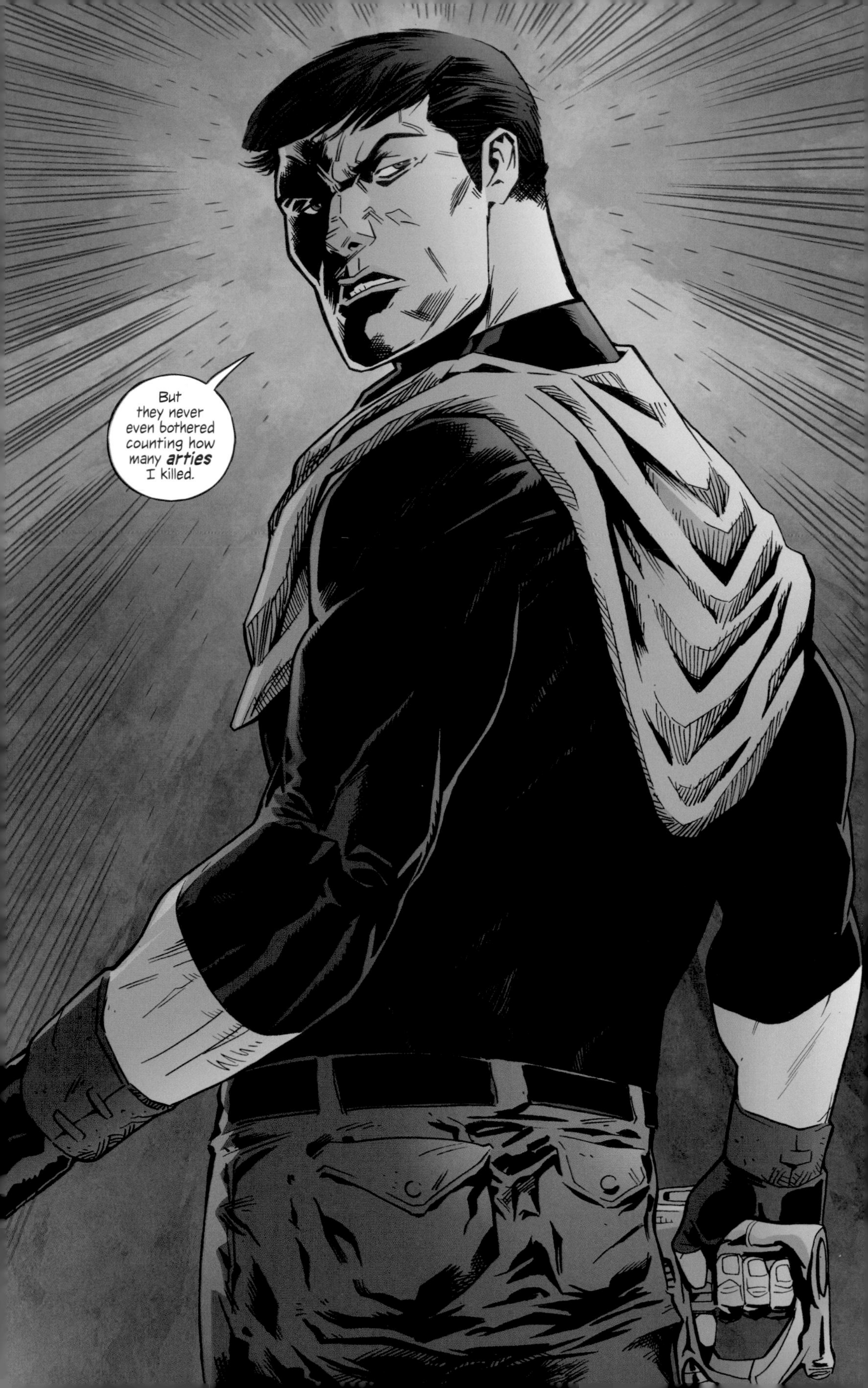
But they never even bothered counting how many **arties** I killed.

CHAPTER III

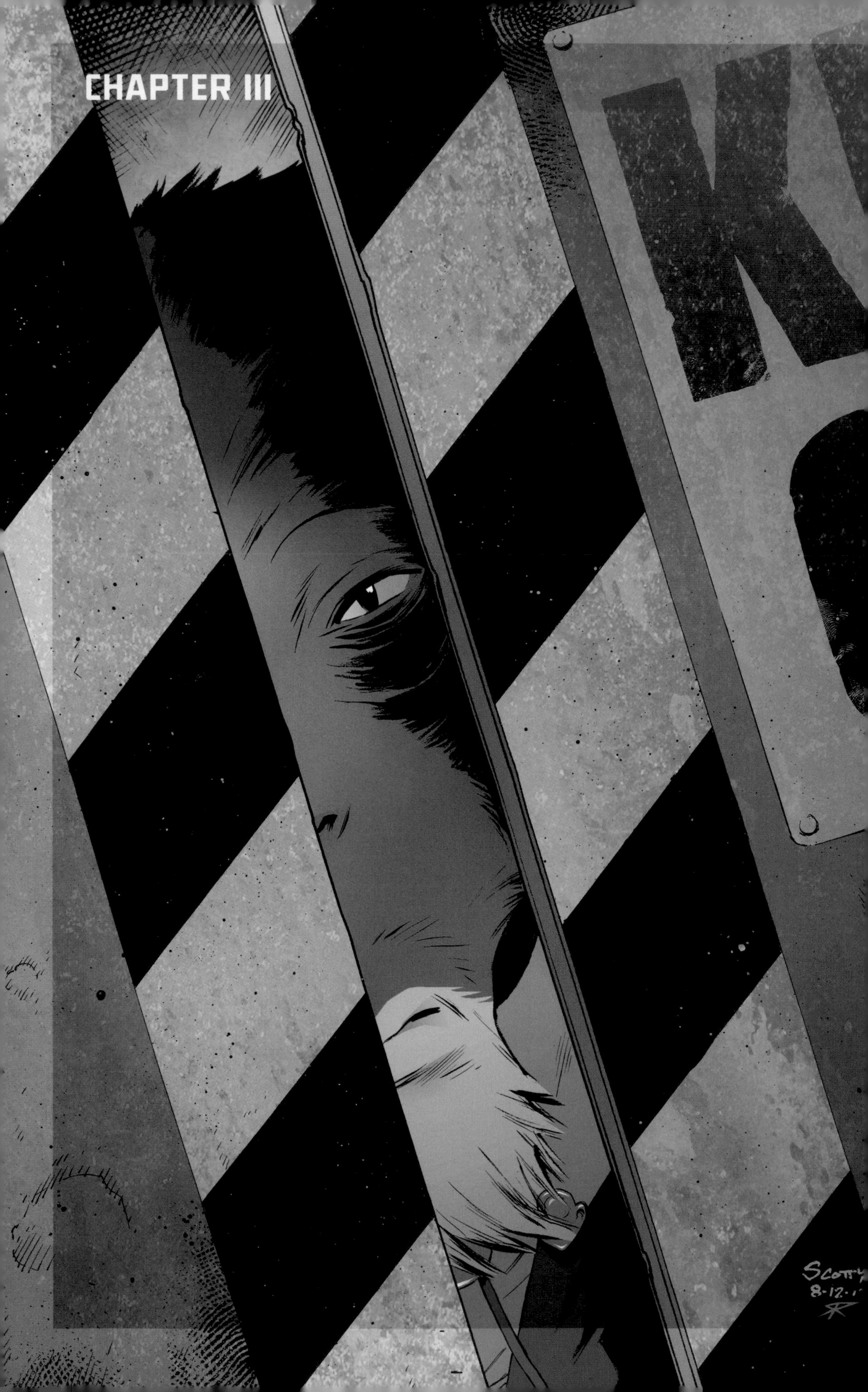

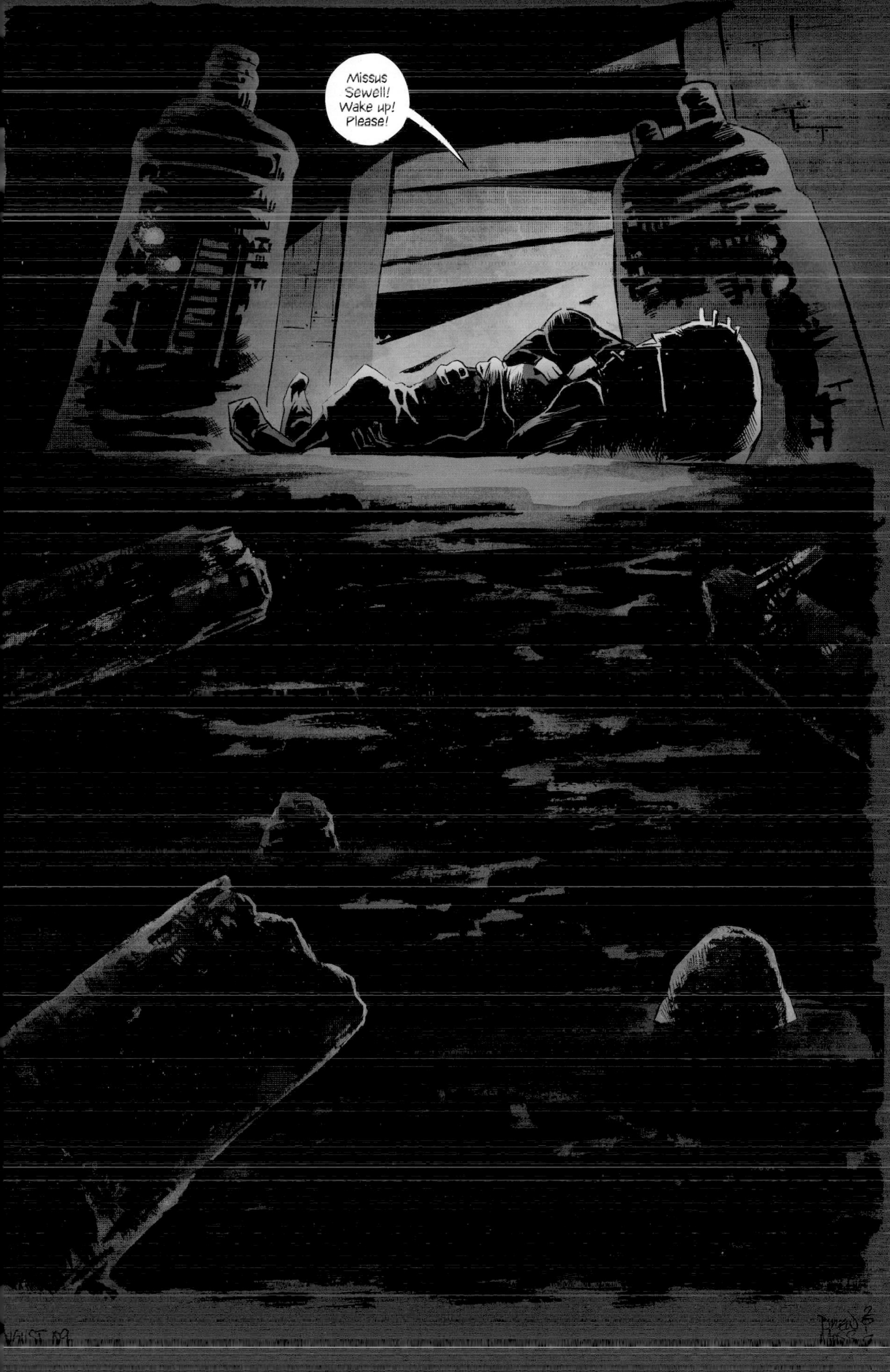
Missus Sewell! Wake up! Please!

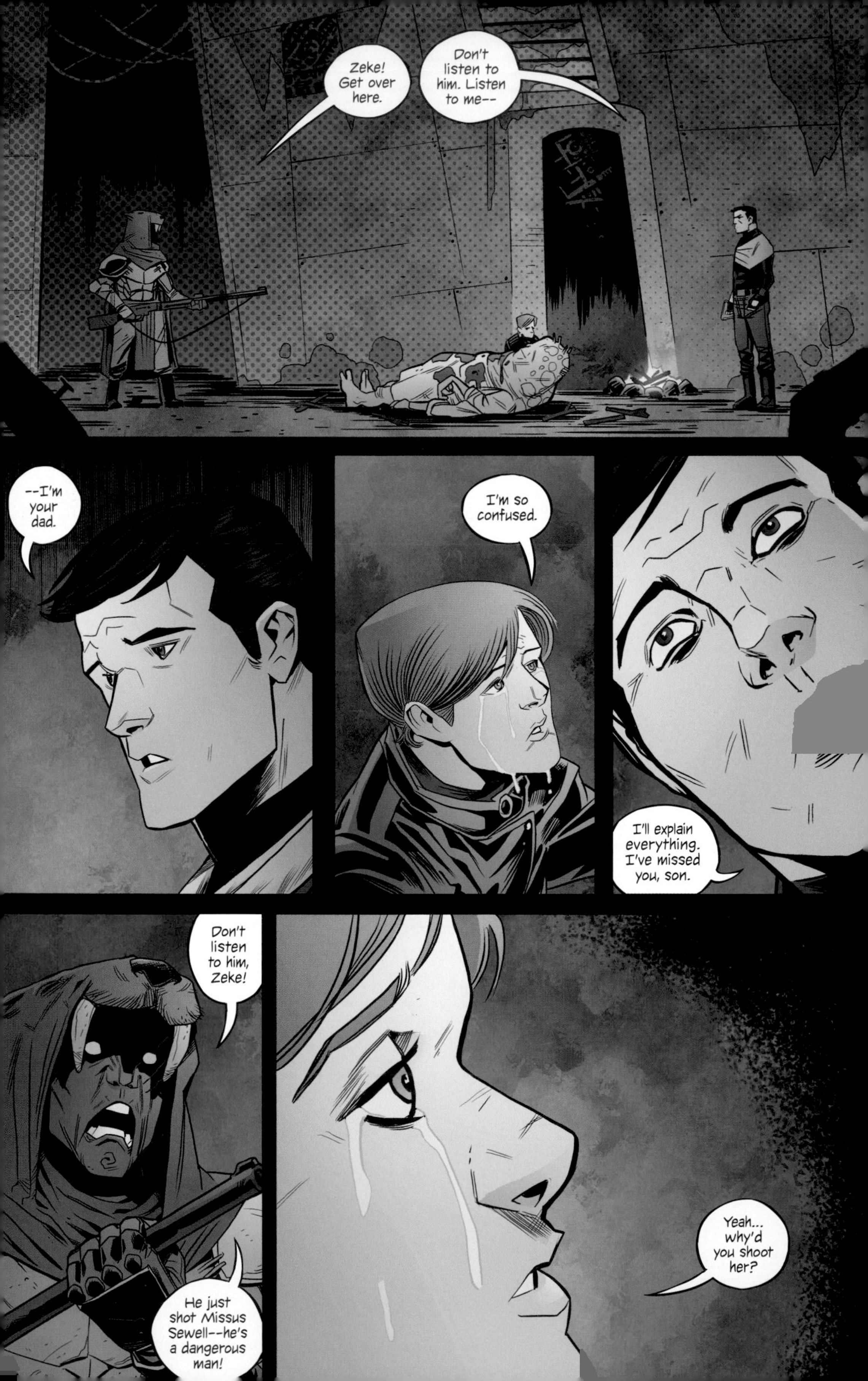
Zeke! Get over here.
Don't listen to him. Listen to me--
--I'm your dad.
I'm so confused.
I'll explain everything. I've missed you, son.
Don't listen to him, Zeke!
He just shot Missus Sewell--he's a dangerous man!
Yeah... why'd you shoot her?

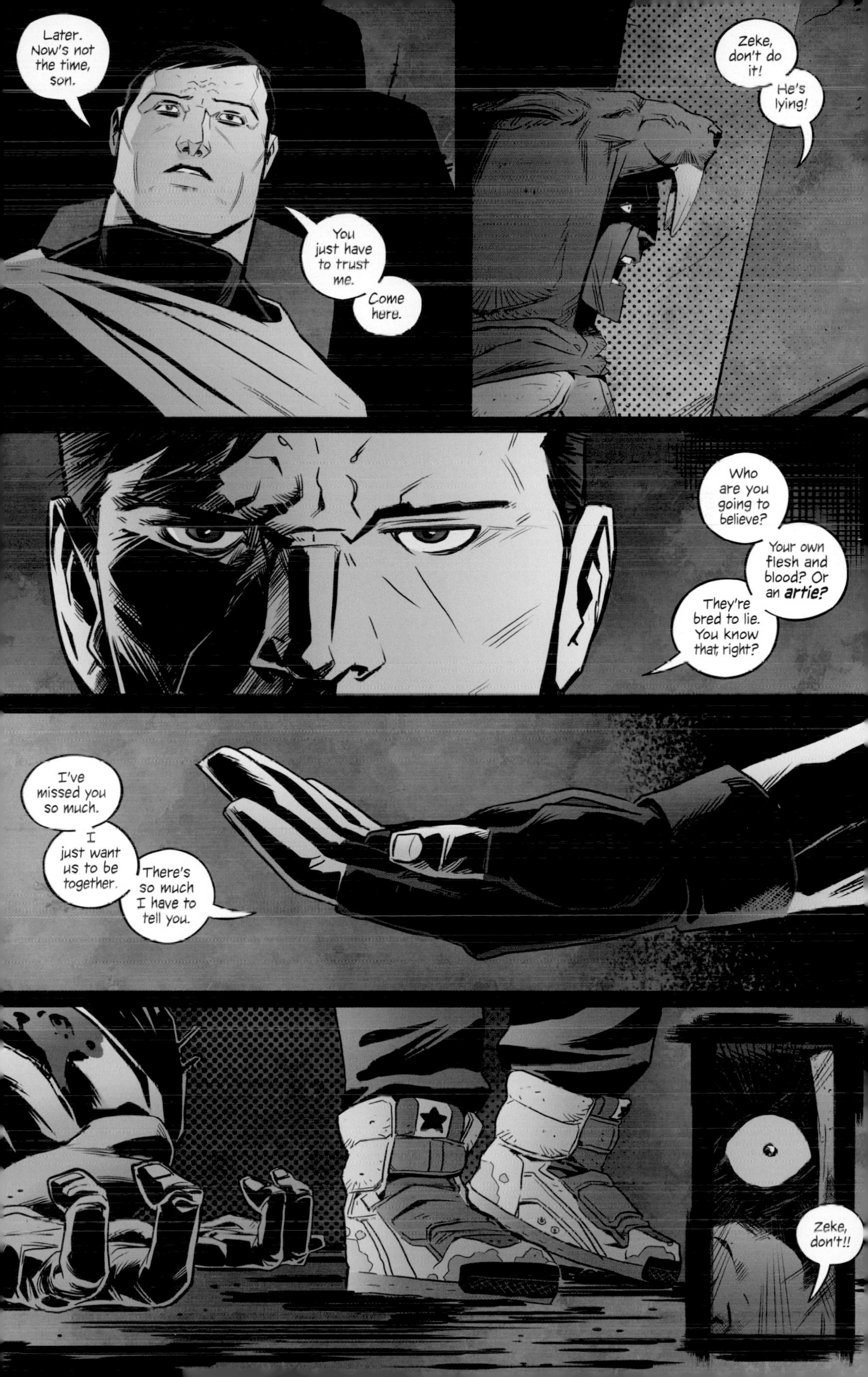
Later. Now's not the time, son.
You just have to trust me.
Come here.
Zeke, don't do it!
He's lying!
Who are you going to believe?
Your own flesh and blood? Or an ***artie?***
They're bred to lie. You know that, right?
I've missed you so much.
I just want us to be together.
There's so much I have to tell you.
Zeke, don't!!

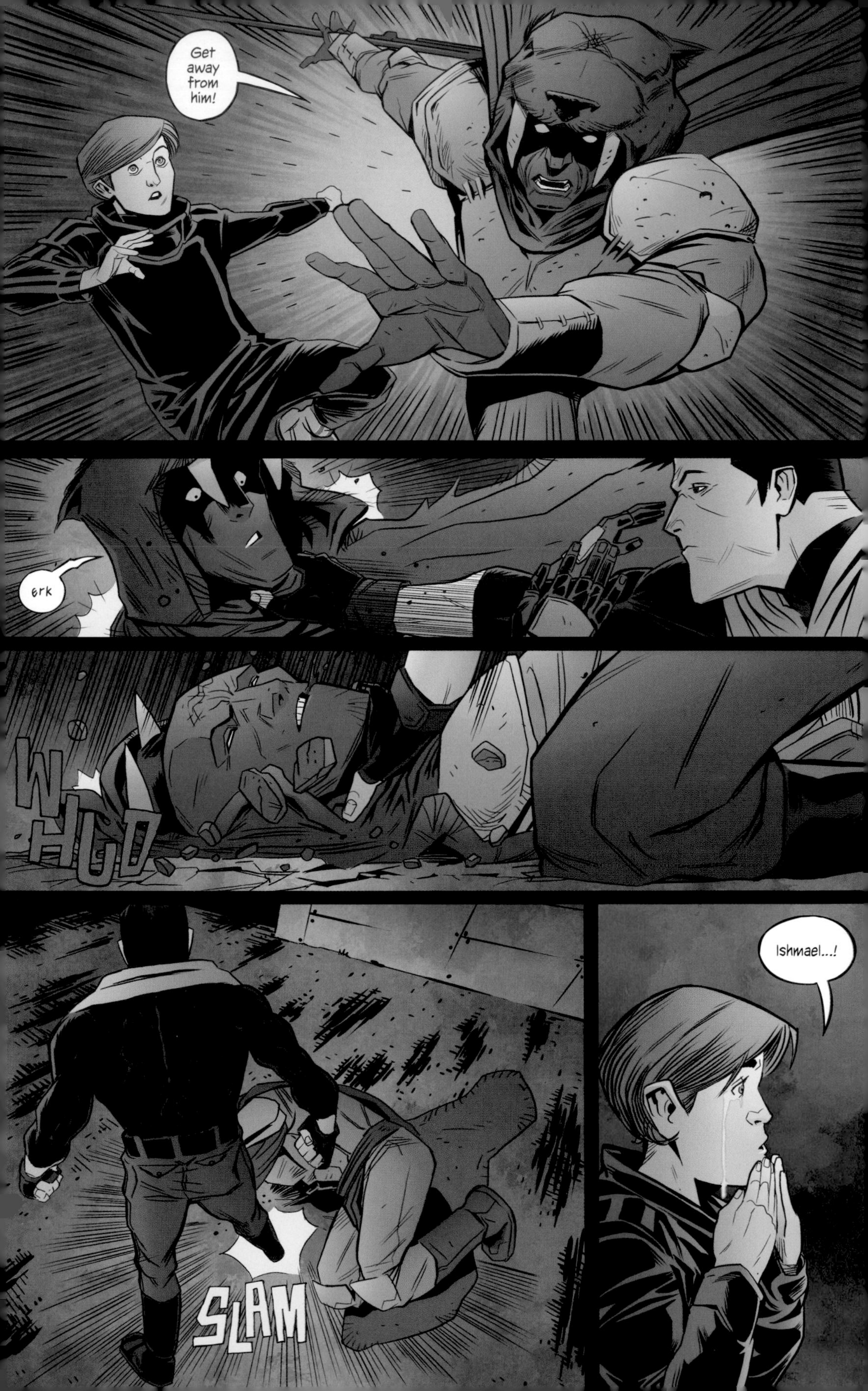
Get away from him!
Erk
WHUD
SLAM
Ishmael...!

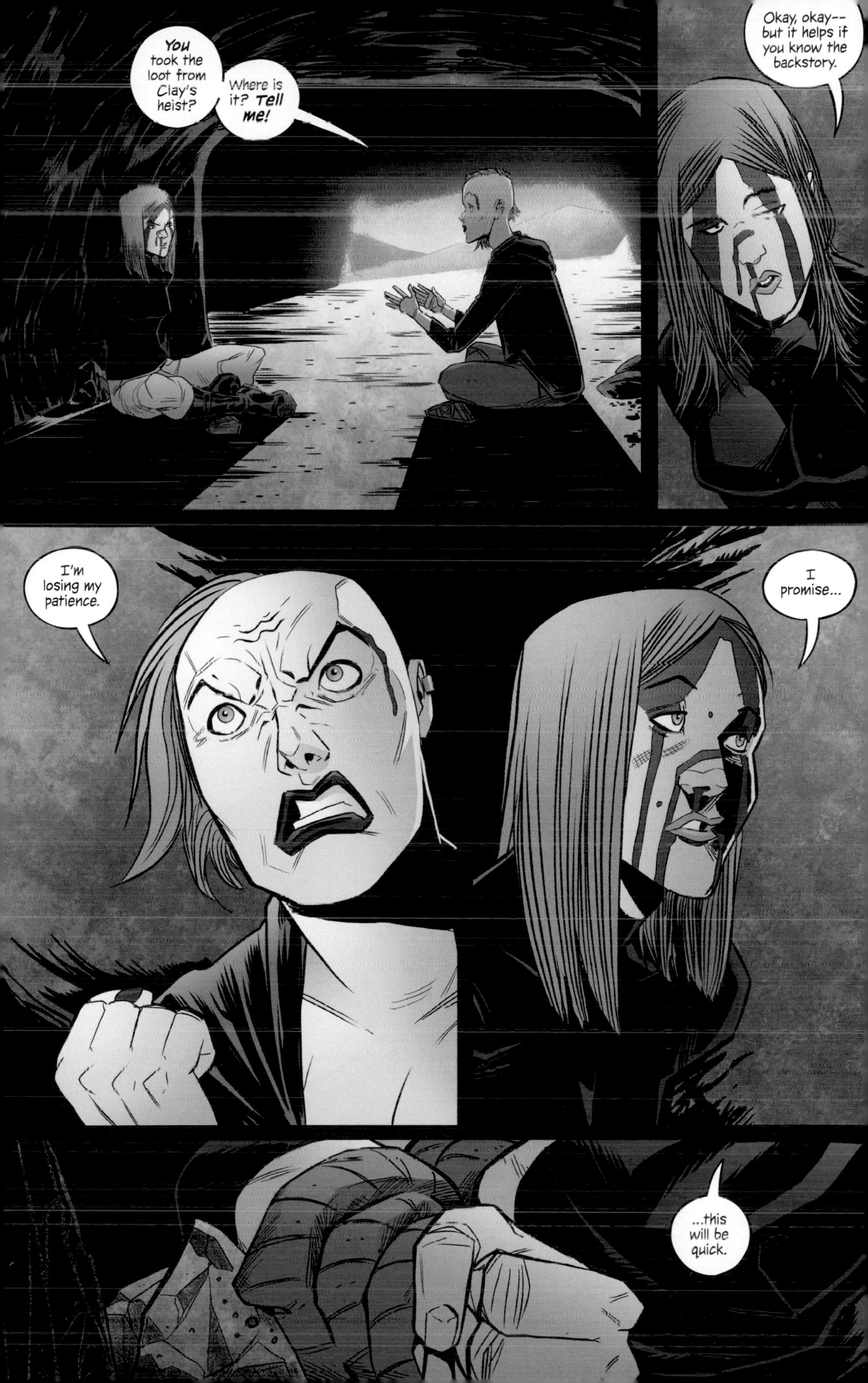
You took the loot from Clay's heist?
Where is it? Tell me!
Okay, okay--but it helps if you know the backstory.
I'm losing my patience.
I promise...
...this will be quick.

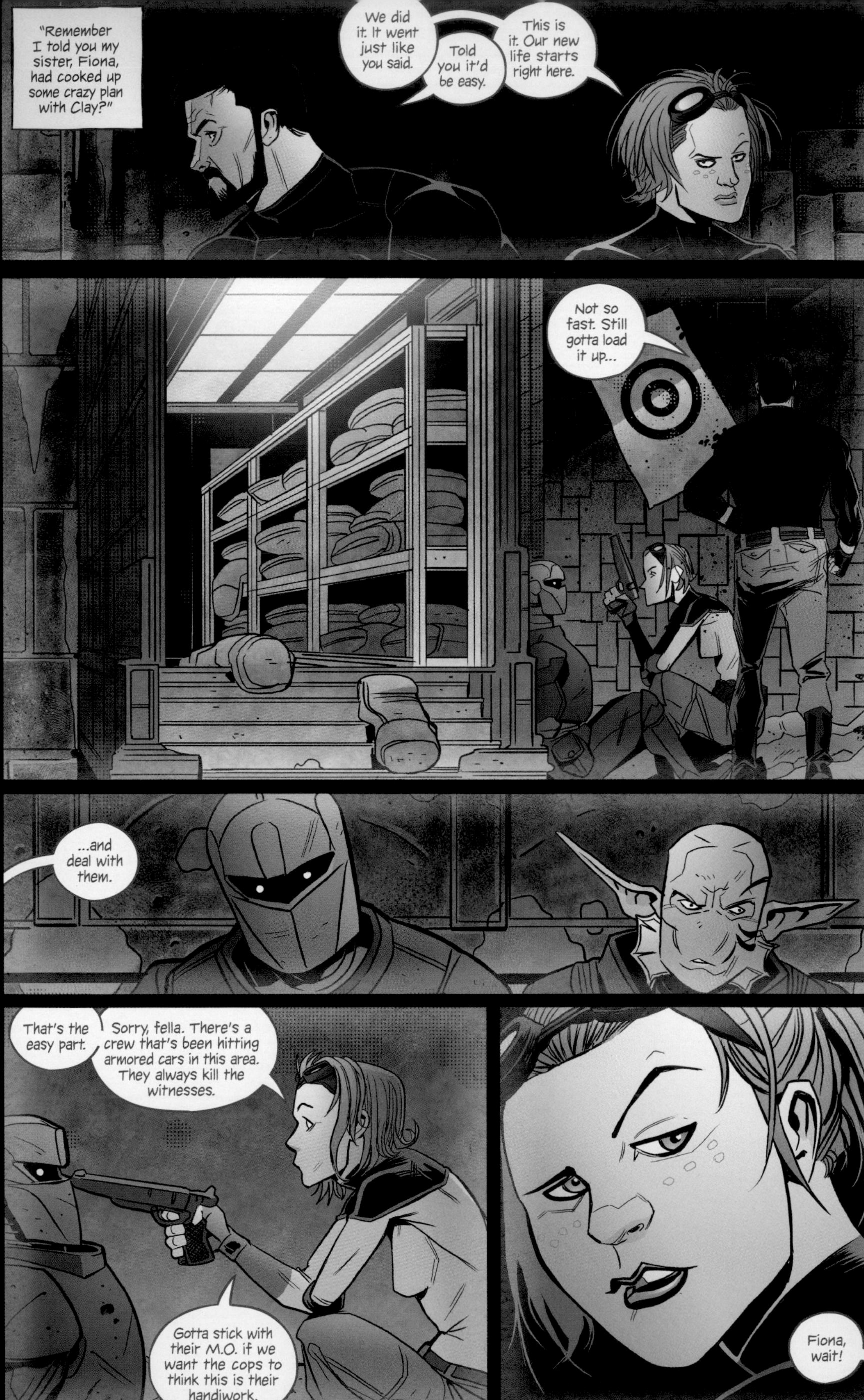
"Remember I told you my sister, Fiona, had cooked up some crazy plan with Clay?"
We did it. It went just like you said.
Told you it'd be easy.
This is it. Our new life starts right here.
Not so fast. Still gotta load it up...
...and deal with them.
That's the easy part.
Sorry, fella. There's a crew that's been hitting armored cars in this area. They always kill the witnesses.
Gotta stick with their M.O. if we want the cops to think this is their handiwork.
Fiona, wait!

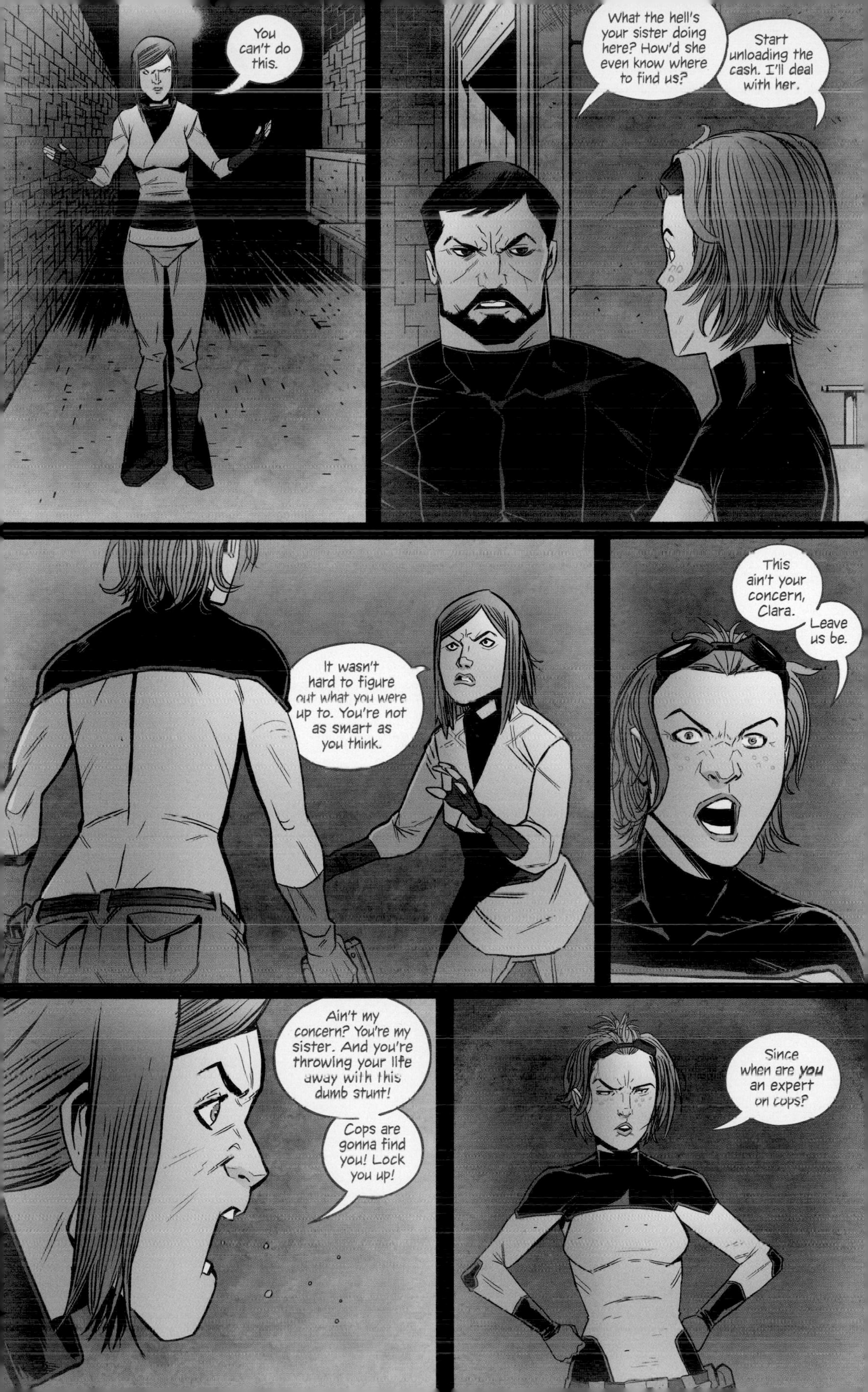
You can't do this.
What the hell's your sister doing here? How'd she even know where to find us?
Start unloading the cash. I'll deal with her.
It wasn't hard to figure out what you were up to. You're not as smart as you think.
This ain't your concern, Clara.
Leave us be.
Ain't my concern? You're my sister. And you're throwing your life away with this dumb stunt!
Cops are gonna find you! Lock you up!
Since when are *you* an expert on cops?

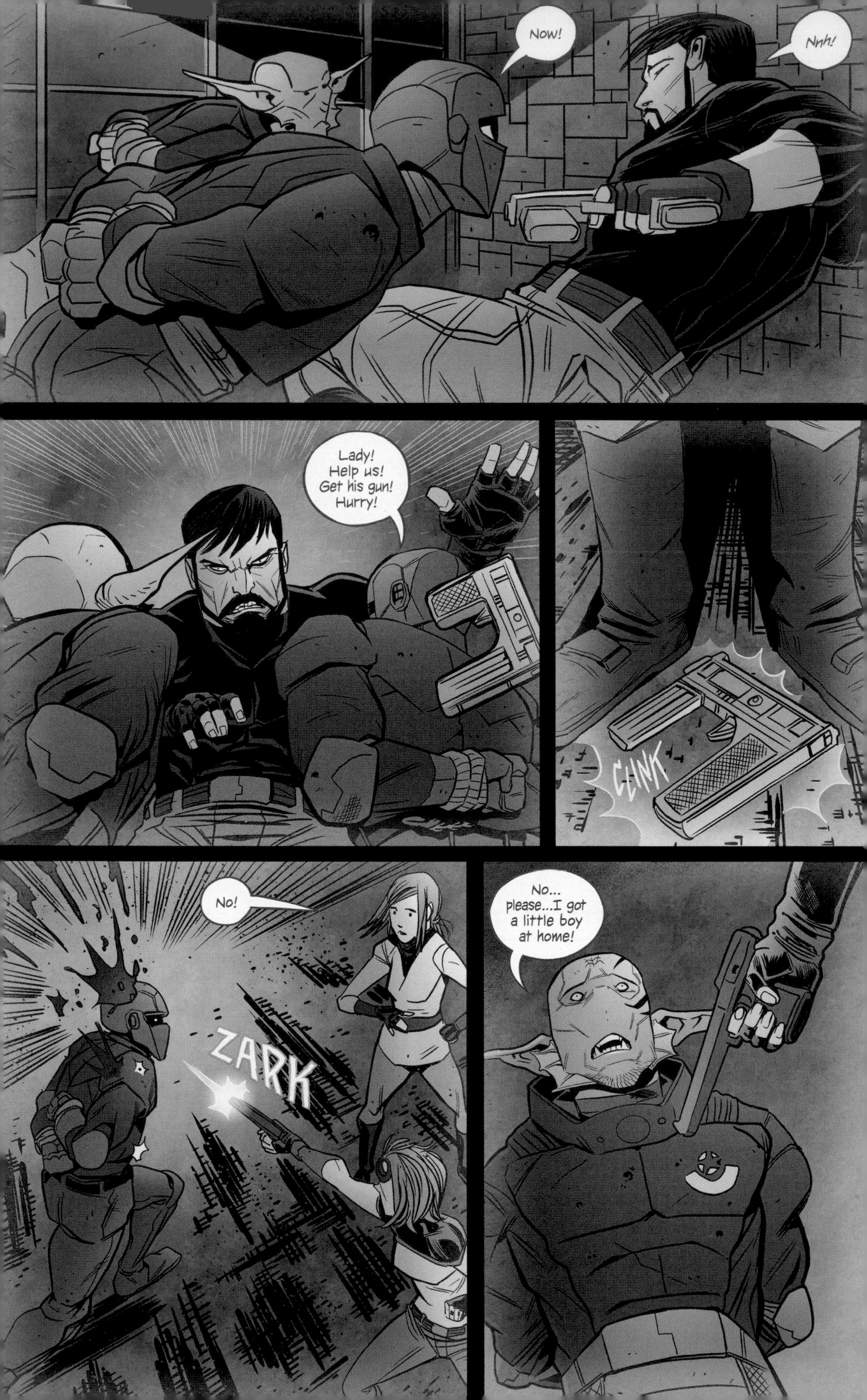
Now!
Nnh!
Lady! Help us! Get his gun! Hurry!
CLINK
No!
ZARK
No... please...I got a little boy at home!

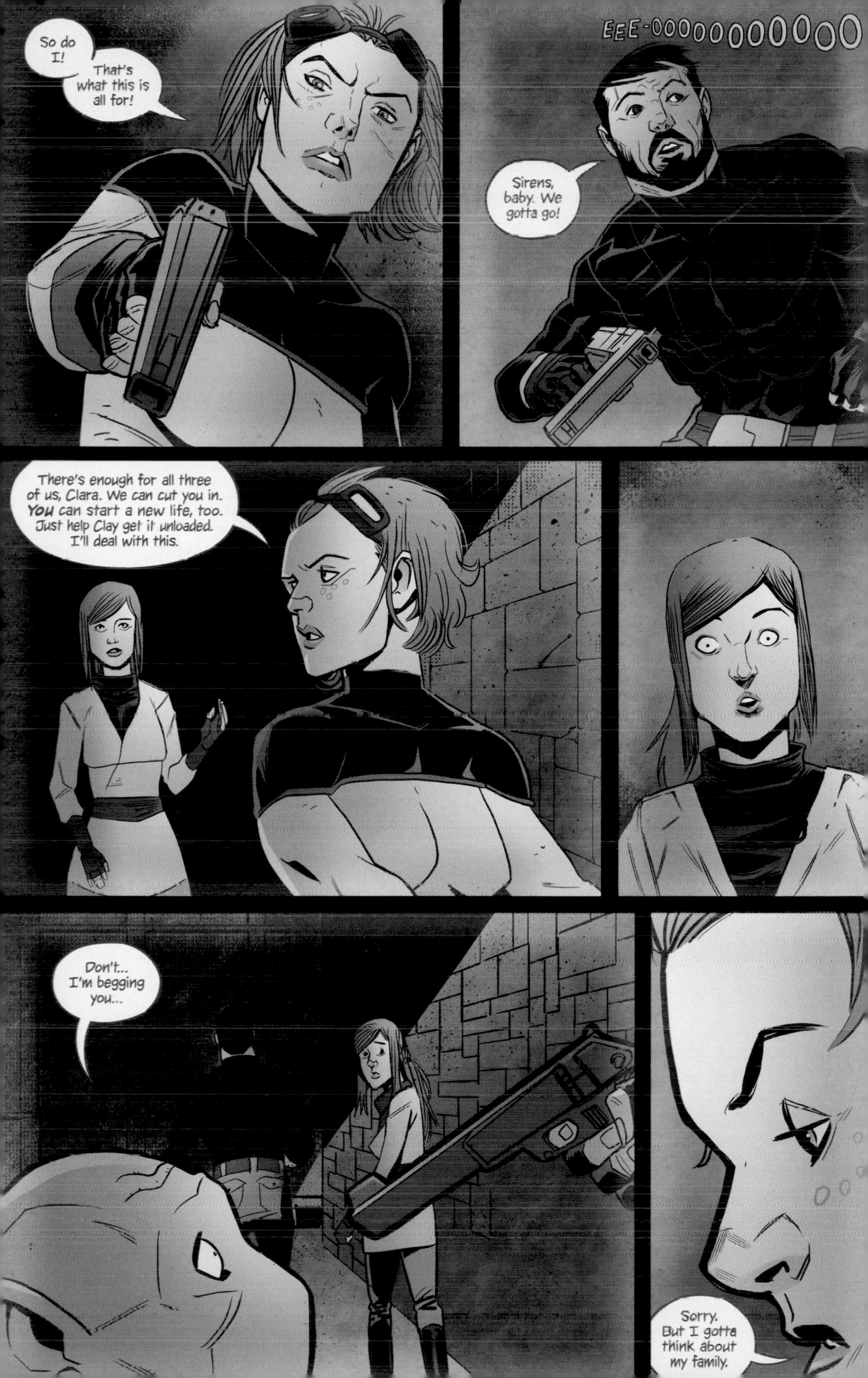
So do I!
That's what this is all for!
EEE-OOOOOOOOOOO
Sirens, baby. We gotta go!
There's enough for all three of us, Clara. We can cut you in. **You** can start a new life, too. Just help Clay get it unloaded. I'll deal with this.
Don't... I'm begging you...
Sorry. But I gotta think about my family.

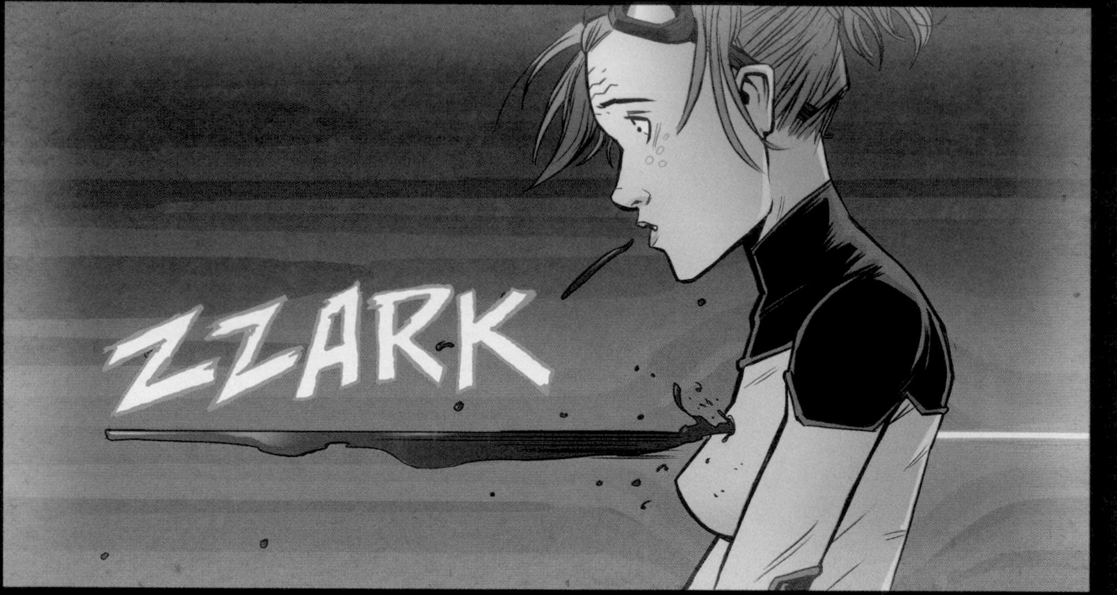
ZZARK

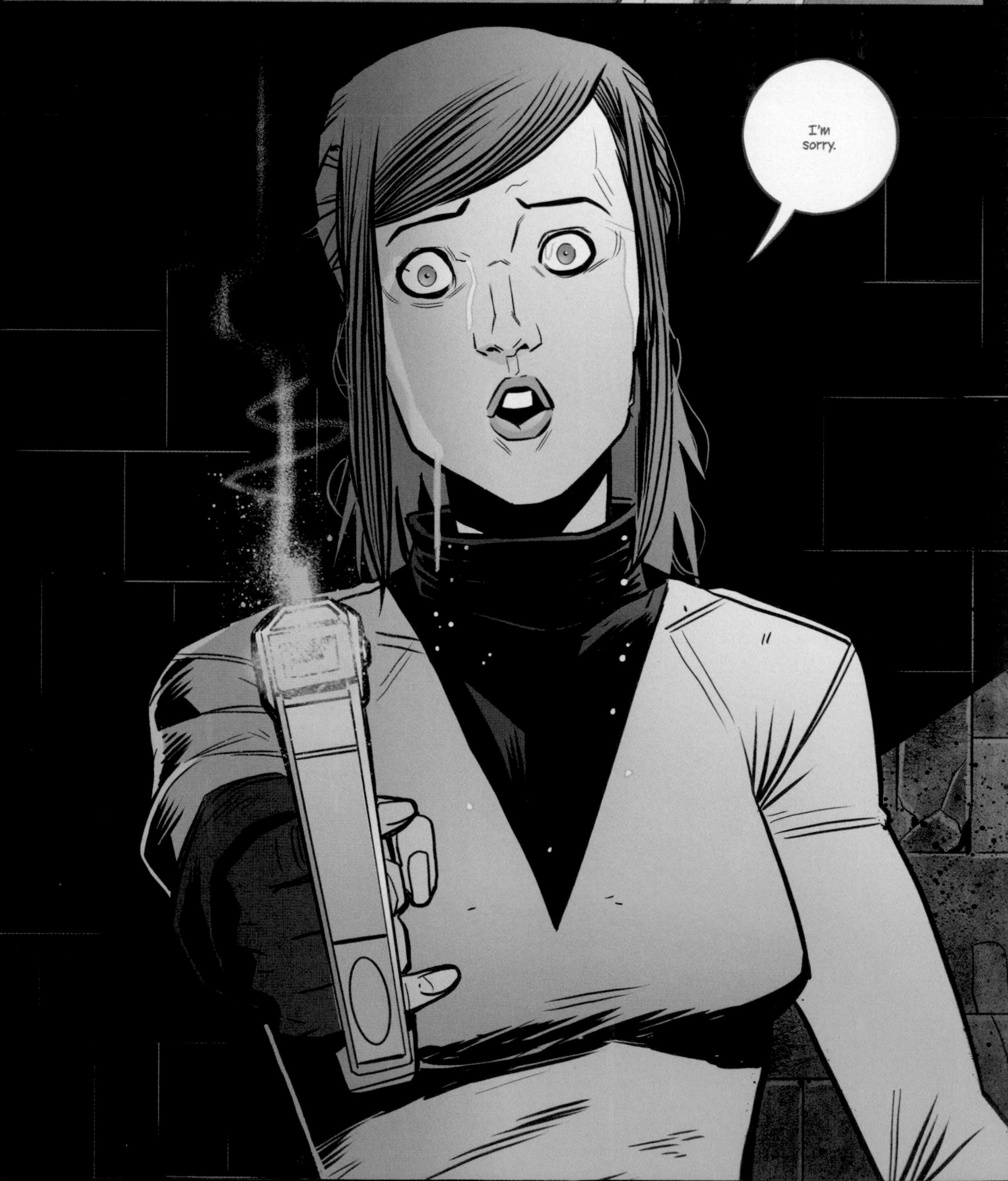
I'm sorry.

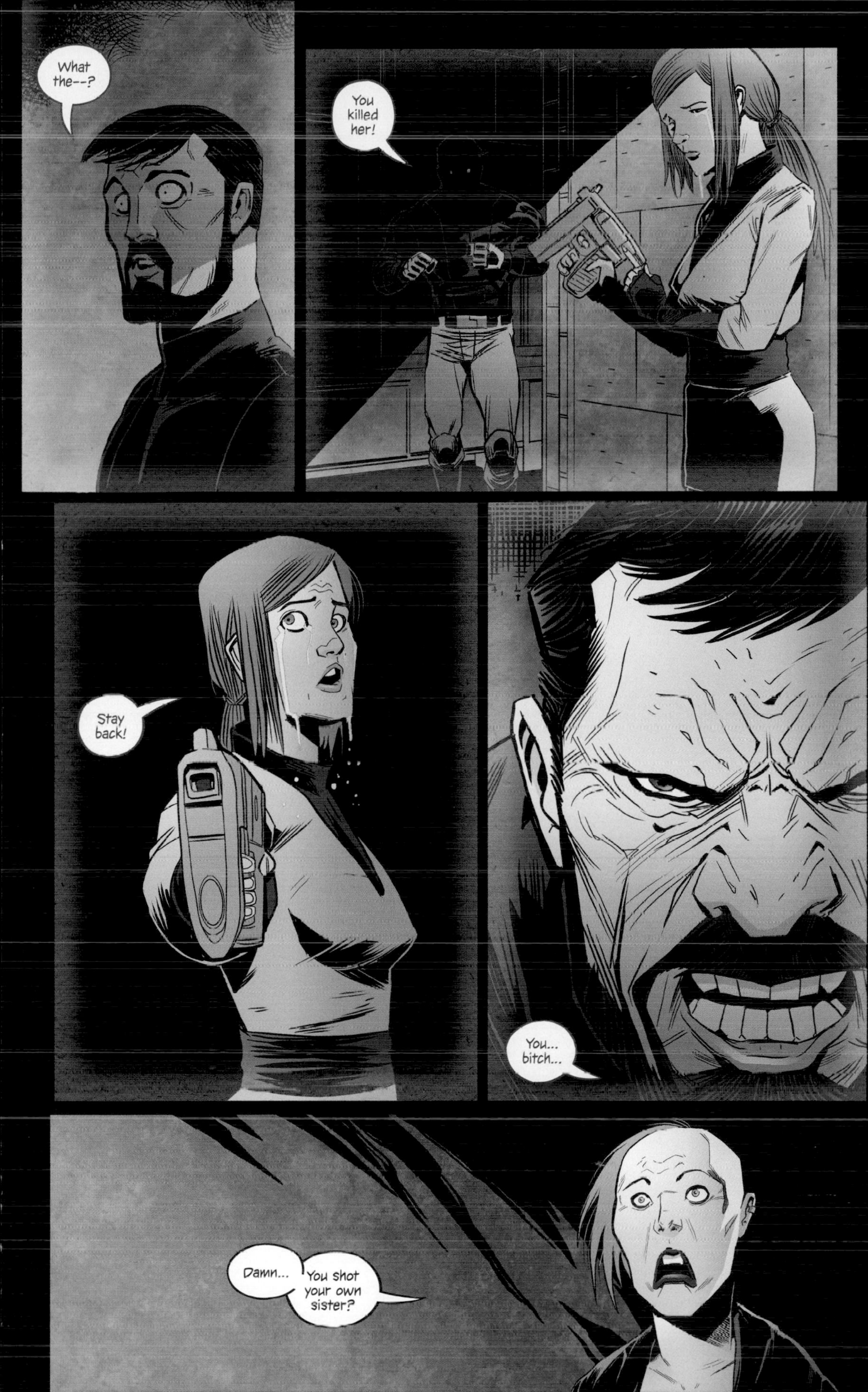
What the--?
You killed her!
Stay back!
You... bitch...
Damn...
You shot your own sister?

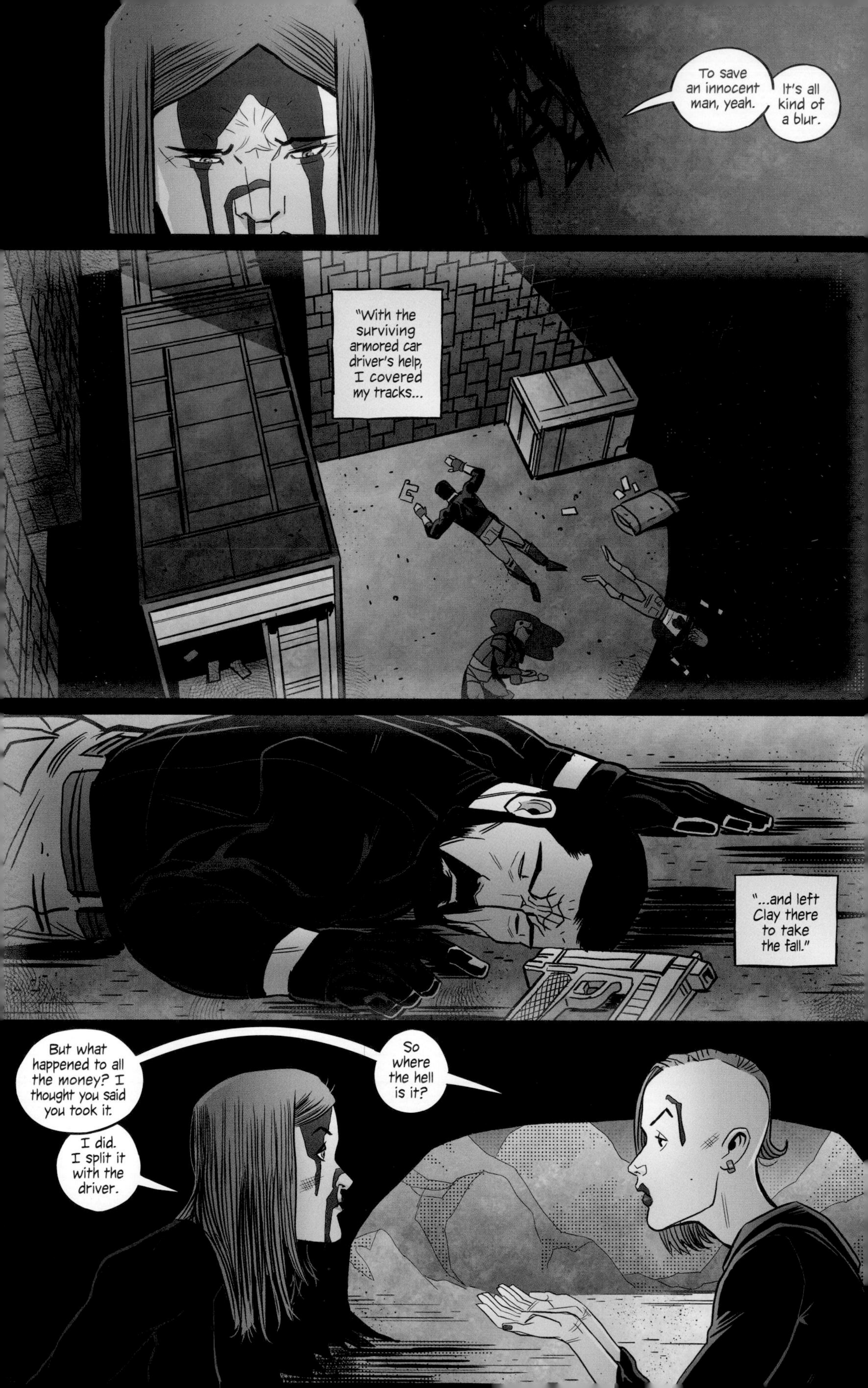
To save an innocent man, yeah.
It's all kind of a blur.
"With the surviving armored car driver's help, I covered my tracks...
"...and left Clay there to take the fall."
But what happened to all the money? I thought you said you took it.
So where the hell is it?
I did. I split it with the driver.

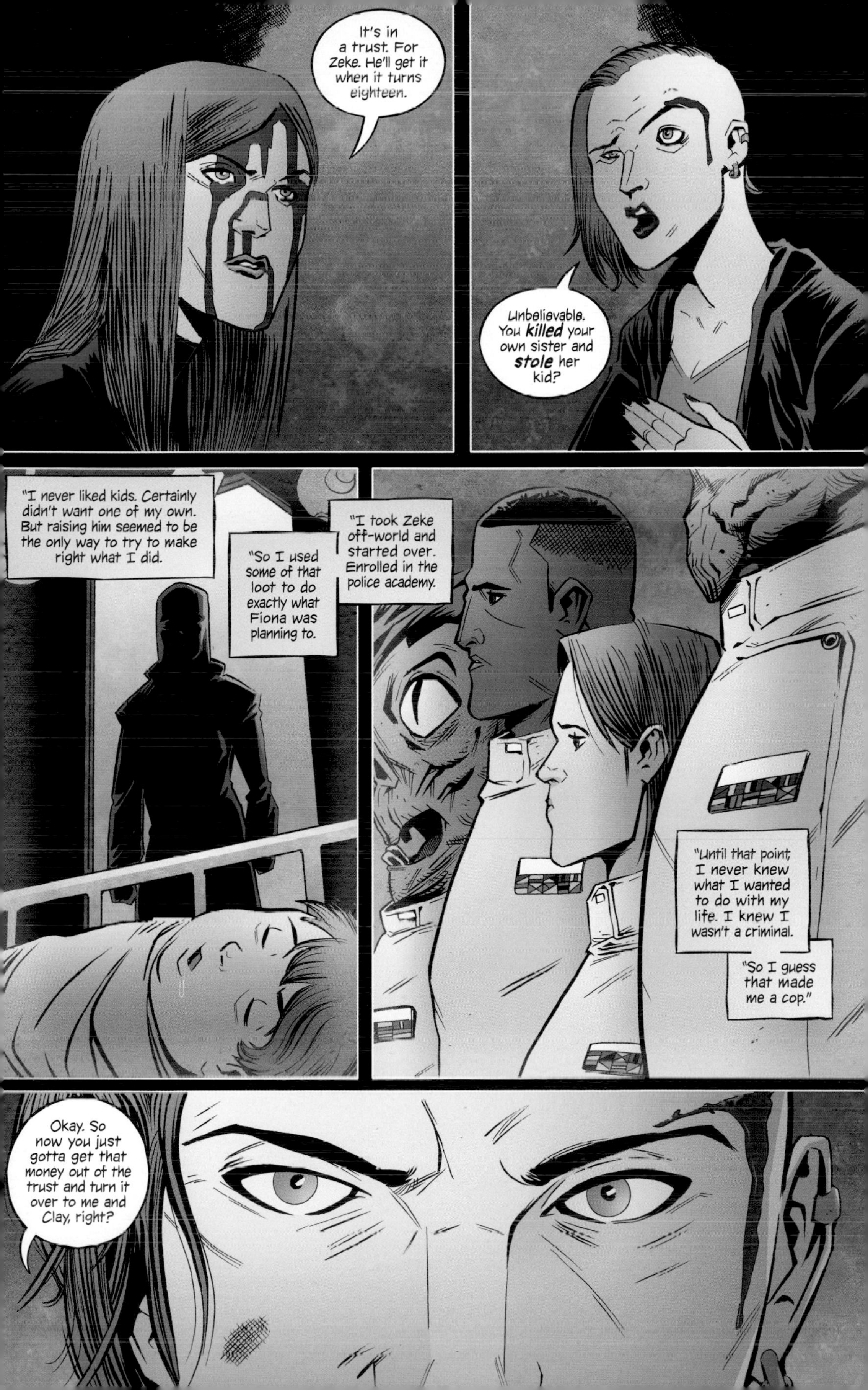
It's in a trust. For Zeke. He'll get it when it turns eighteen.
Unbelievable. You **killed** your own sister and **stole** her kid?
"I never liked kids. Certainly didn't want one of my own. But raising him seemed to be the only way to try to make right what I did.
"So I used some of that loot to do exactly what Fiona was planning to.
"I took Zeke off-world and started over. Enrolled in the police academy.
"Until that point, I never knew what I wanted to do with my life. I knew I wasn't a criminal.
"So I guess that made me a cop."
Okay. So now you just gotta get that money out of the trust and turn it over to me and Clay, right?

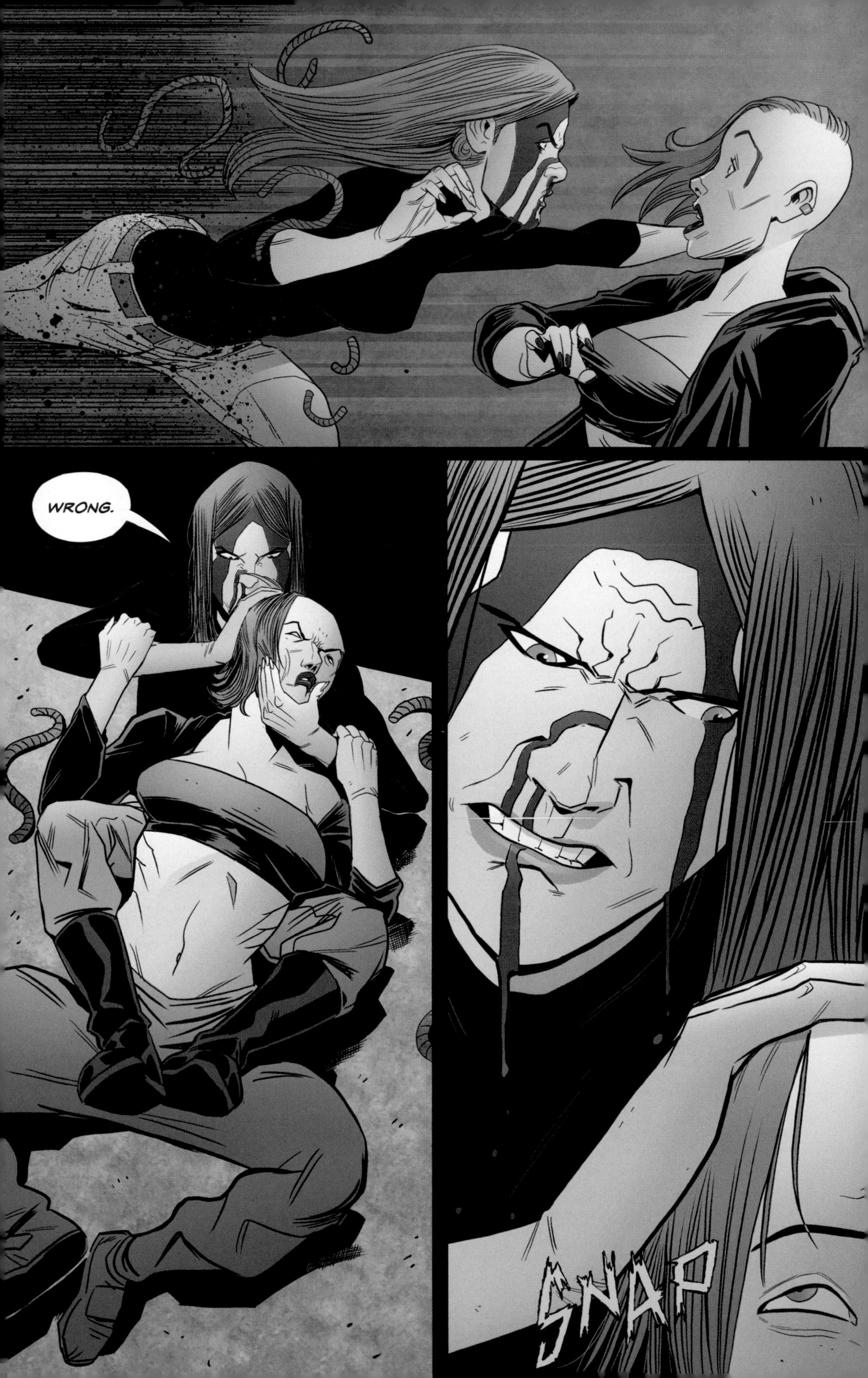
WRONG.
SNAP

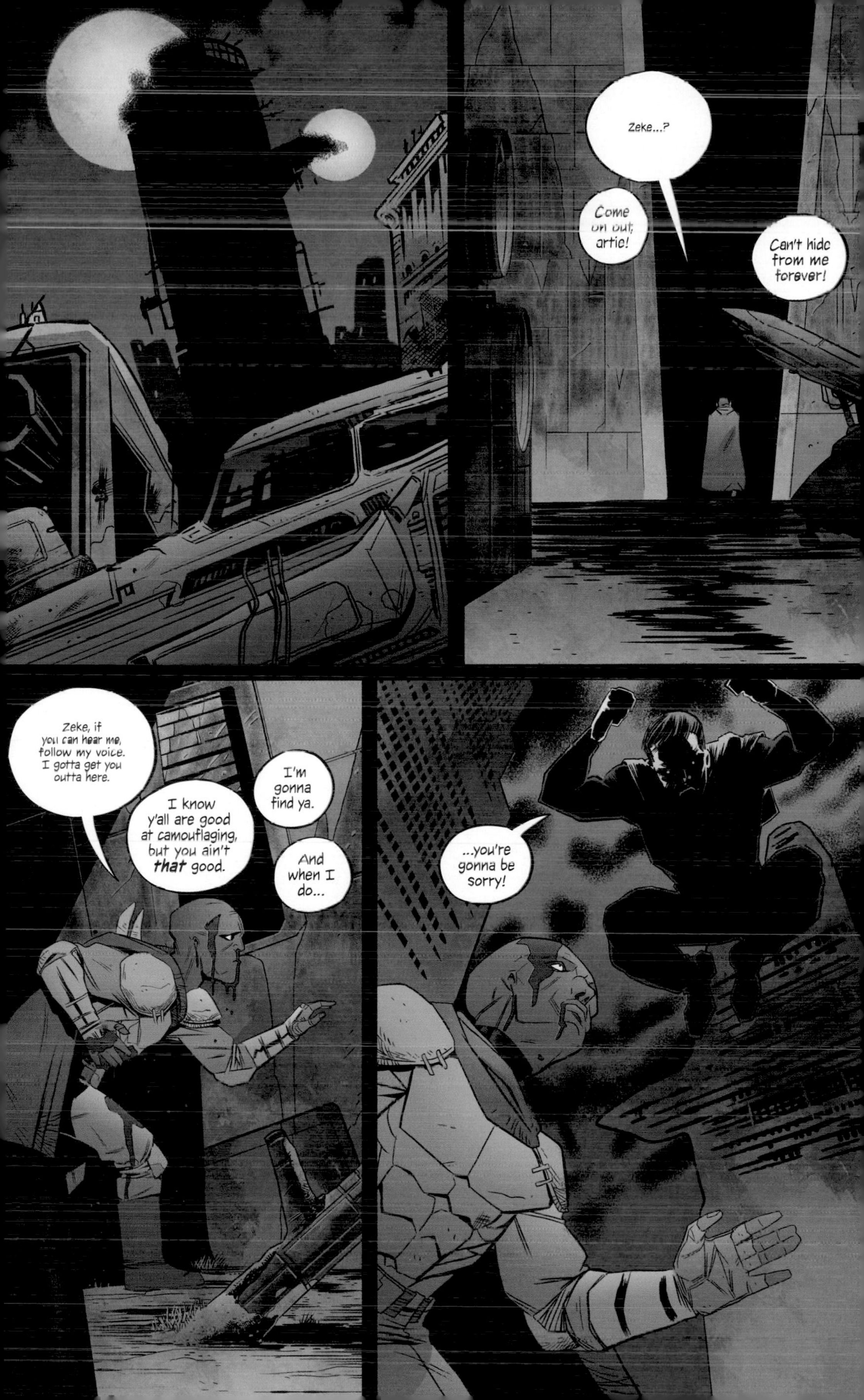
Zeke...?
Come on out, artie!
Can't hide from me forever!
Zeke, if you can hear me, follow my voice. I gotta get you outta here.
I know y'all are good at camouflaging, but you ain't **that** good.
I'm gonna find ya.
And when I do...
...you're gonna be sorry!

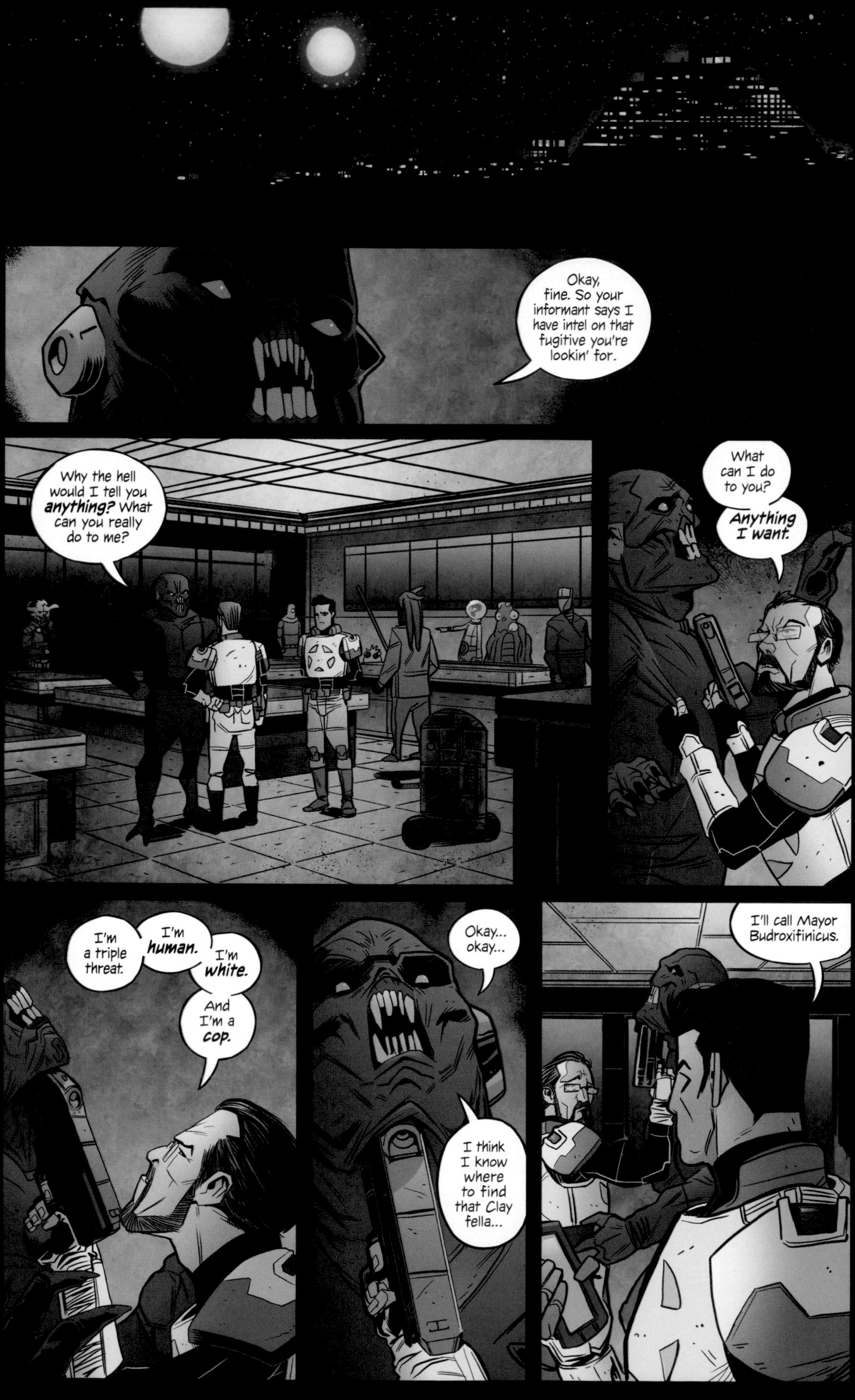
Okay, fine. So your informant says I have intel on that fugitive you're lookin' for.
Why the hell would I tell you **anything?** What can you really do to me?
What can I do to you?
Anything I want.
I'm a triple threat.
I'm **human.**
I'm **white.**
And I'm a **cop.**
Okay... okay...
I think I know where to find that Clay fella...
I'll call Mayor Budroxifinicus.

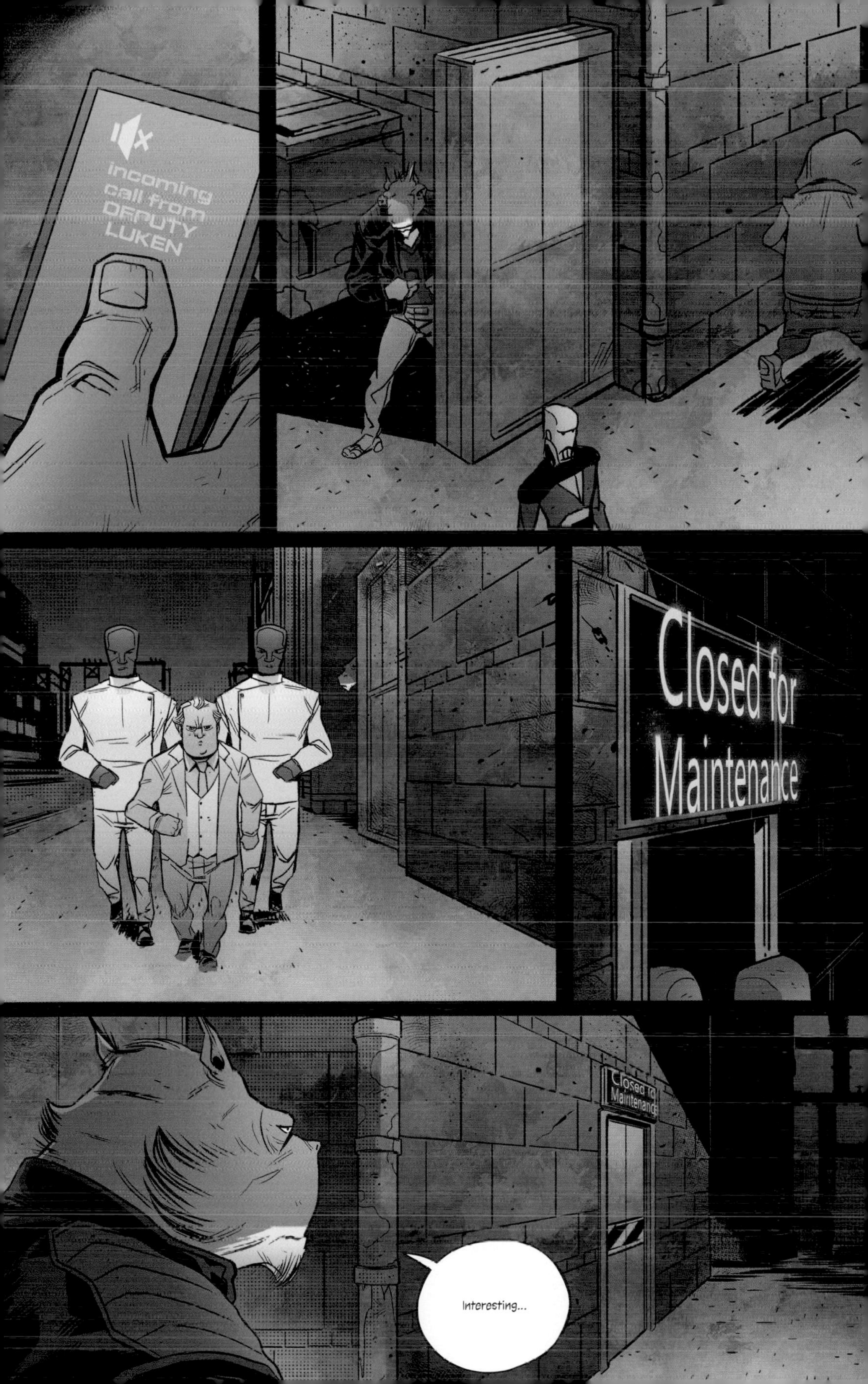
incoming call from DEPUTY LUKEN
Closed for Maintenance
Closed for Maintenance
Interesting...

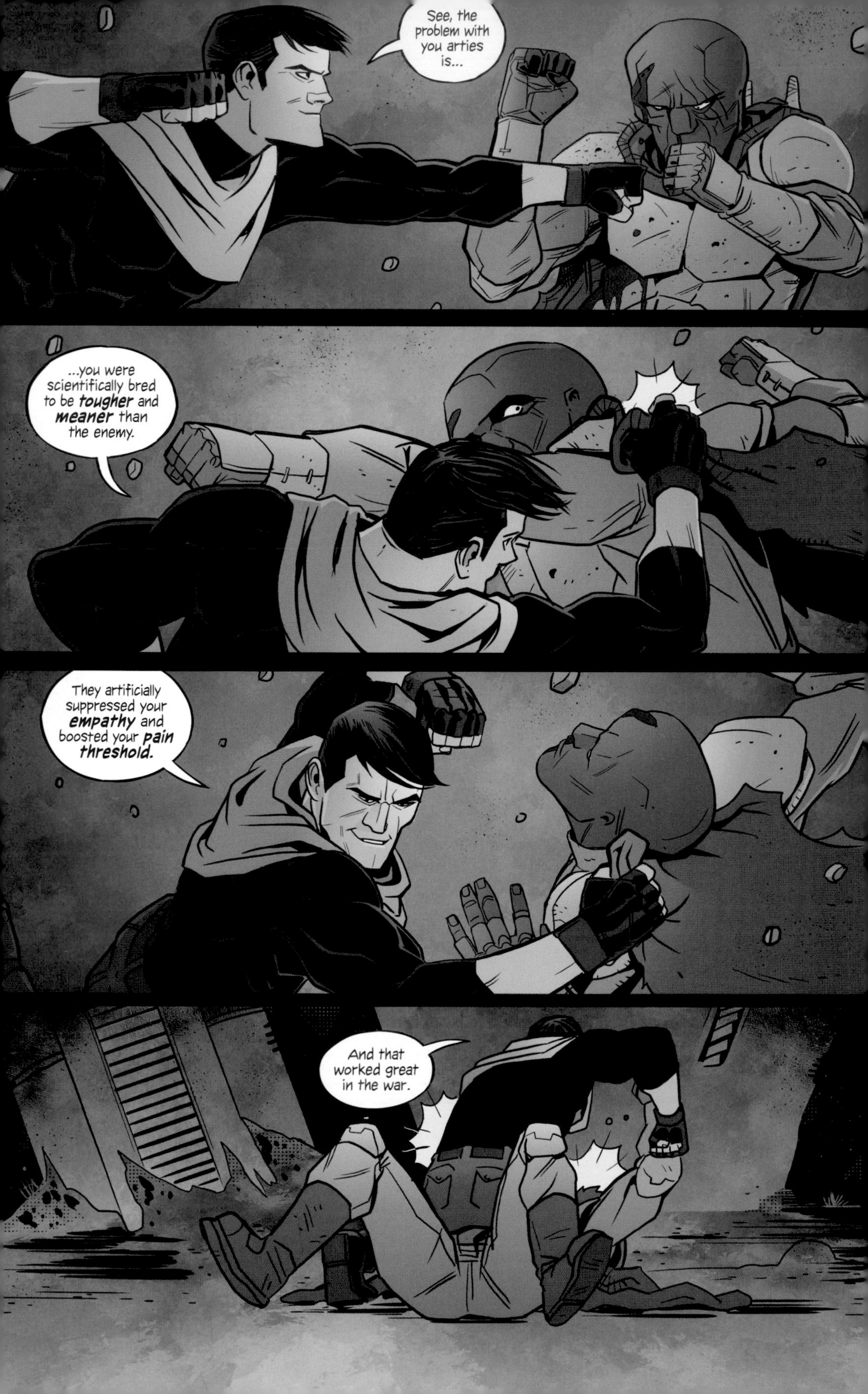
See, the problem with you arties is...
...you were scientifically bred to be **tougher** and **meaner** than the enemy.
They artificially suppressed your **empathy** and boosted your **pain threshold.**
And that worked great in the war.

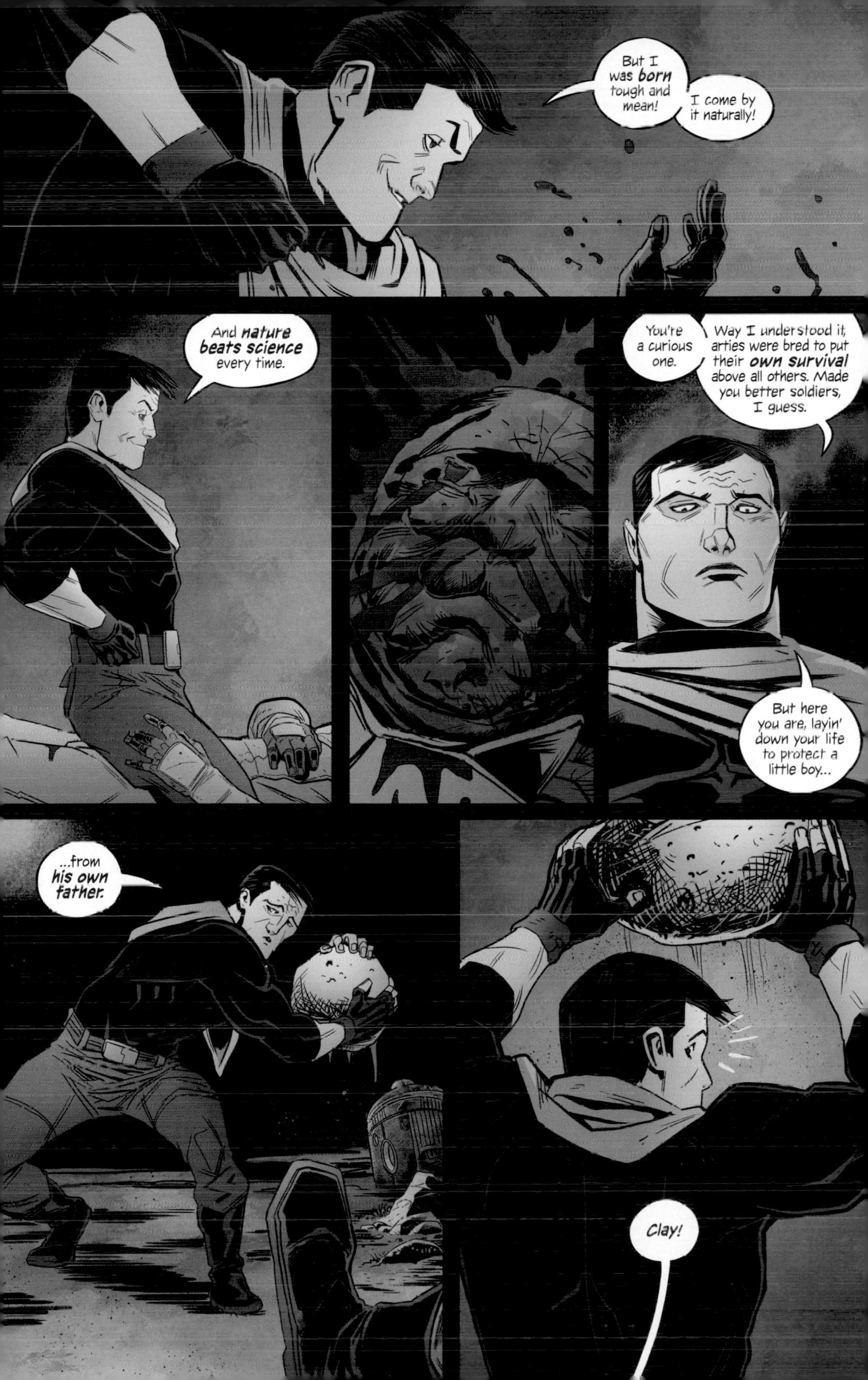
But I was born tough and mean!
I come by it naturally!
And nature beats science every time.
You're a curious one.
Way I understood it, arties were bred to put their own survival above all others. Made you better soldiers, I guess.
But here you are, layin' down your life to protect a little boy...
...from his own father.
Clay!

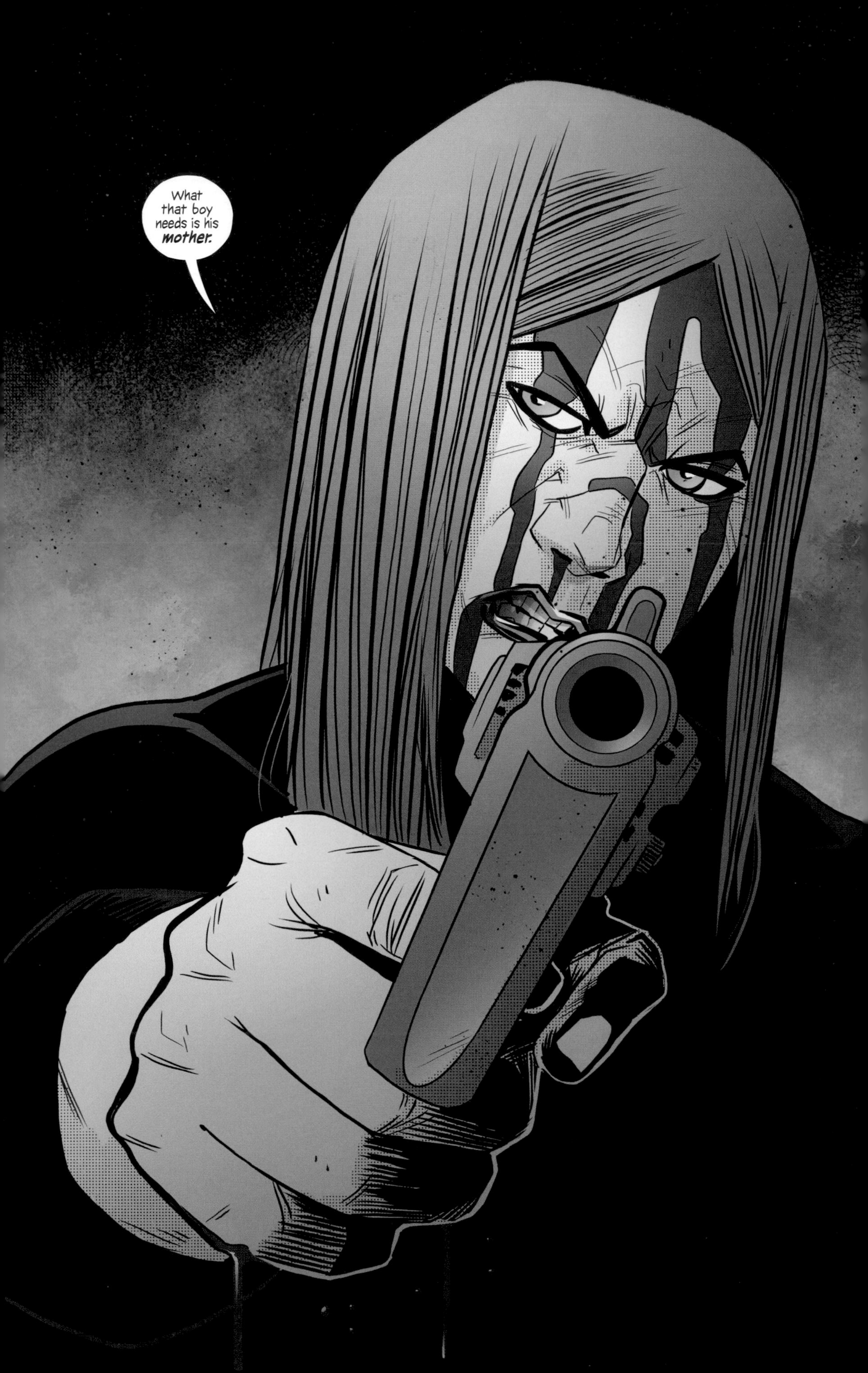
What that boy needs is his *mother.*

CHAPTER IV

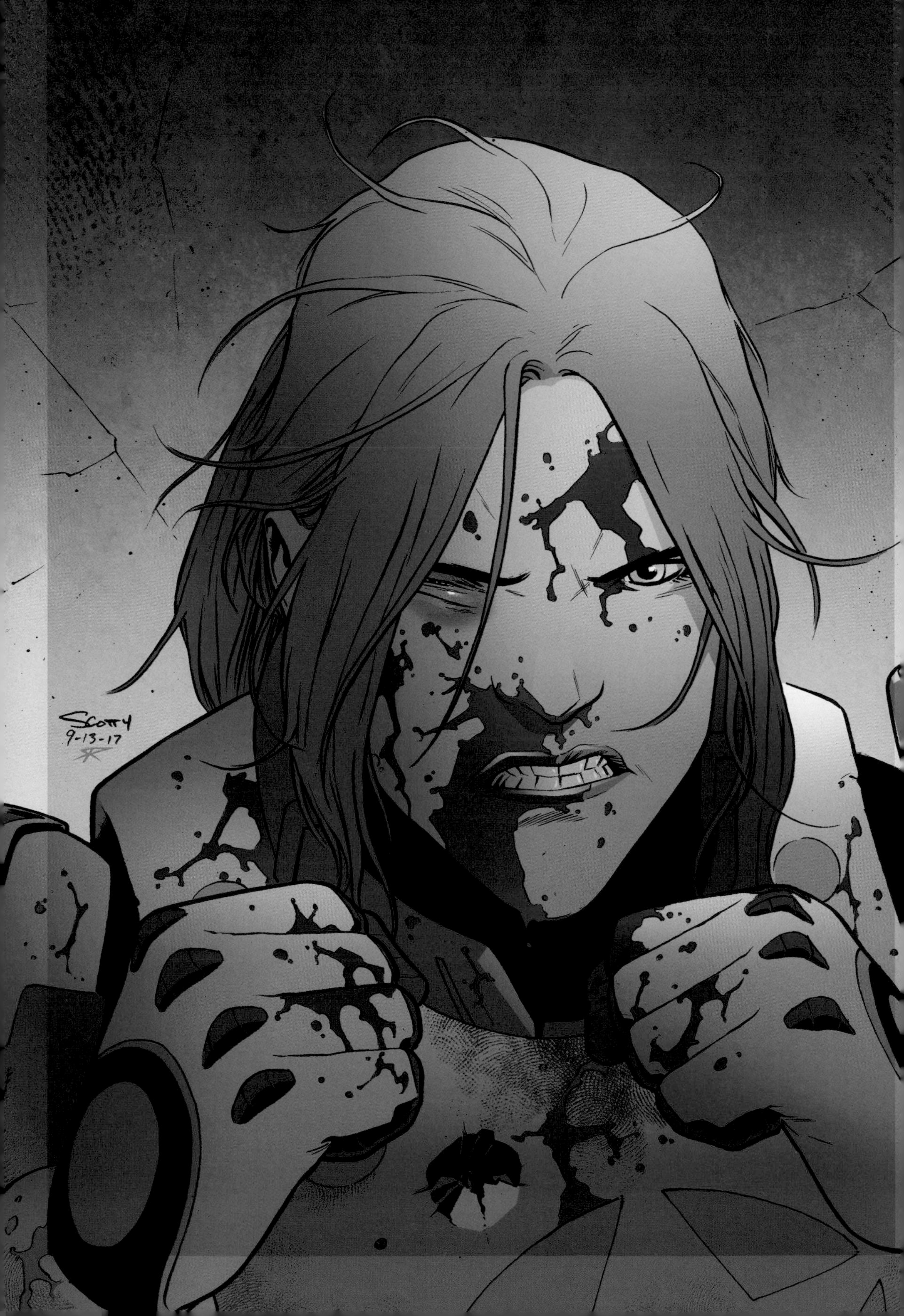
SCOTTY
9-13-17

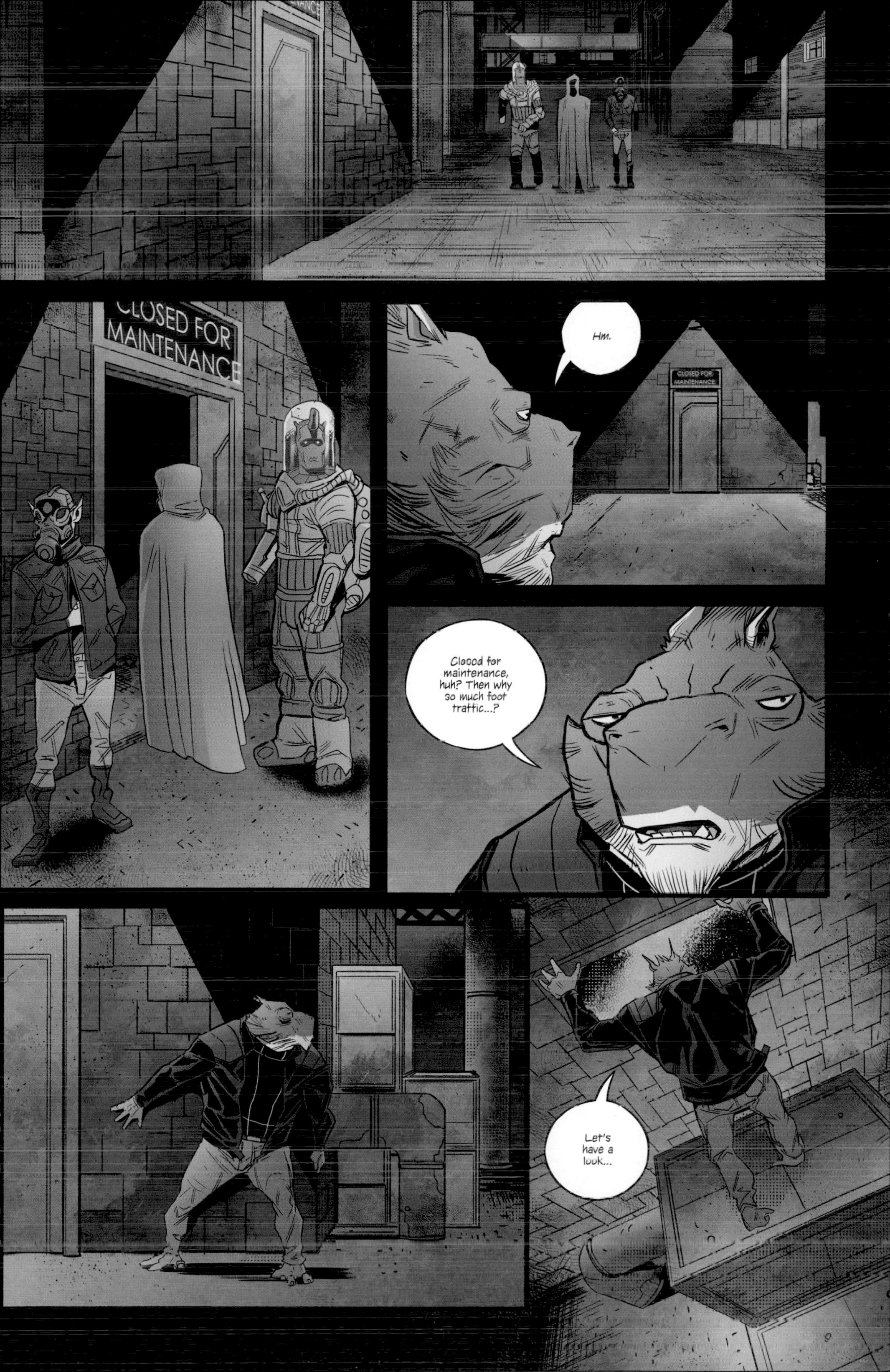
CLOSED FOR MAINTENANCE
Hm.
CLOSED FOR MAINTENANCE
Closed for maintenance, huh? Then why so much foot traffic...?
Let's have a look...

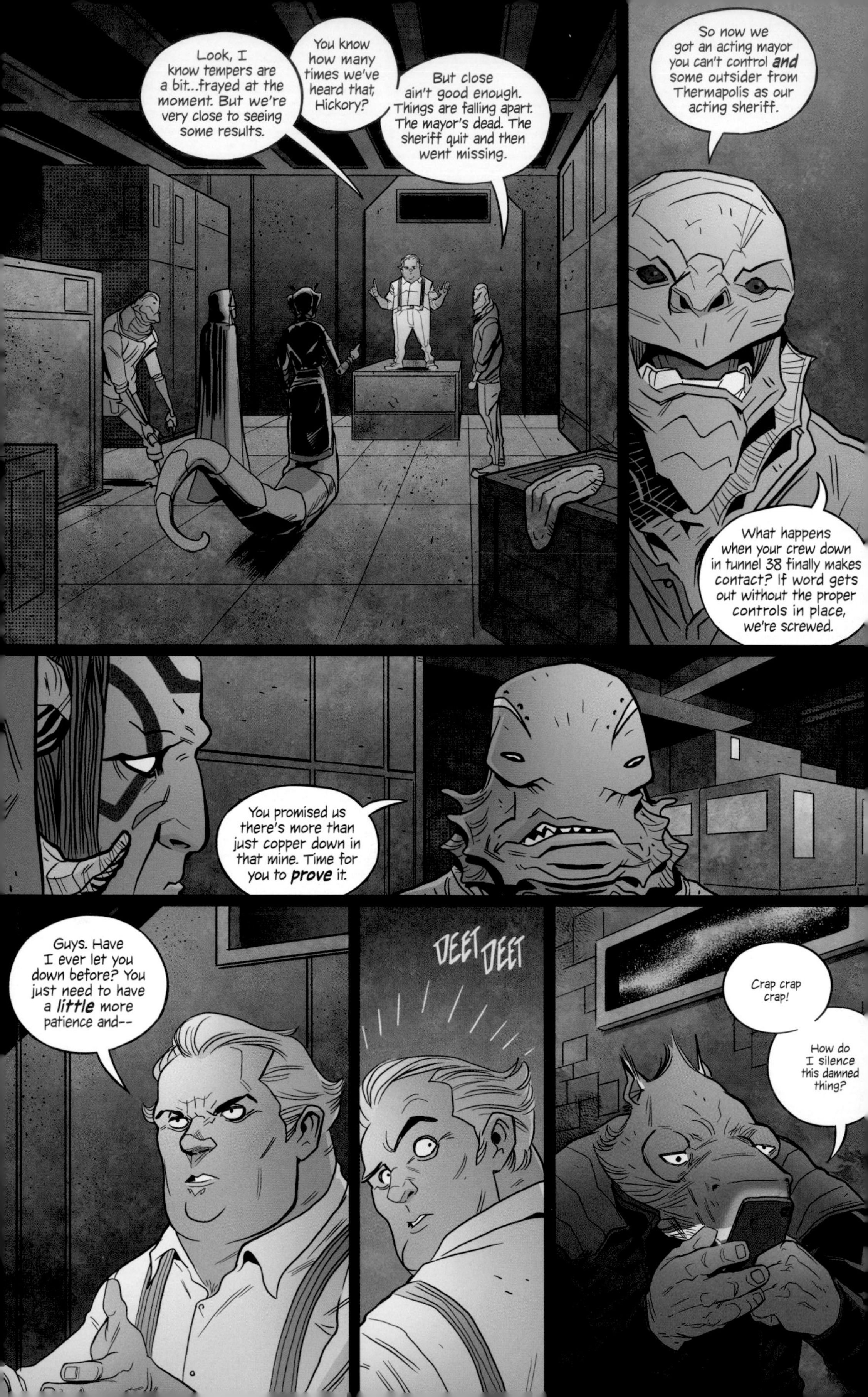

Look, I know tempers are a bit...frayed at the moment. But we're very close to seeing some results.
You know how many times we've heard that, Hickory?
But close ain't good enough. Things are falling apart. The mayor's dead. The sheriff quit and then went missing.
So now we got an acting mayor you can't control and some outsider from Thermapolis as our acting sheriff.
What happens when your crew down in tunnel 38 finally makes contact? If word gets out without the proper controls in place, we're screwed.
You promised us there's more than just copper down in that mine. Time for you to prove it.
Guys. Have I ever let you down before? You just need to have a little more patience and--
DEET DEET
Crap crap crap!
How do I silence this damned thing?

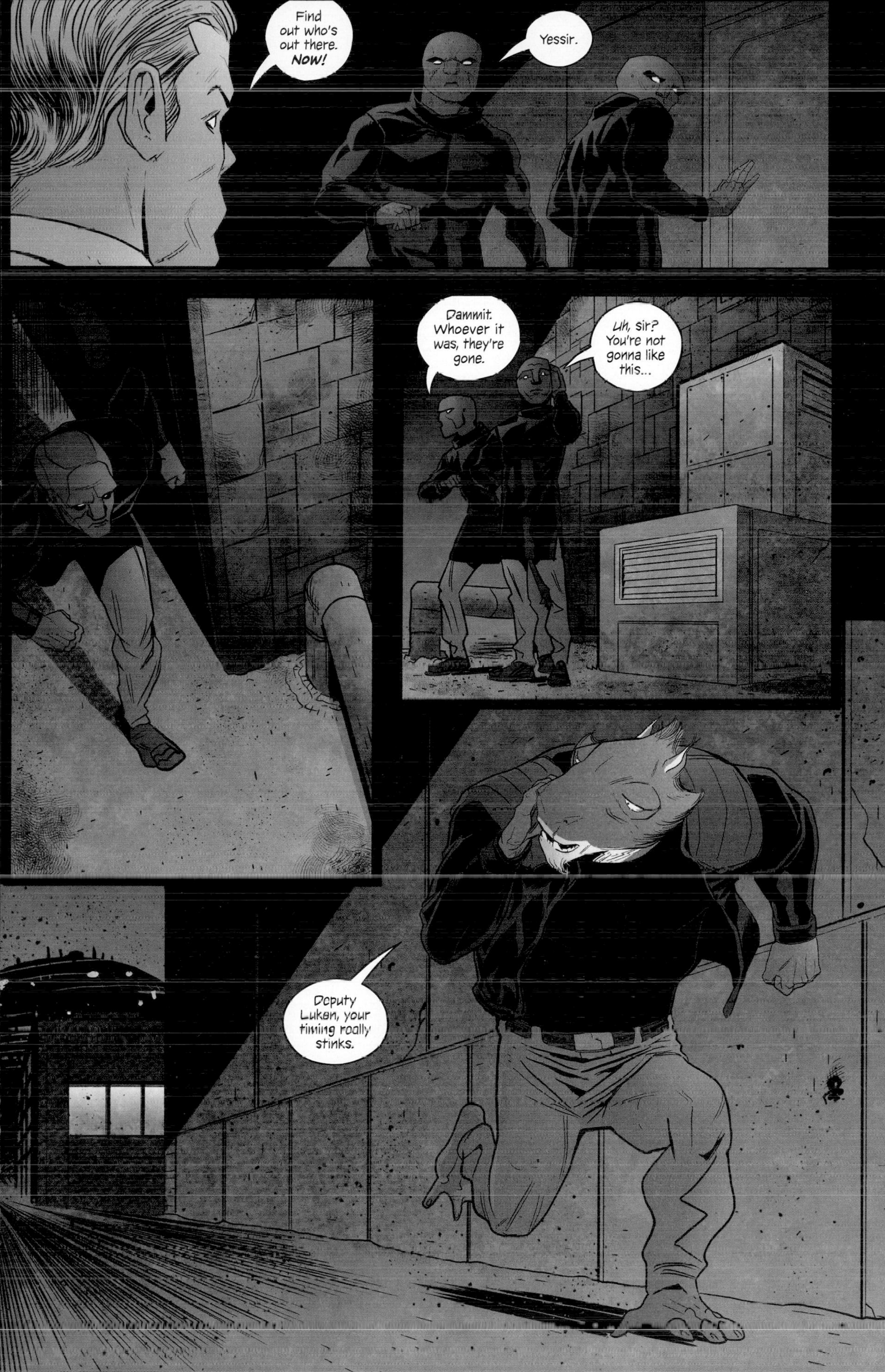
Find out who's out there. NOW!
Yessir.
Dammit. Whoever it was, they're gone.
Uh, sir? You're not gonna like this...
Deputy Luken, your timing really stinks.

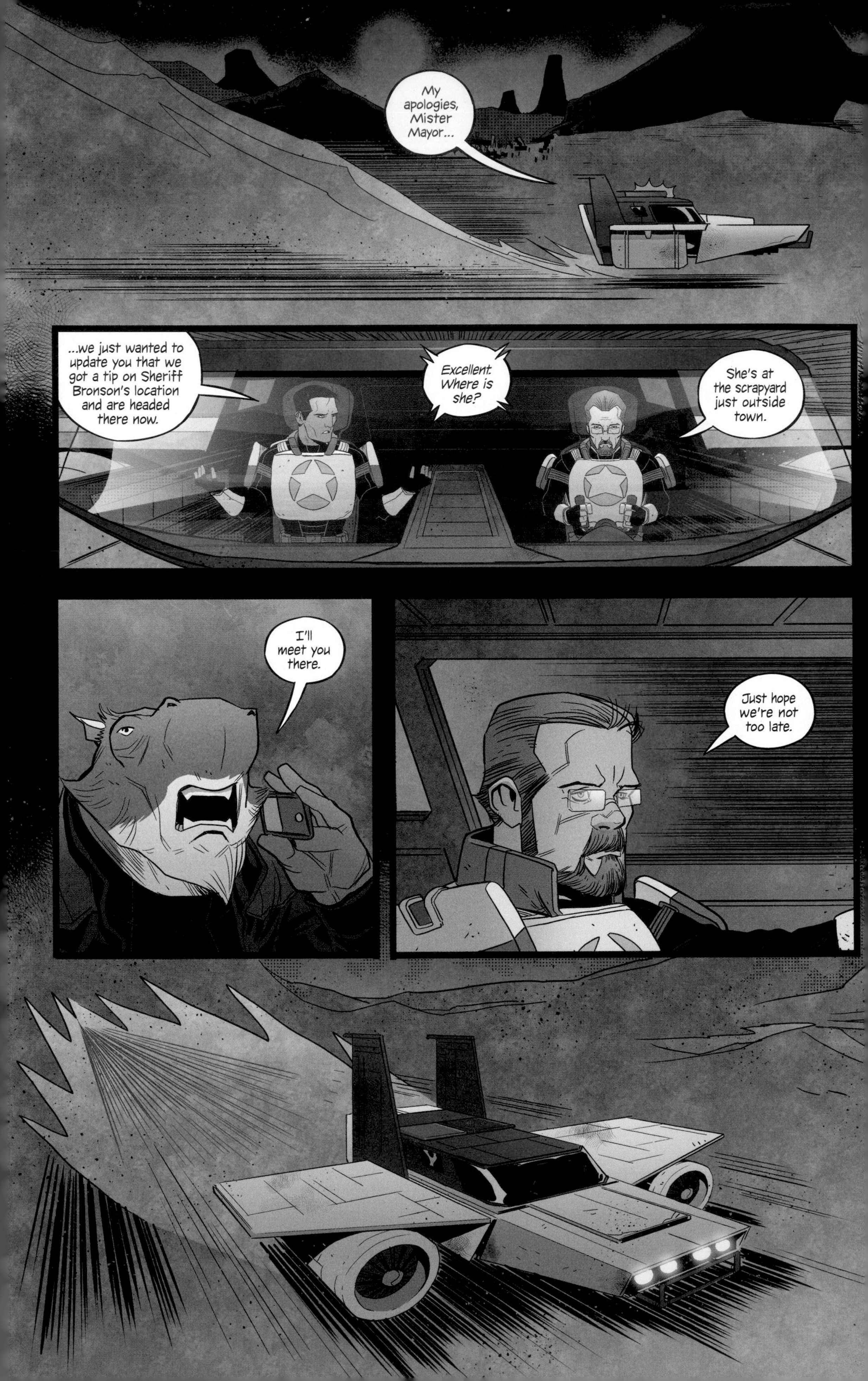
My apologies, Mister Mayor...
...we just wanted to update you that we got a tip on Sheriff Bronson's location and are headed there now.
Excellent. Where is she?
She's at the scrapyard just outside town.
I'll meet you there.
Just hope we're not too late.

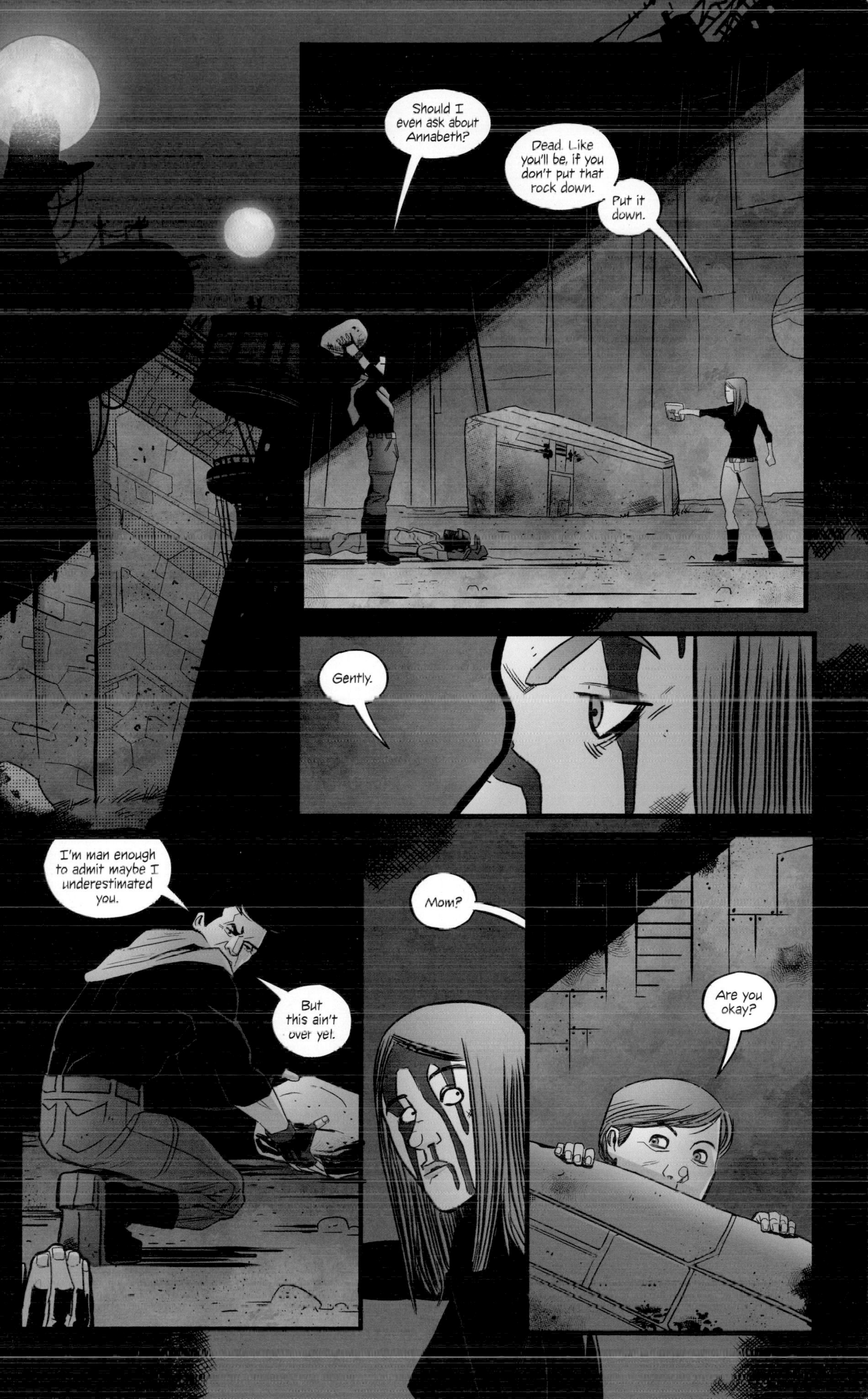
Should I even ask about Annabeth?
Dead. Like you'll be, if you don't put that rock down.
Put it down.
Gently.
I'm man enough to admit maybe I underestimated you.
But this ain't over yet.
Mom?
Are you okay?

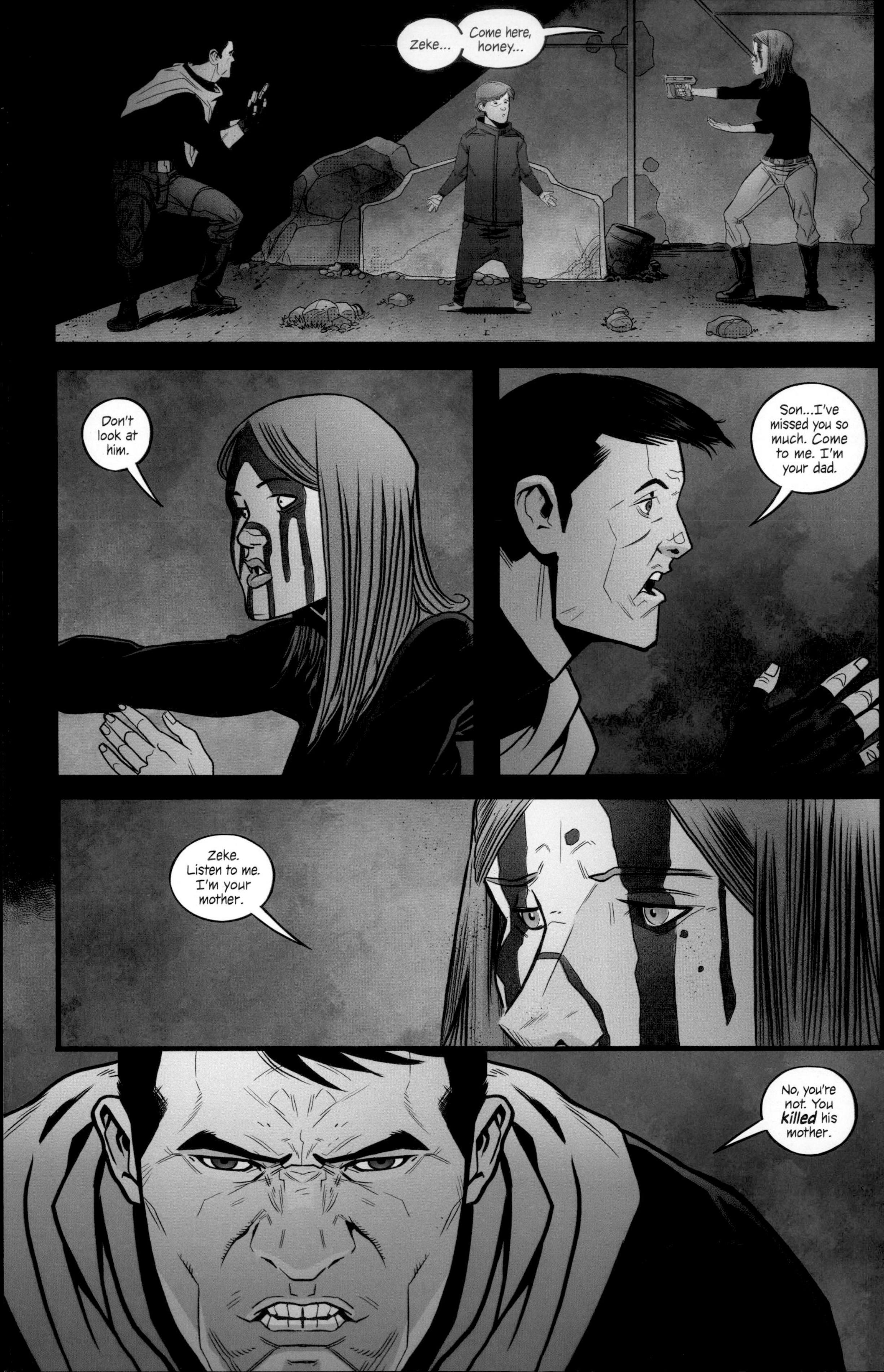
Zeke...
Come here, honey...
Don't look at him.
Son...I've missed you so much. Come to me. I'm your dad.
Zeke. Listen to me. I'm your mother.
No, you're not. You *killed* his mother.

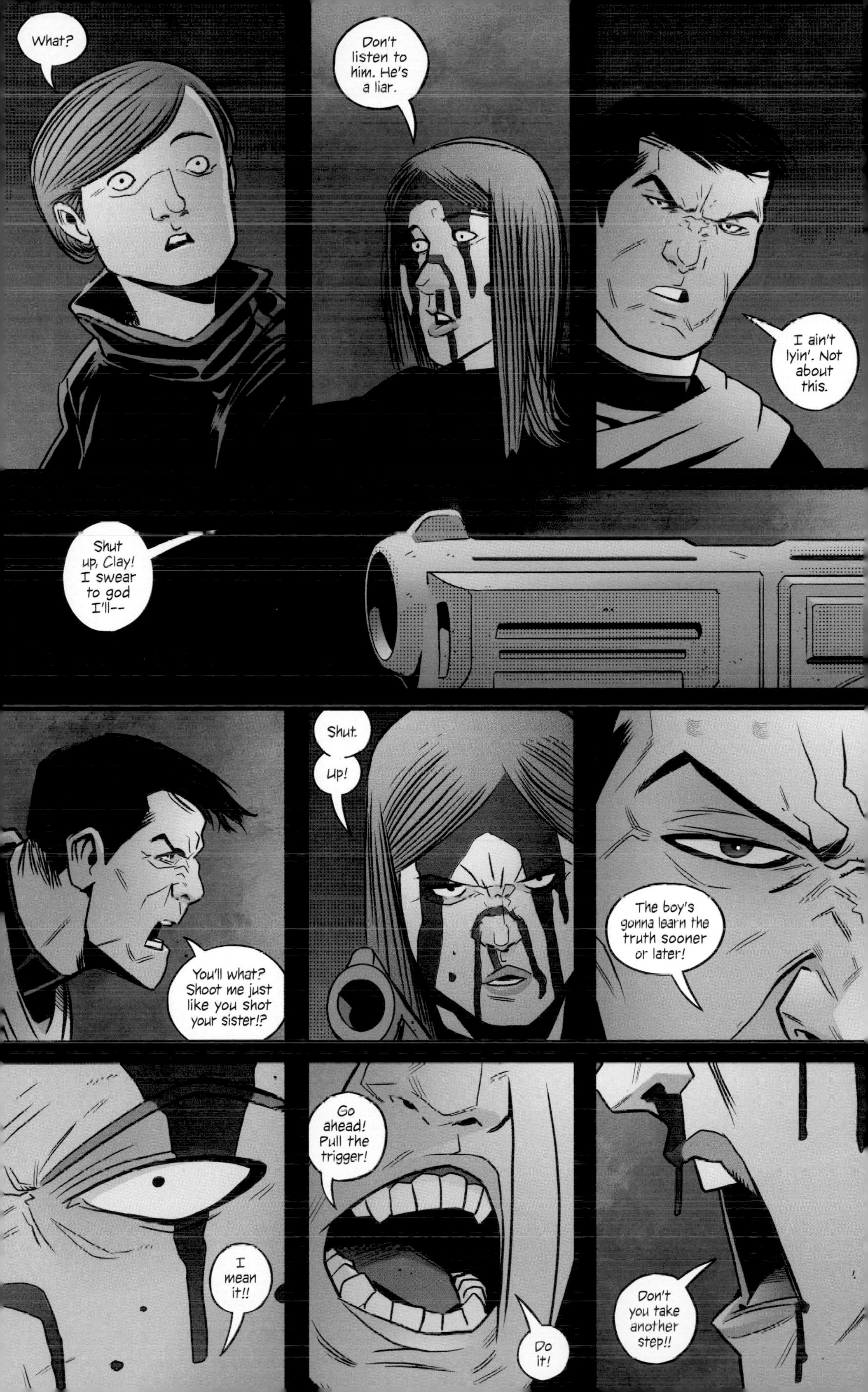
What?
Don't listen to him. He's a liar.
I ain't lyin'. Not about this.
Shut up, Clay! I swear to god I'll--
You'll what? Shoot me just like you shot your sister!?
Shut.
Up!
The boy's gonna learn the truth sooner or later!
I mean it!!
Go ahead! Pull the trigger!
Do it!
Don't you take another step!!

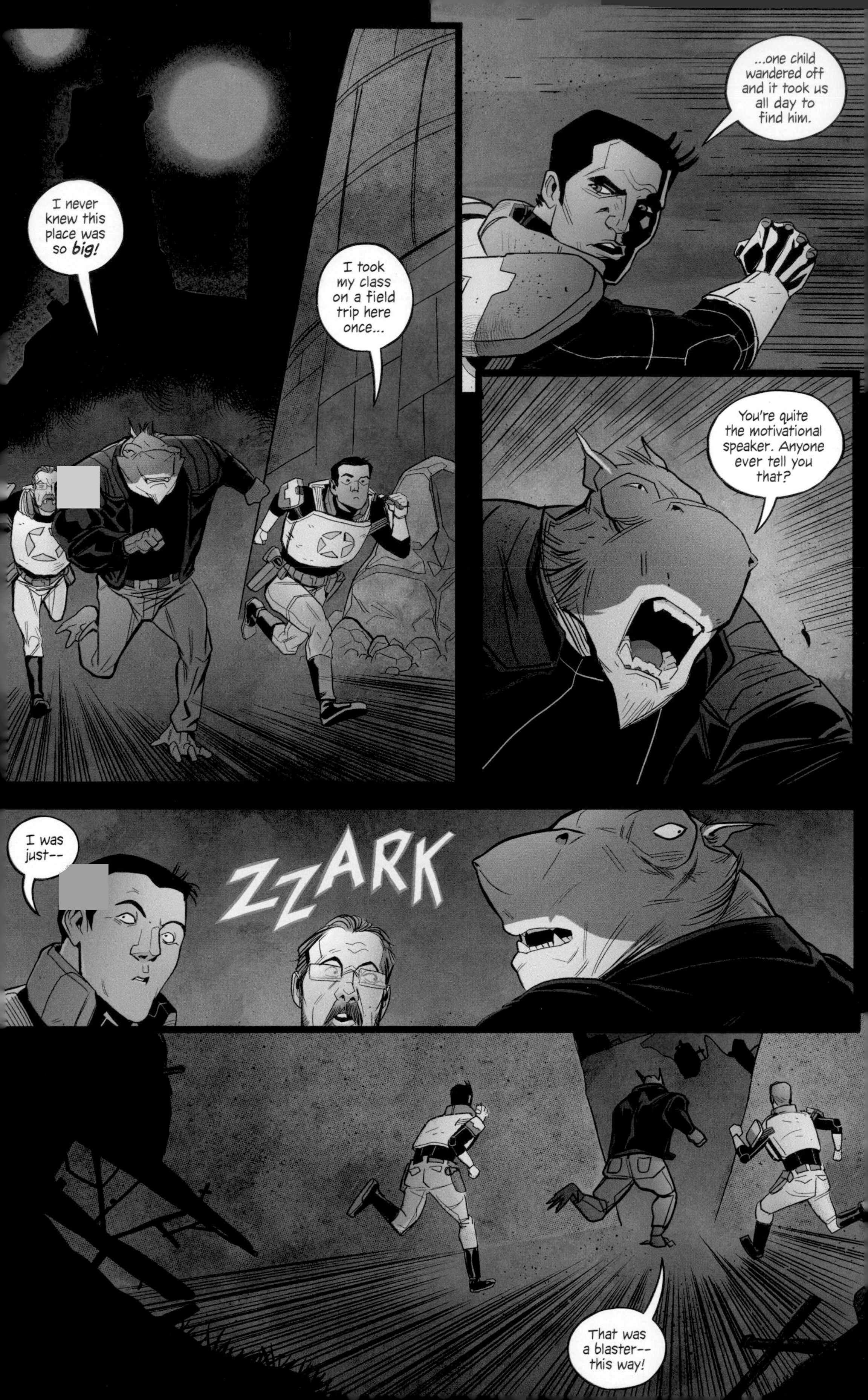
I never knew this place was so *big!*
I took my class on a field trip here once...
...one child wandered off and it took us all day to find him.
You're quite the motivational speaker. Anyone ever tell you that?
I was just--
ZZARK
That was a blaster-- this way!

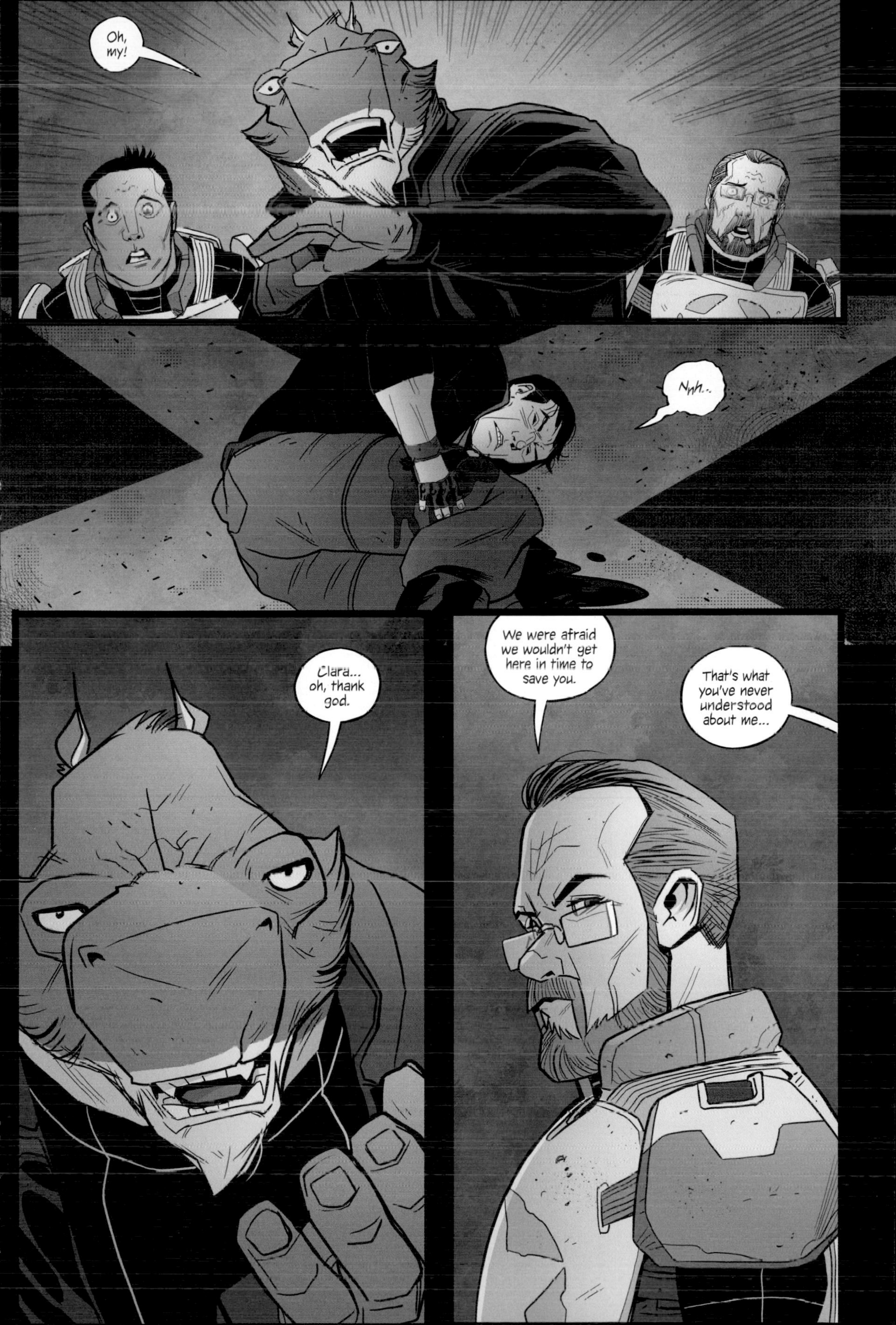
Oh, my!
Nnh...
Clara... oh, thank god.
We were afraid we wouldn't get here in time to save you.
That's what you've never understood about me...

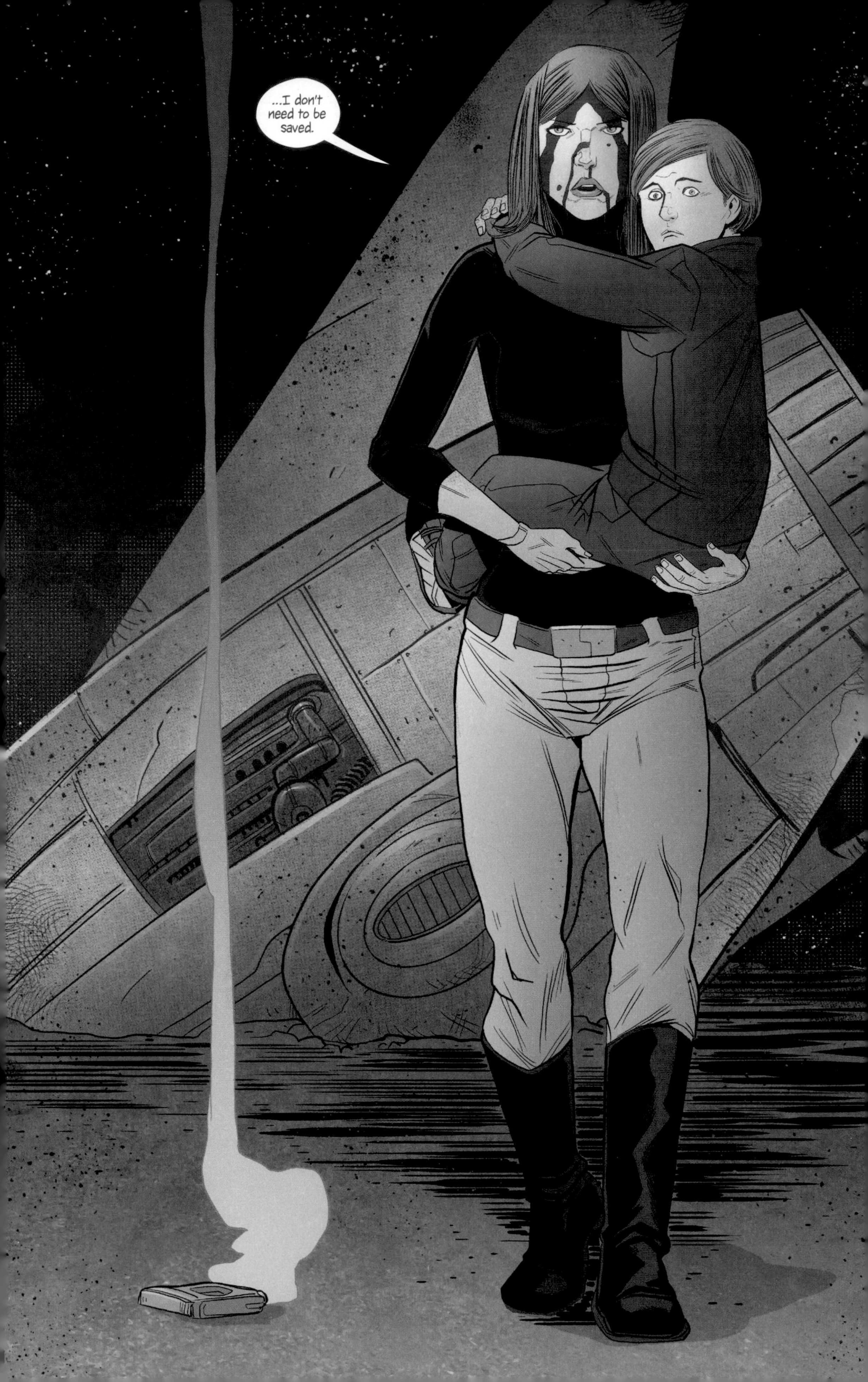
...I don't need to be saved.

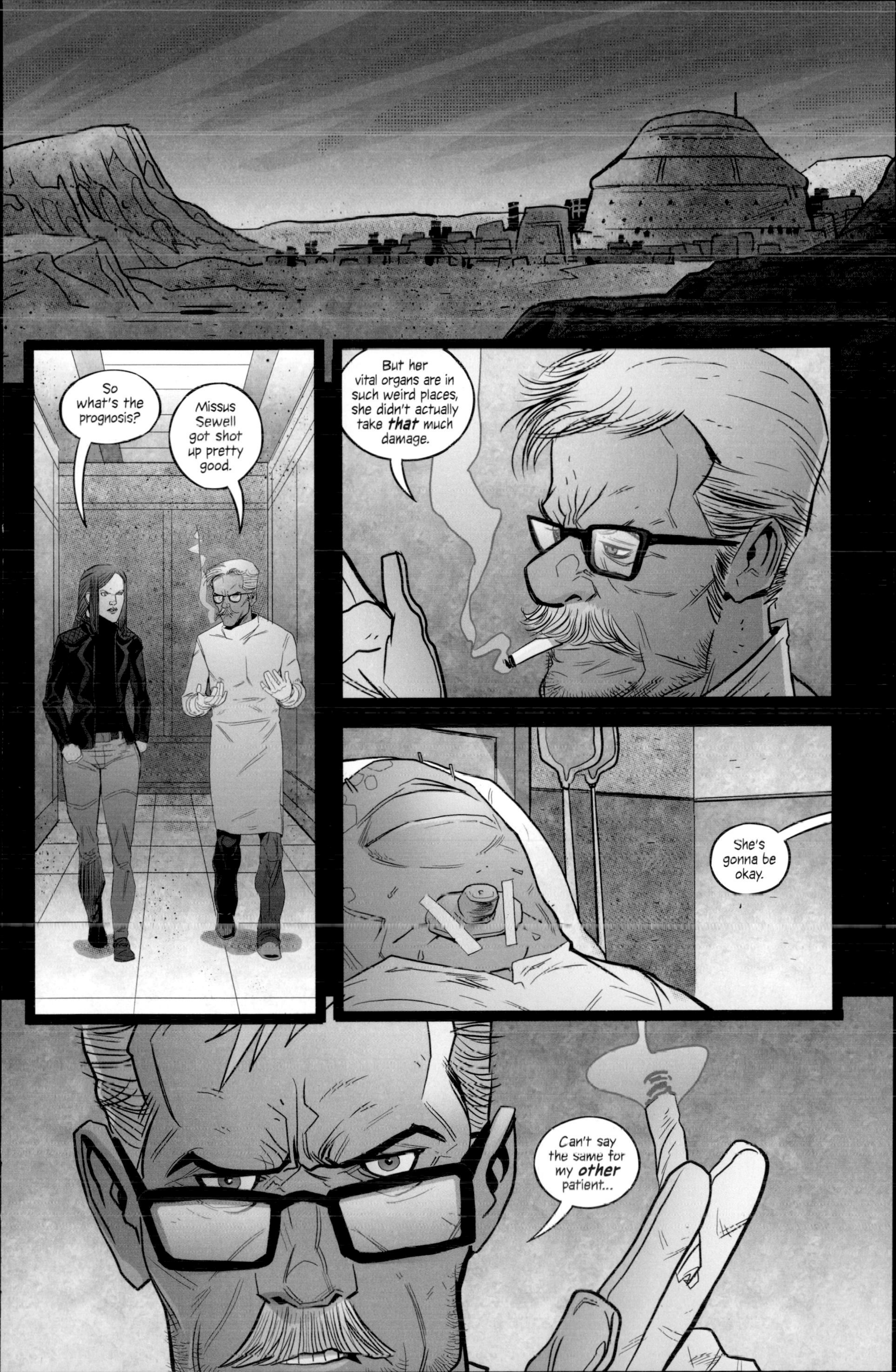
So what's the prognosis?
Missus Sewell got shot up pretty good.
But her vital organs are in such weird places, she didn't actually take *that* much damage.
She's gonna be okay.
Can't say the same for my *other* patient...

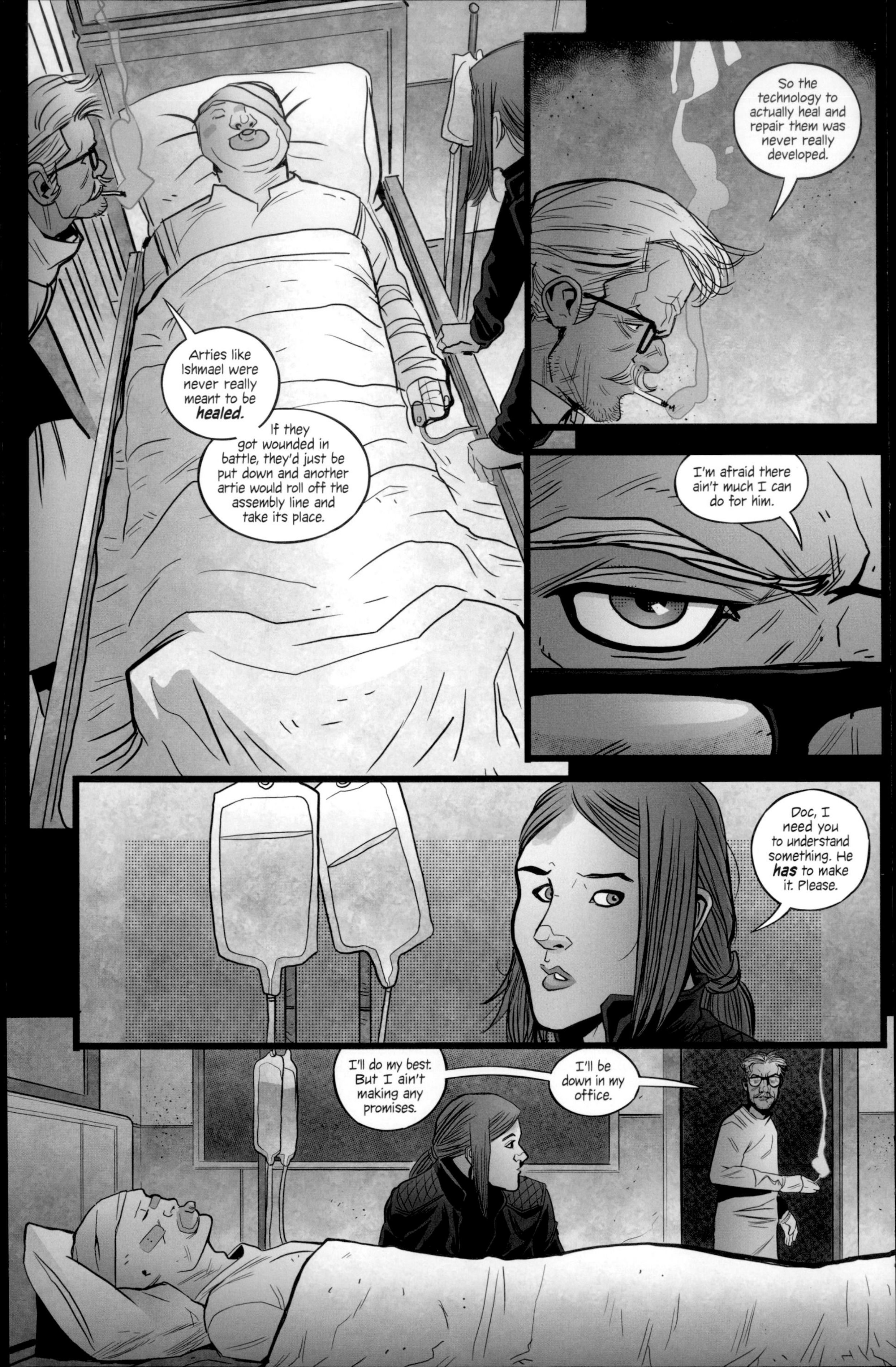
Arties like Ishmael were never really meant to be **healed.**
If they got wounded in battle, they'd just be put down and another artie would roll off the assembly line and take its place.
So the technology to actually heal and repair them was never really developed.
I'm afraid there ain't much I can do for him.
Doc, I need you to understand something. He **has** to make it. Please.
I'll do my best. But I ain't making any promises.
I'll be down in my office.

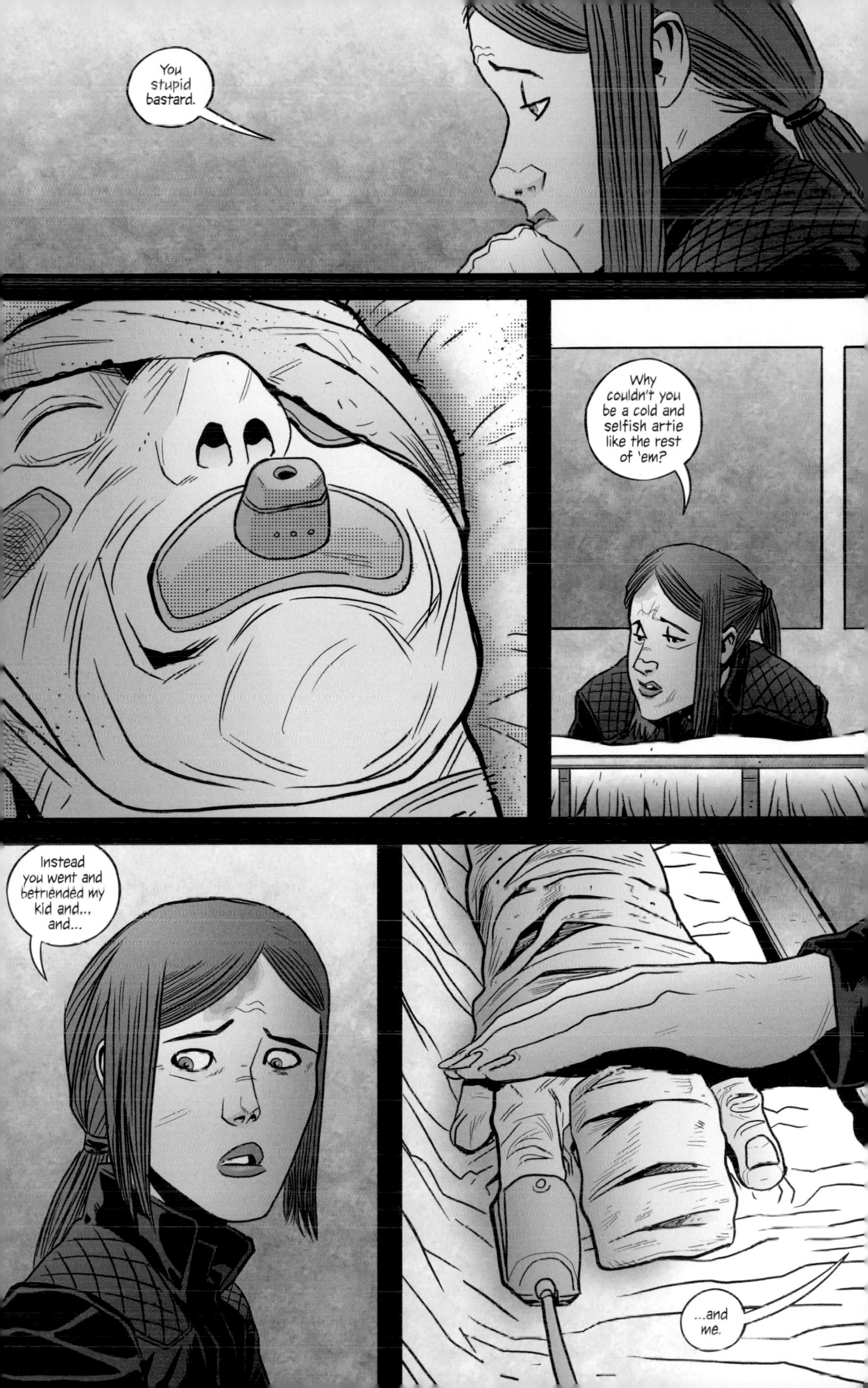

You stupid bastard.
Why couldn't you be a cold and selfish artie like the rest of 'em?
Instead you went and befriended my kid and... and...
...and me.

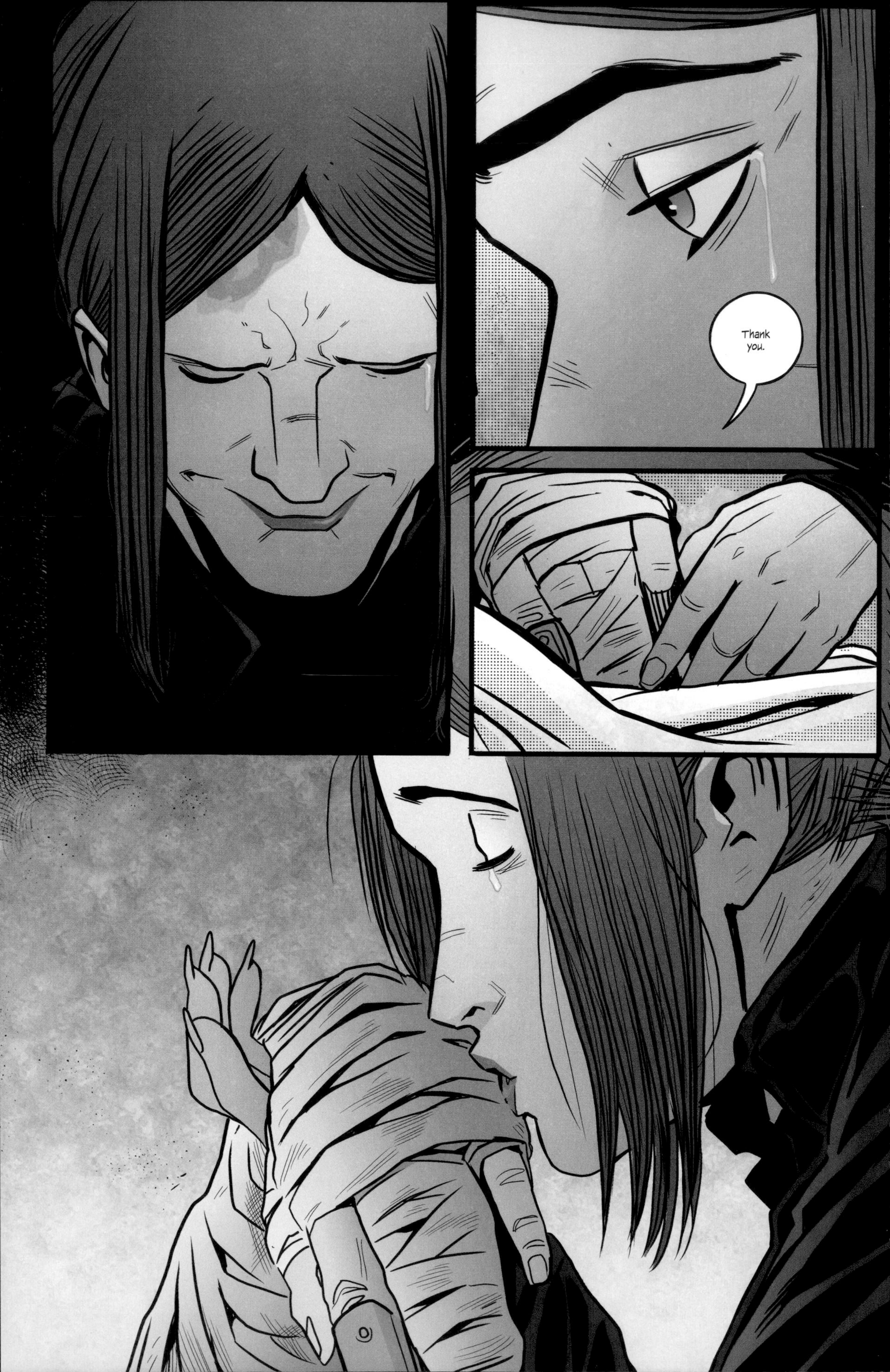
Thank you.

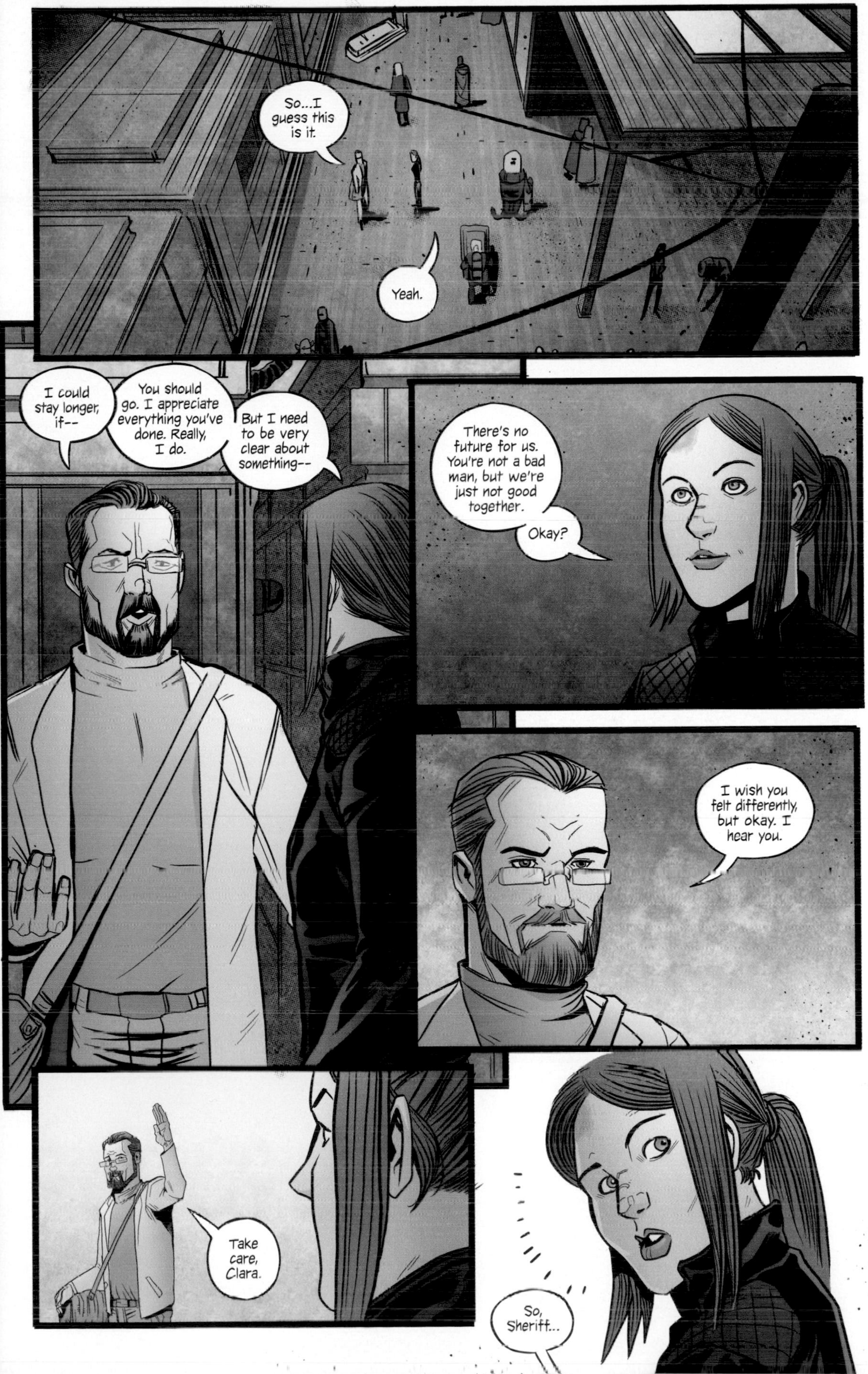
So...I guess this is it.
Yeah.
I could stay longer, if--
You should go. I appreciate everything you've done. Really, I do.
But I need to be very clear about something--
There's no future for us. You're not a bad man, but we're just not good together.
Okay?
I wish you felt differently, but okay. I hear you.
Take care, Clara.
So, Sheriff...

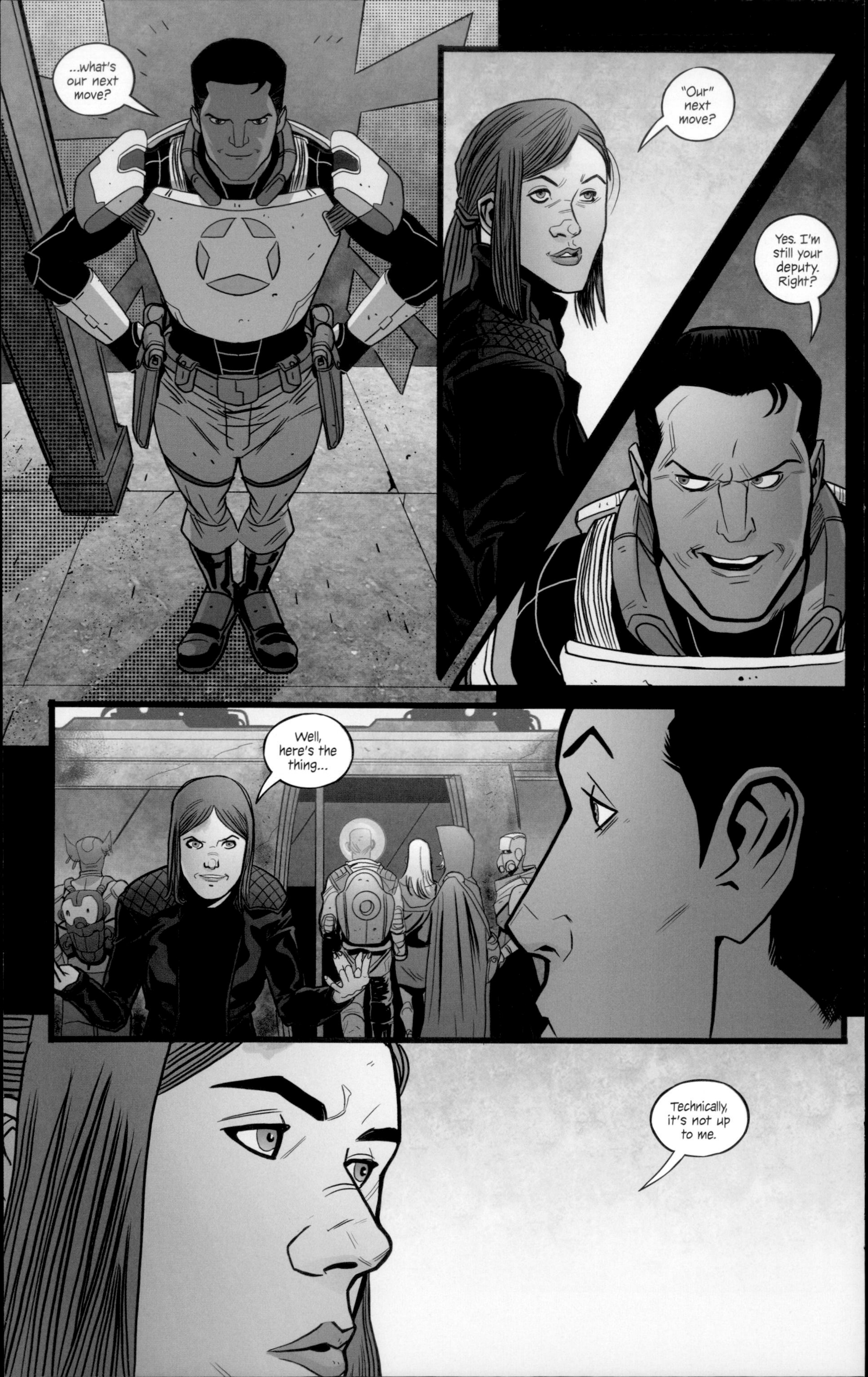
...what's our next move?
"Our" next move?
Yes. I'm still your deputy. Right?
Well, here's the thing...
Technically, it's not up to me.

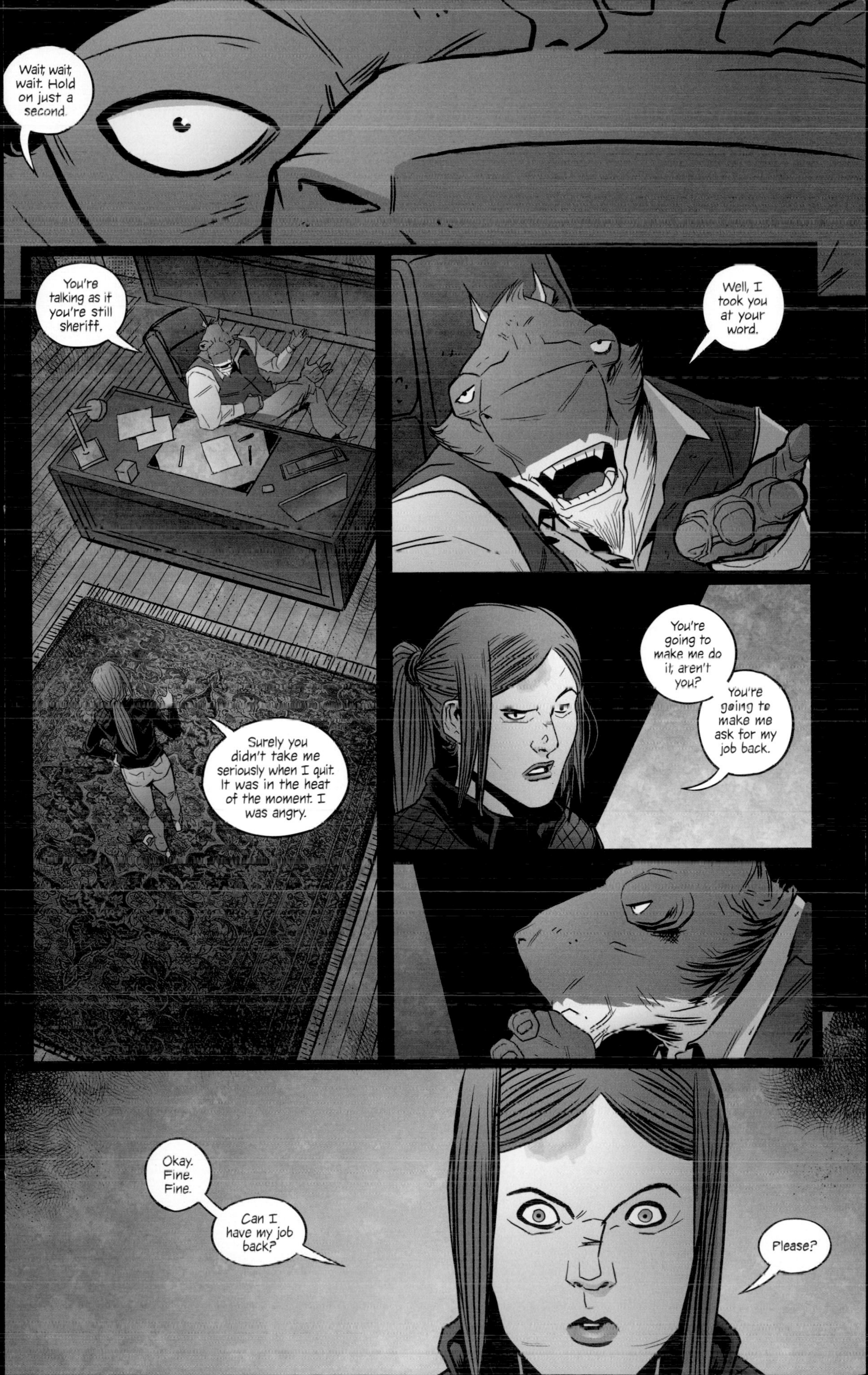
Wait, wait, wait. Hold on just a second.
You're talking as if you're still sheriff.
Well, I took you at your word.
Surely you didn't take me seriously when I quit. It was in the heat of the moment. I was angry.
You're going to make me do it, aren't you?
You're going to make me ask for my job back.
Okay. Fine. Fine.
Can I have my job back?
Please?

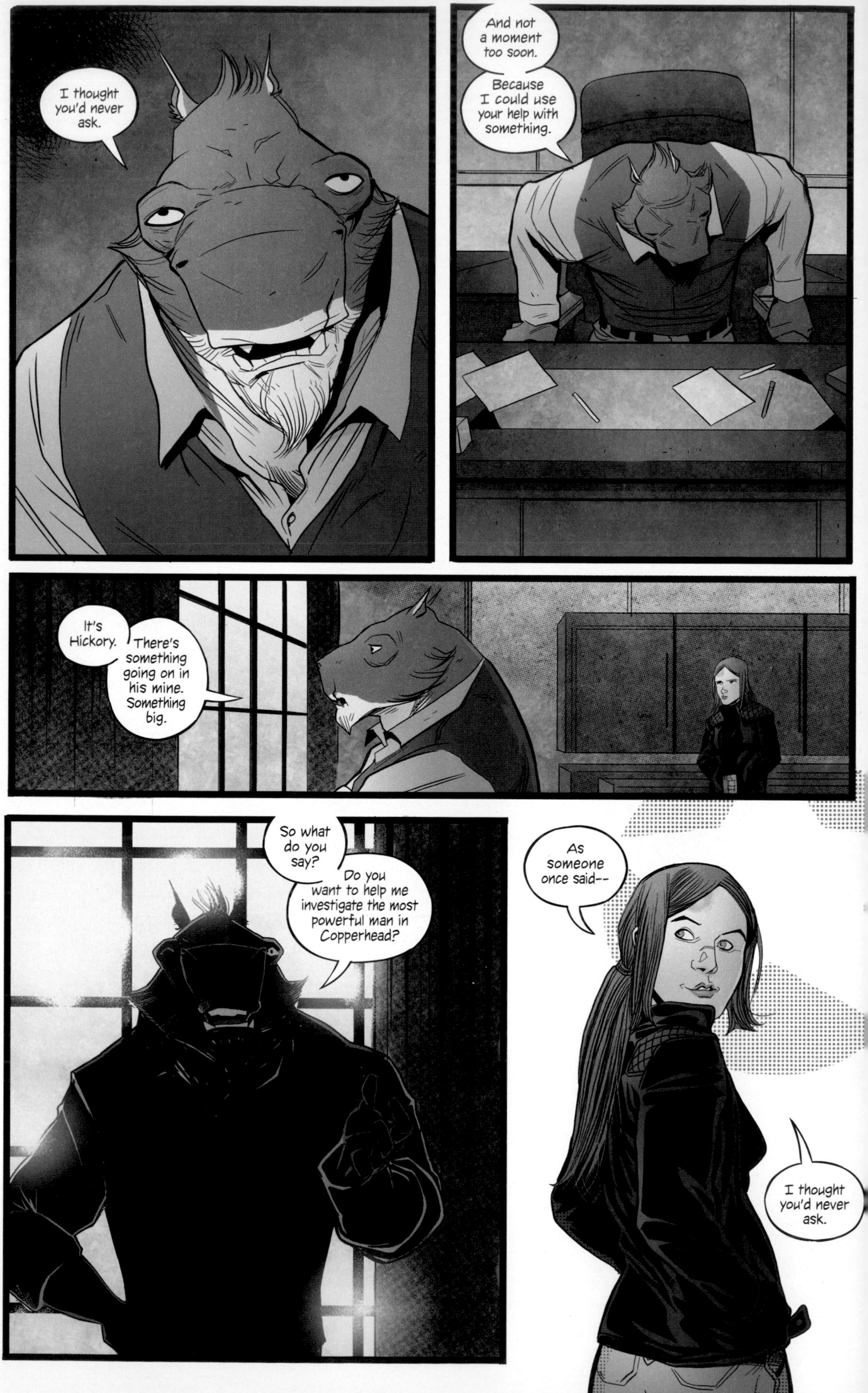
I thought you'd never ask.
And not a moment too soon.
Because I could use your help with something.
It's Hickory.
There's something going on in his mine. Something big.
So what do you say?
Do you want to help me investigate the most powerful man in Copperhead?
As someone once said--
I thought you'd never ask.

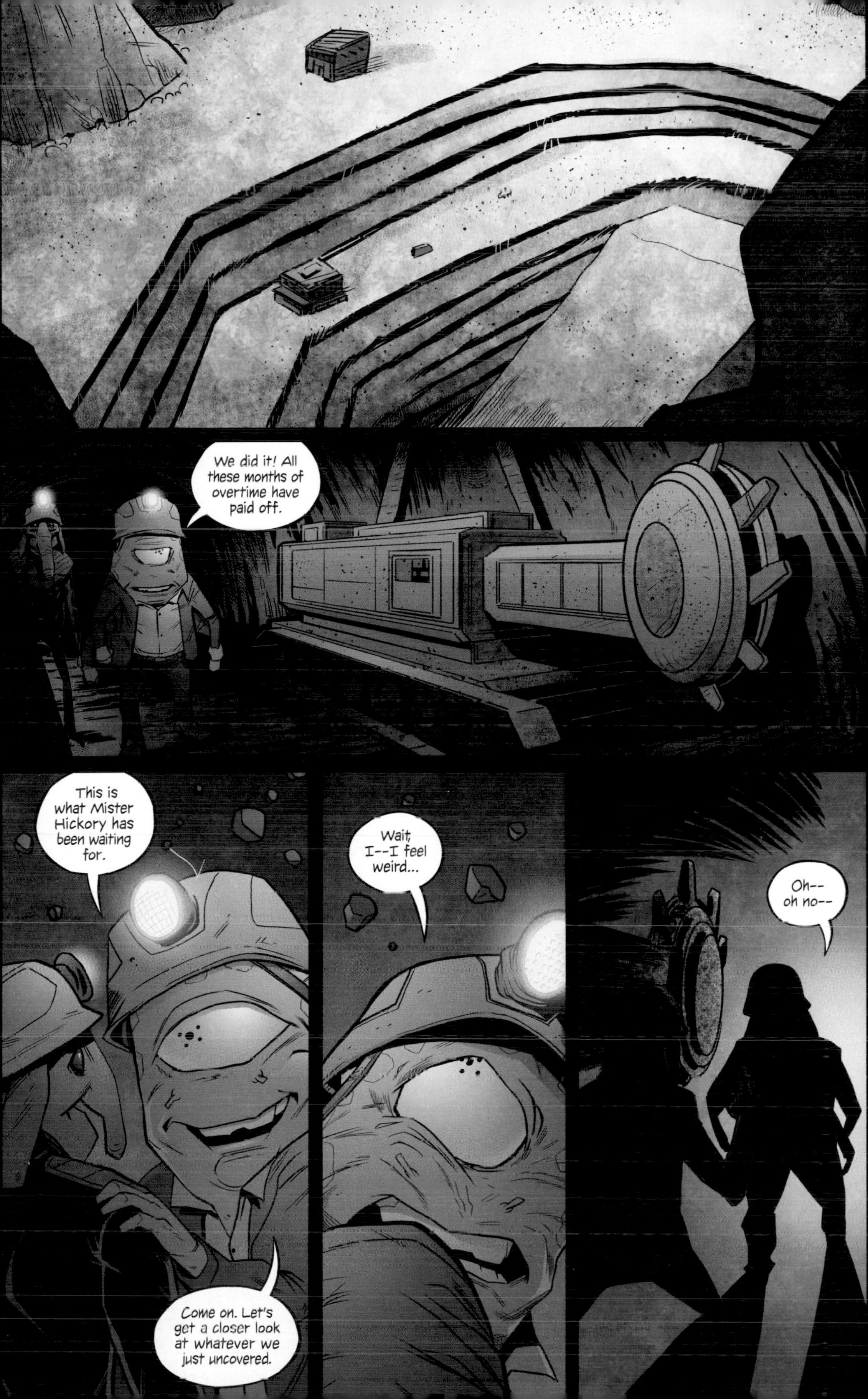
We did it! All these months of overtime have paid off.
This is what Mister Hickory has been waiting for.
Come on. Let's get a closer look at whatever we just uncovered.
Wait, I--I feel weird...
Oh-- oh no--

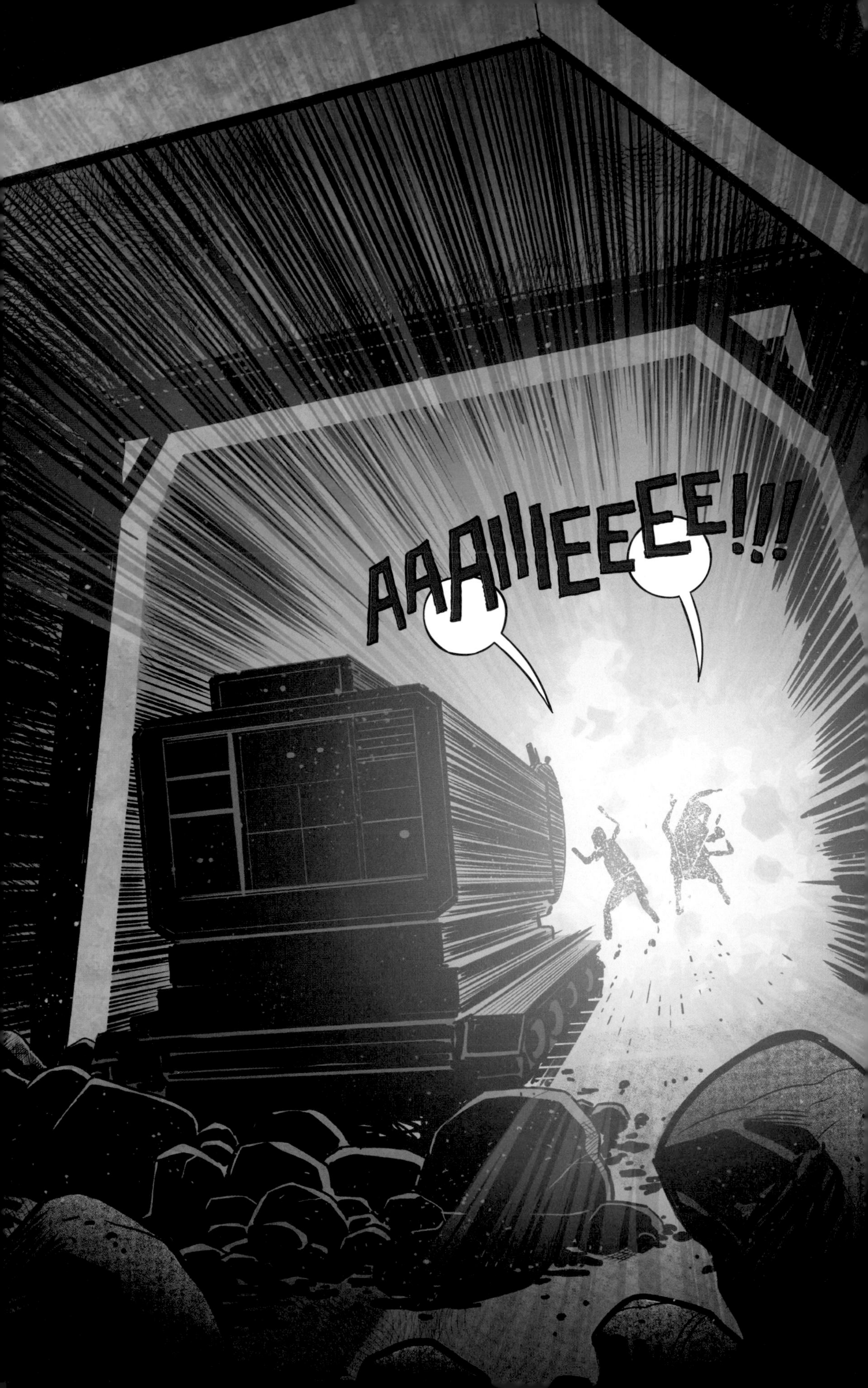
AAAIIIEEEEE!!!

TO BE
CONTINUED

BONUS CONTENT

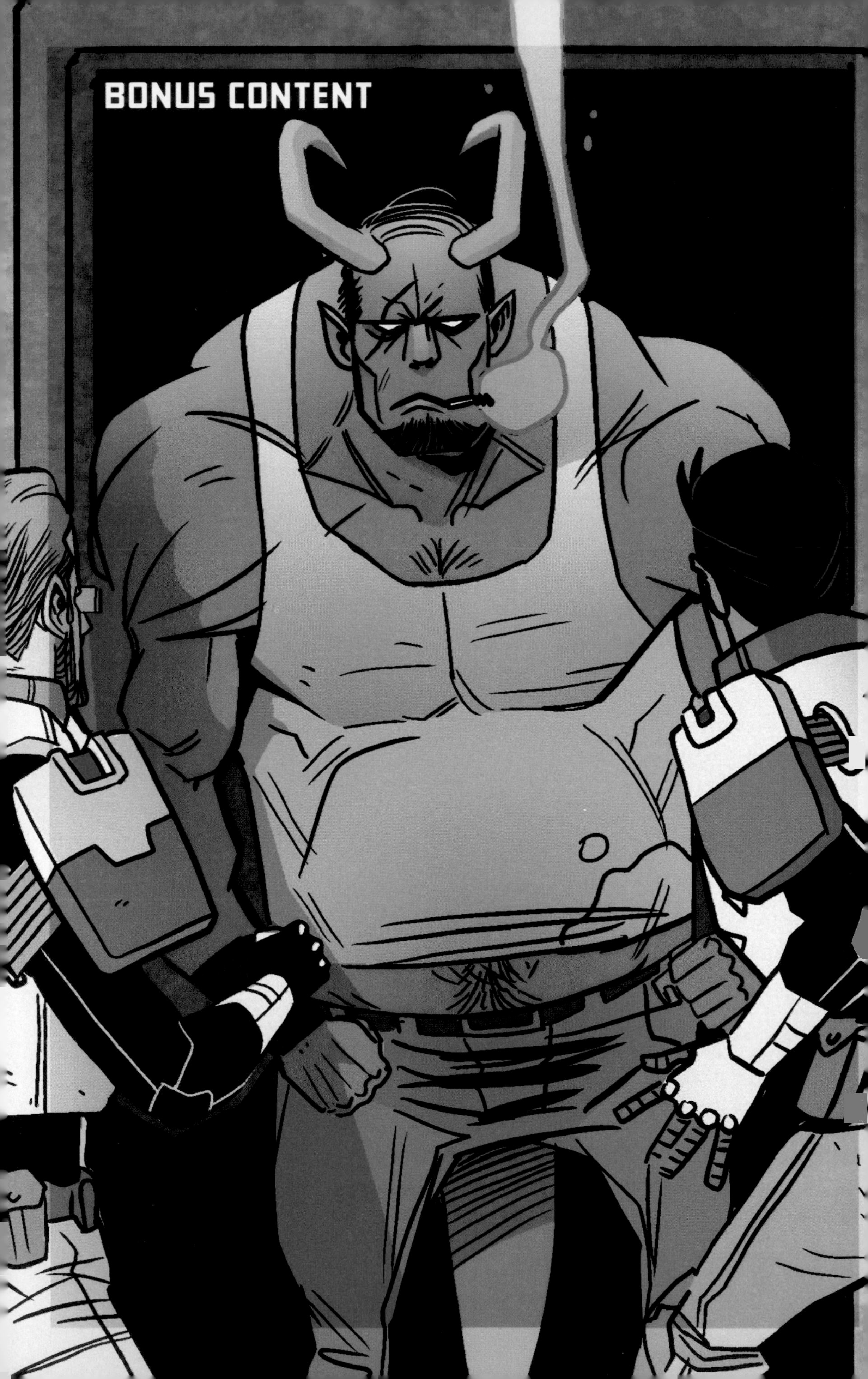

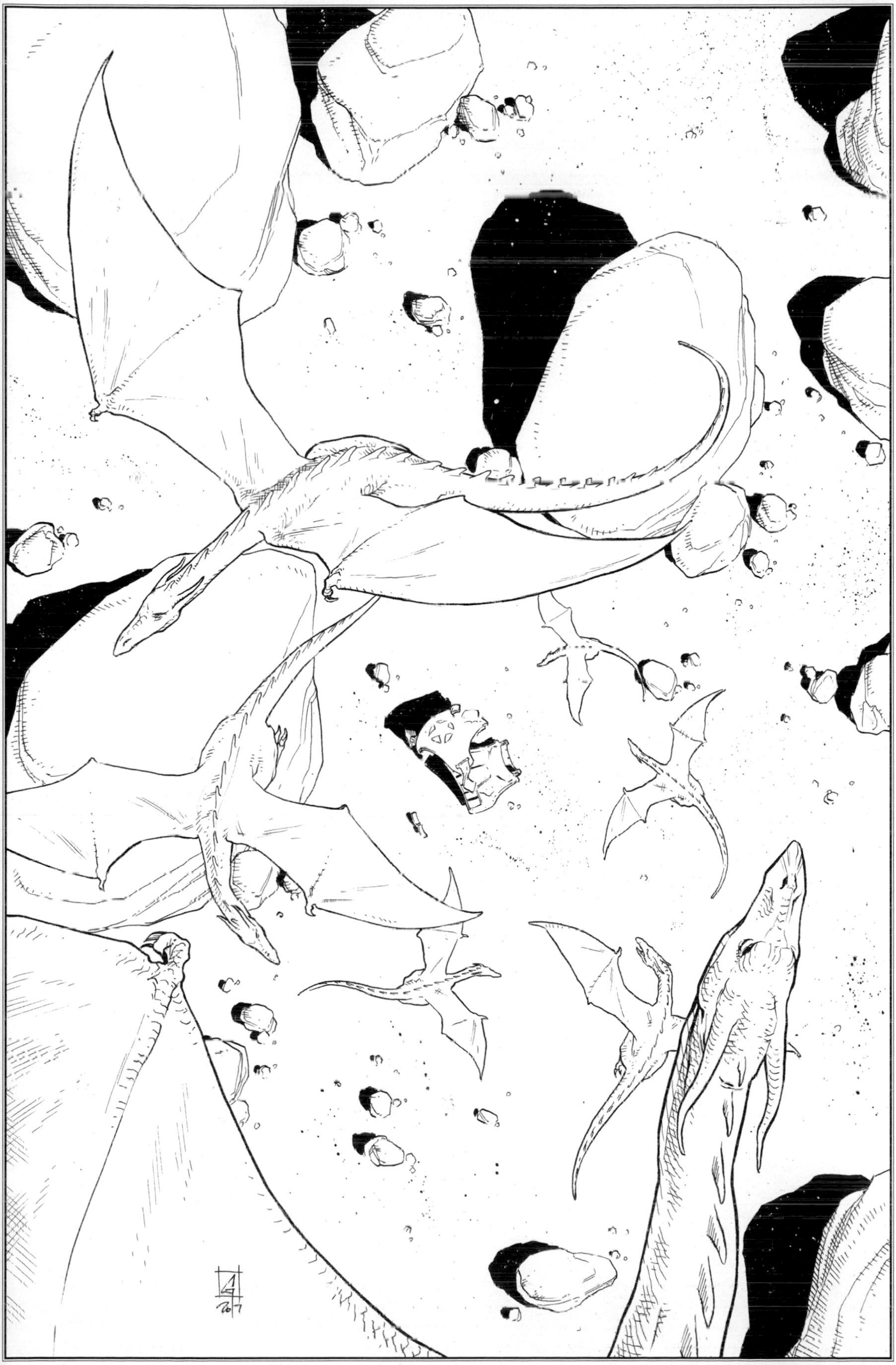

Inks by Scott Godlewski

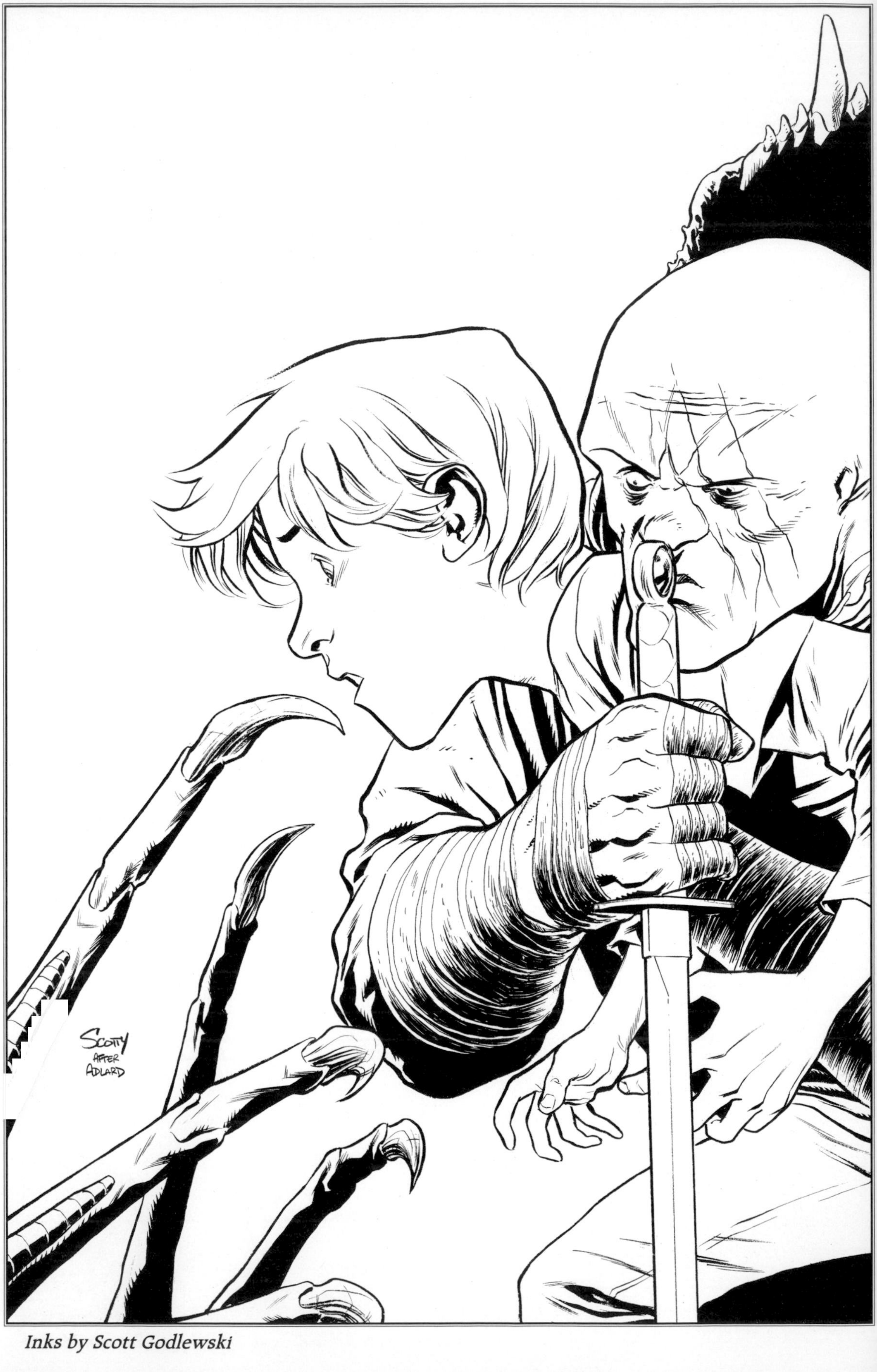
SCOTTY
AFTER
ADLARD

Inks by Scott Godlewski

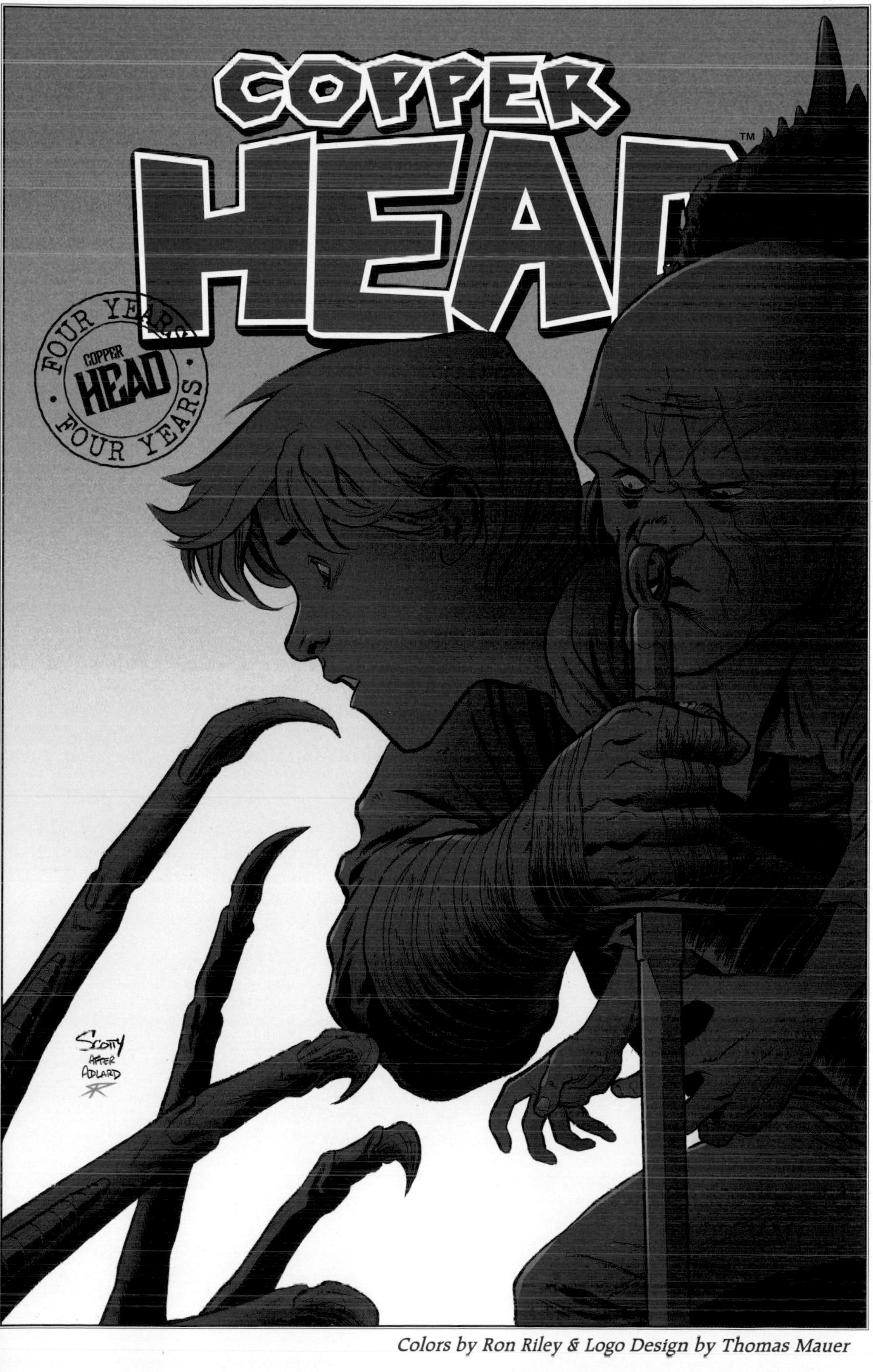
COPPER
HEAD
FOUR YEARS
COPPER
HEAD
FOUR YEARS
SCOTTY
AFTER
ADLARD
Colors by Ron Riley & Logo Design by Thomas Mauer

ISSUE 16 COVER DEVELOPMENT PROCESS

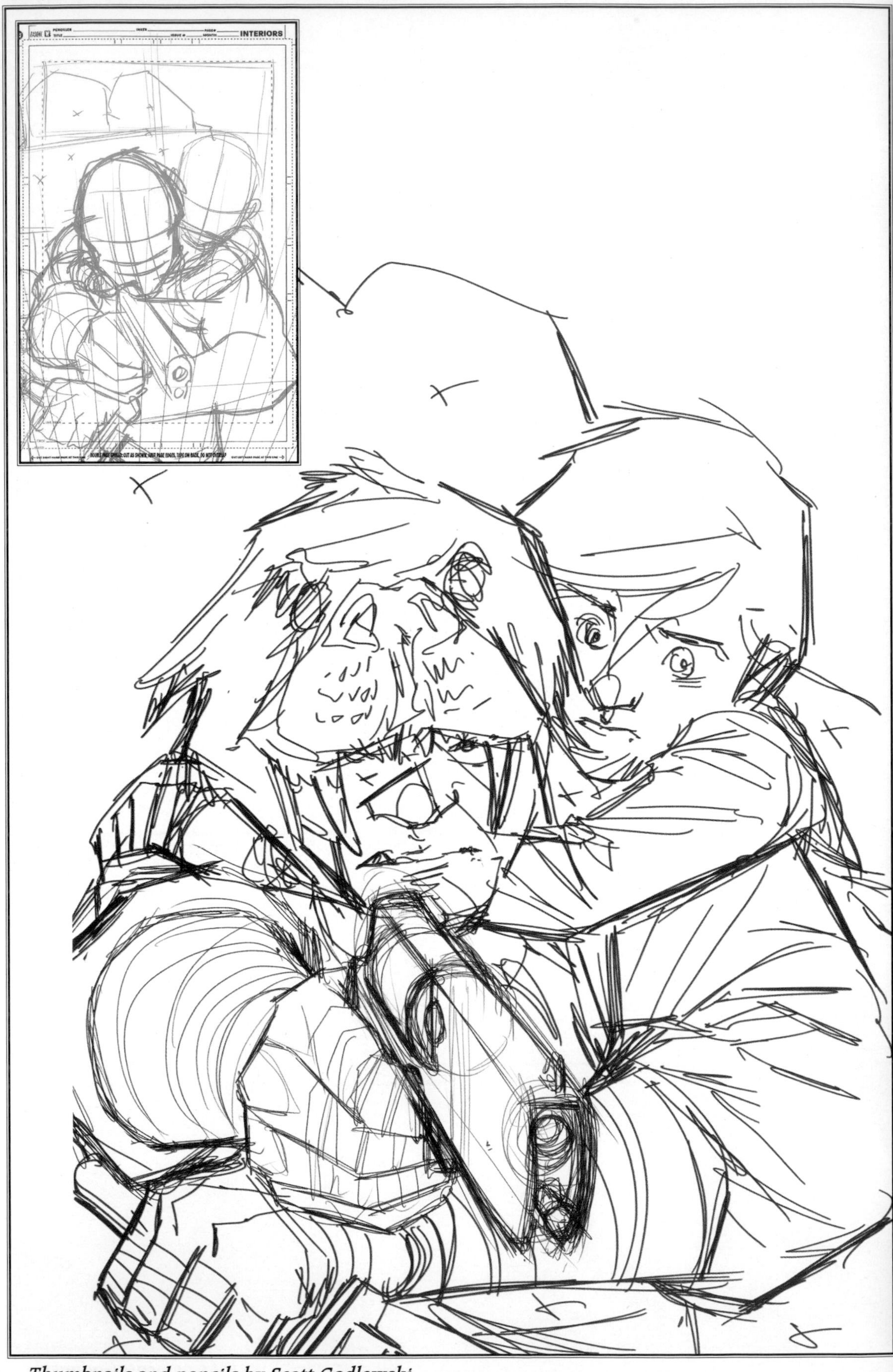
INTERIORS

Thumbnails and pencils by Scott Godlewski

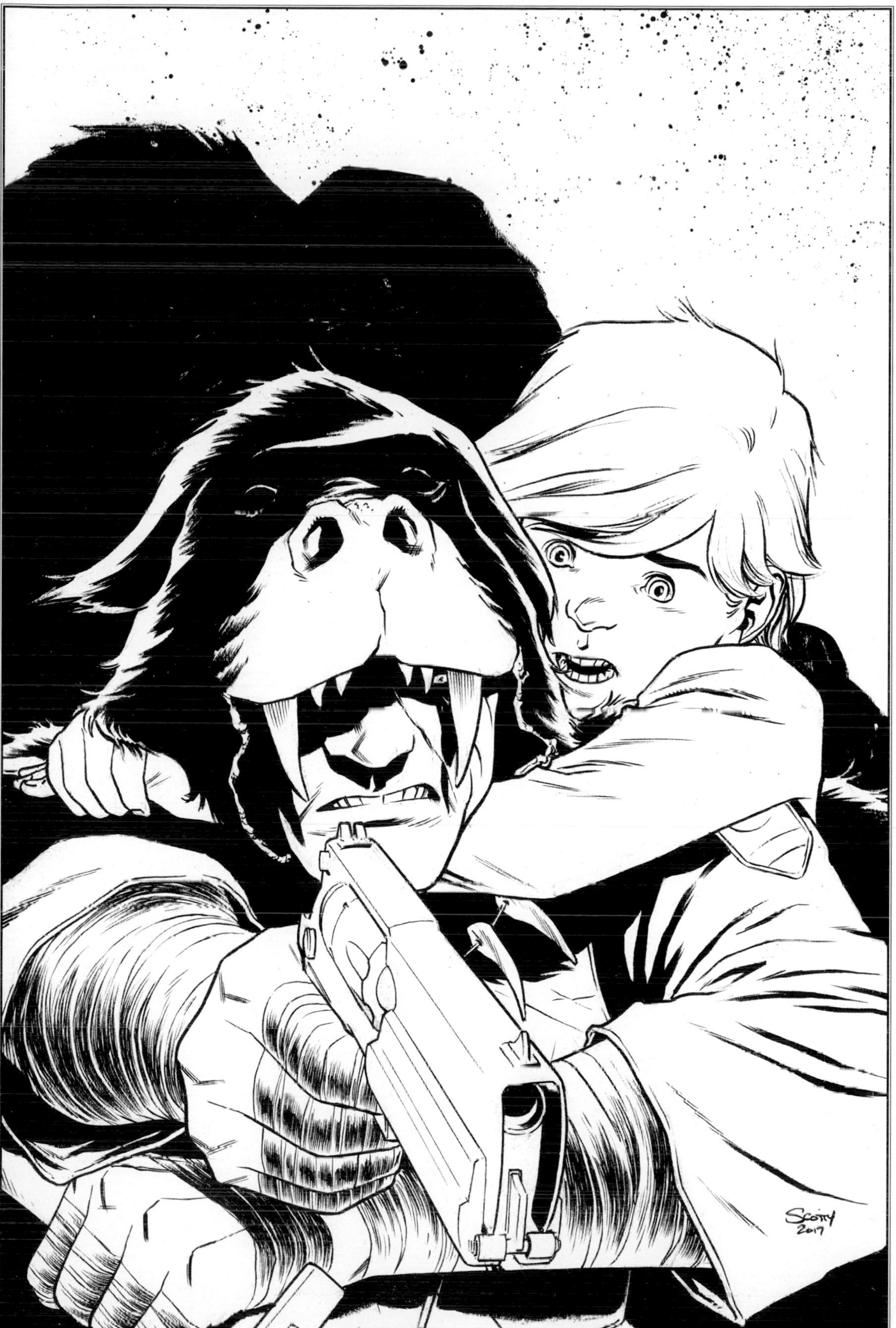
SCOTTY
2017
Inks by Scott Godlewski

ISSUE 17 COVER DEVELOPMENT PROCESS

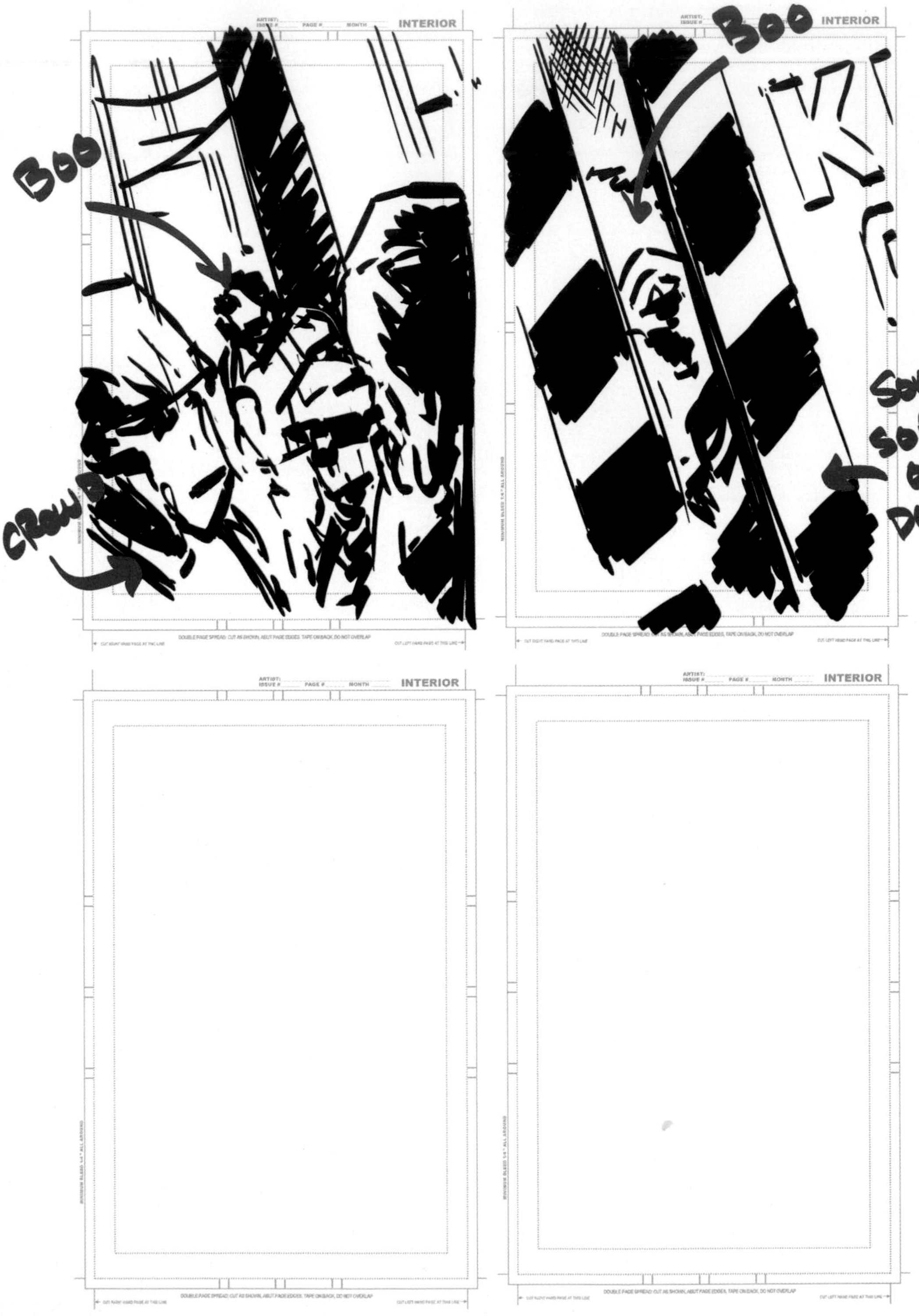
INTERIOR
BOO
CROWD
INTERIOR
BOO
SOME SORT OF DOOR
INTERIOR
INTERIOR

Thumbnails by Scott Godlewski

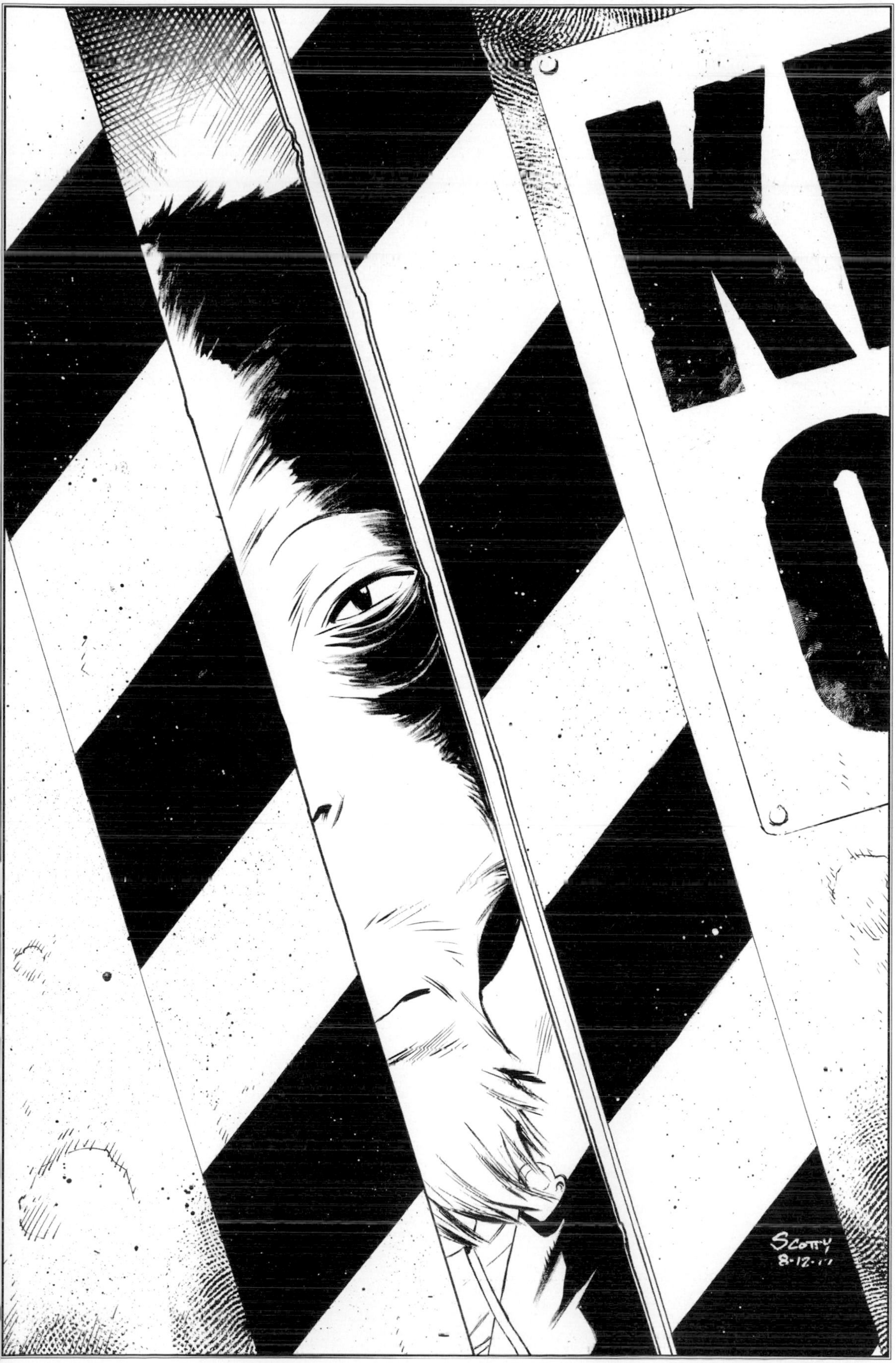
SCOTTY
8-12-11

Inks by Scott Godlewski

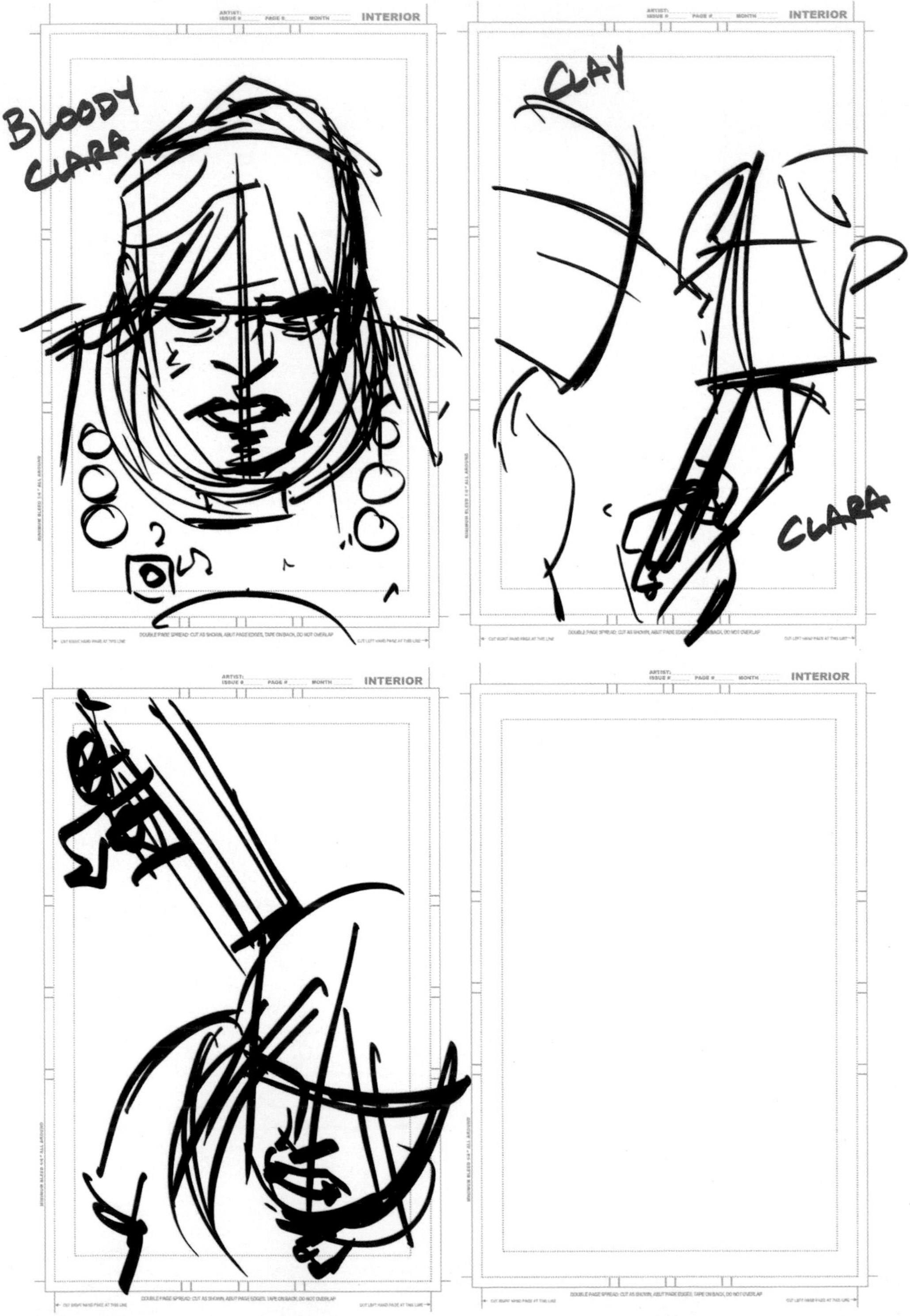
INTERIOR
BLOODY CLARA
INTERIOR
CLAY
CLARA
INTERIOR
INTERIOR

Thumbnails by Scott Godlewski

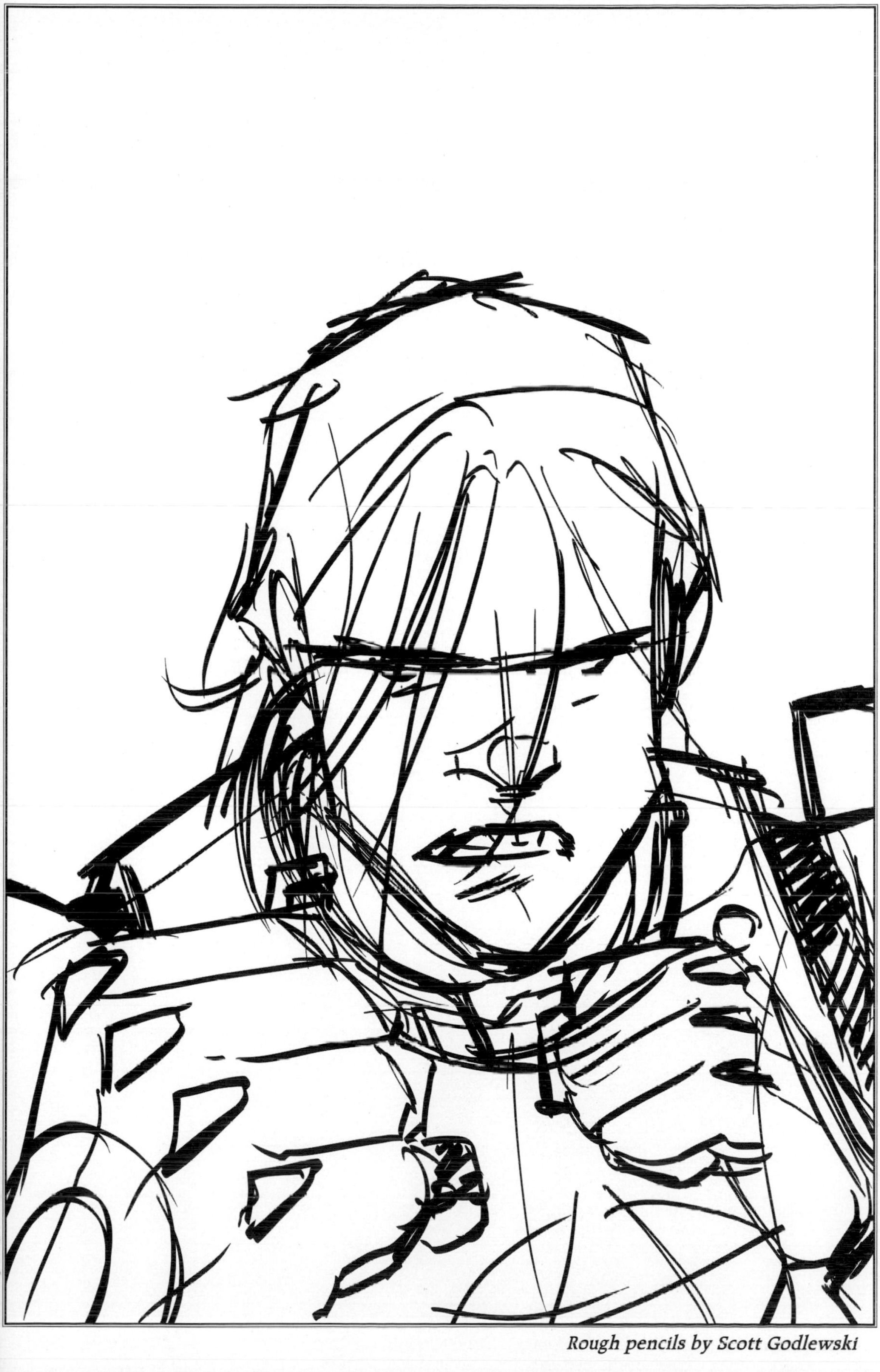

Rough pencils by Scott Godlewski

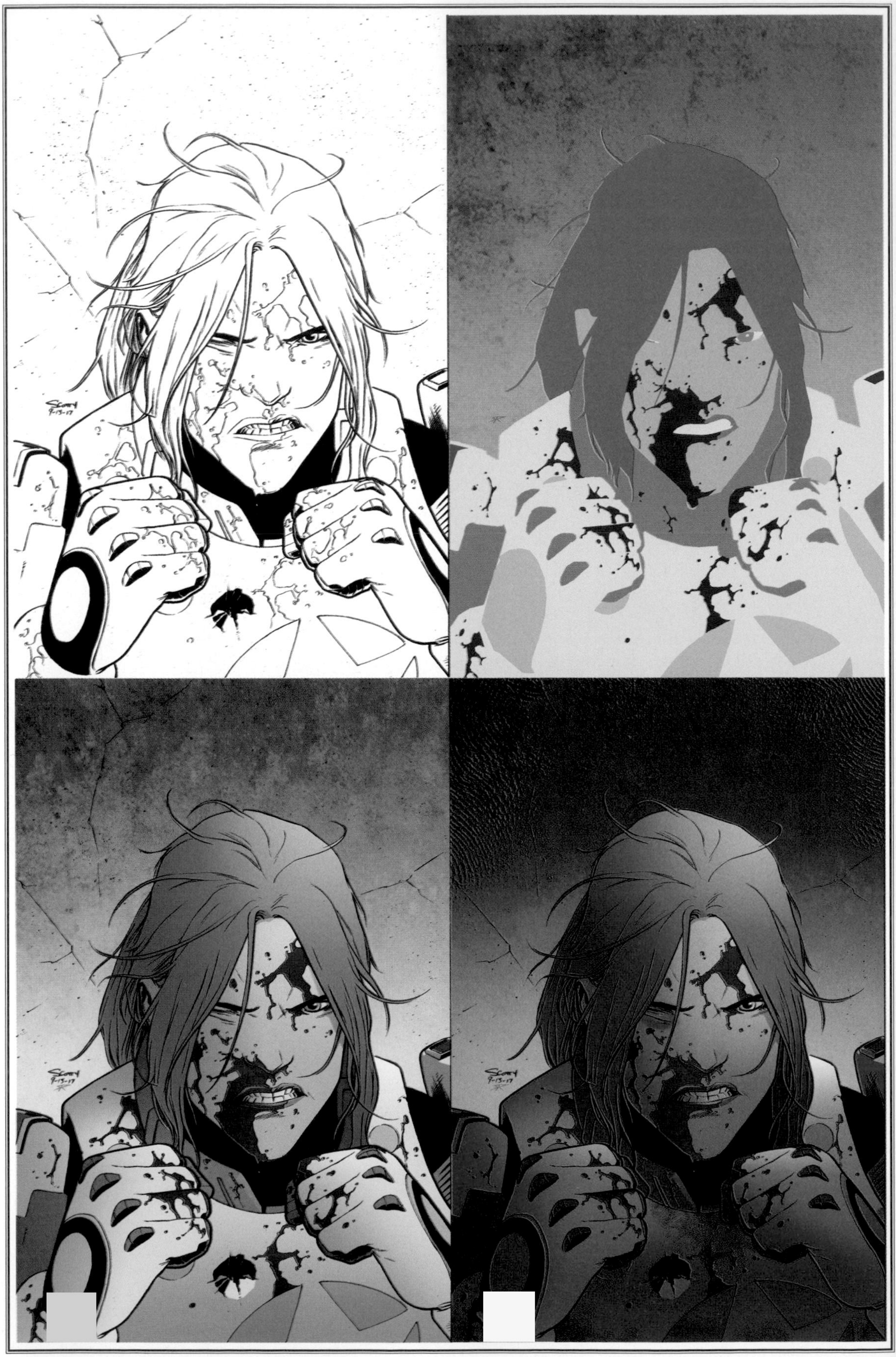

From Scott's inks to Ron's final colors

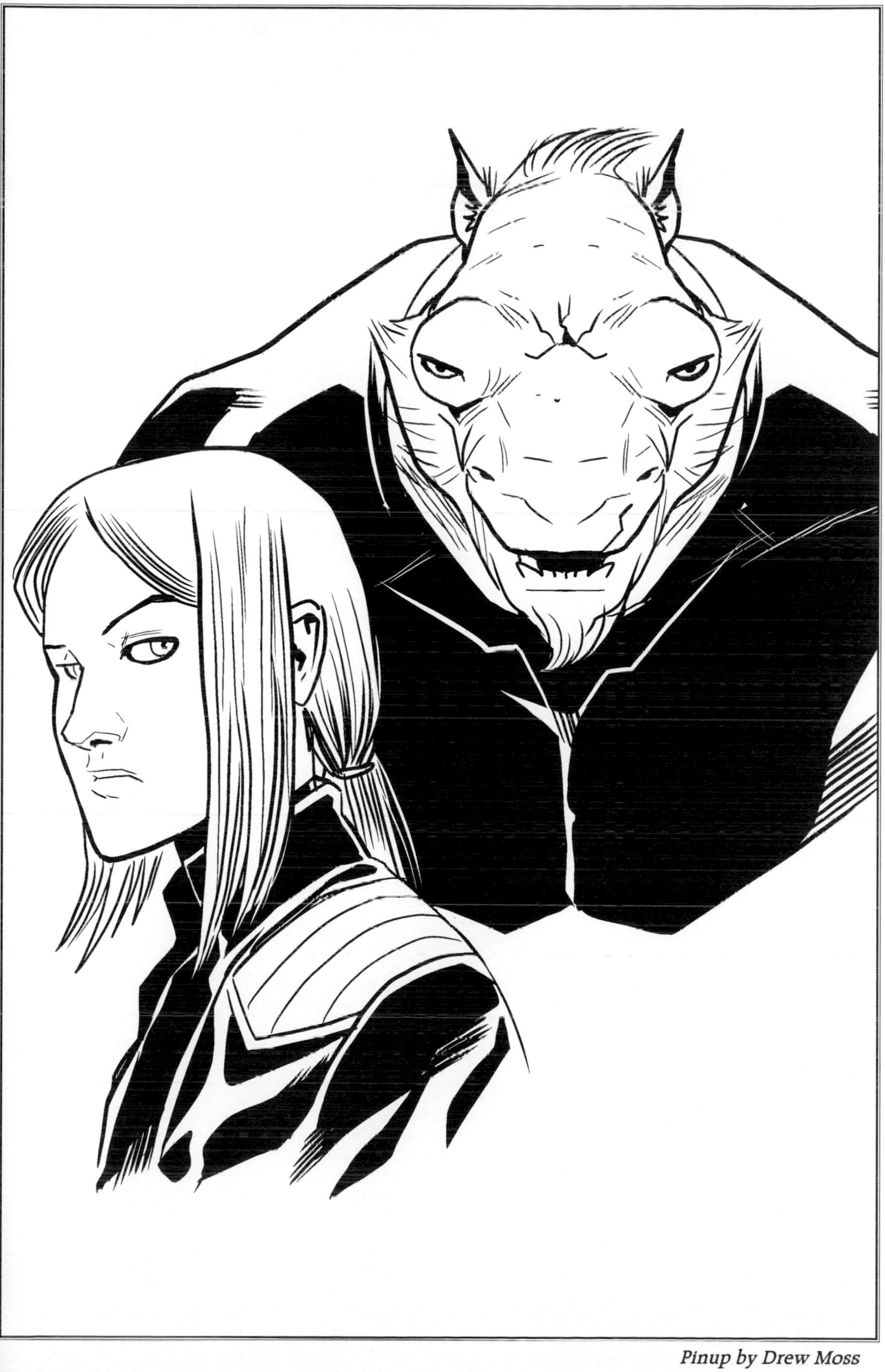

Pinup by Drew Moss

ABOUT THE CREATORS

Jay Faerber was born in Harvey's Lake, PA and got his start at Marvel and DC Comics in the late 1990s, where he worked on such series as THE TITANS, NEW WARRIORS, and GENERATION X. In 2001, he launched NOBLE CAUSES, his first creator-owned series, at Image Comics, which has gone on to garner much critical acclaim. Since then, Faerber has carved out a niche for himself, co-creating DYNAMO 5, NEAR DEATH, POINT OF IMPACT, SECRET IDENTITIES, GRAVEYARD SHIFT, ELSEWHERE, and COPPERHEAD. He also writes for television, most recently on the CBS series ZOO. He lives in Burbank, with his wife, son, dog, and cat. He really loves the Pacific Northwest and 80s television. You can follow him on Twitter @JayFaerber.

Drew Moss is an illustrator based out of southeastern Virginia and has worked for IDW (THE COLONIZED, THE CROW, MASK) Dark Horse (CREEPY), Oni press (TERRIBLE LIZARD, BLOOD FEUD) Image Comics (COPPERHEAD) and various other publishers. Drew enjoys fine cigars and whiskies and spends too much time writing bios. To see more of his work and upcoming projects you can follow him on Twitter @drew_moss or on Instagram @drewerdmoss.

Ron Riley started off colouring Robert Kirkman's TECH JACKET (which is still kicking butt at Image Comics with an all new creative team), then soon after joined the creative team of Mr. Faerber's then-relaunched NOBLE CAUSES. Ron has been Jay's frequent colouring collaborator ever since, most recently on ELSEWHERE. Ron's also been the colour artist on numerous other titles, like ROB ZOMBIE'S SPOOKSHOW INTERNATIONAL, BOOM! Studio's HERO SQUARED and TALENT, among others. Don't follow him on Twitter @thatronriley...unless you're one hip cat.

Thomas Mauer has lent his lettering and design talent to Harvey and Eisner Award nominated and winning titles including Image's POPGUN anthologies and Dark Horse Comics' THE GUNS OF SHADOW VALLEY. Among his recent work are Black Mask Studios' 4 KIDS WALK INTO A BANK, Image Comics' ELSEWHERE, THE BEAUTY, and THE REALM, Skybound's CRUDE, as well as Amazon Studios' NIKO AND THE SWORD OF LIGHT, and the World Food Programme's LIVING LEVEL-3 series. You can follow him on Twitter @thomasmauer.

Scott Godlewski is the co-creator of COPPERHEAD and a freelance illustrator. His past credits include works with Image, BOOM! Studios, Dynamite, Dark Horse, and DC. He is also the co-host of *The Illustrious Gentlemen* podcast. You can find Scott on Twitter @scottygod.

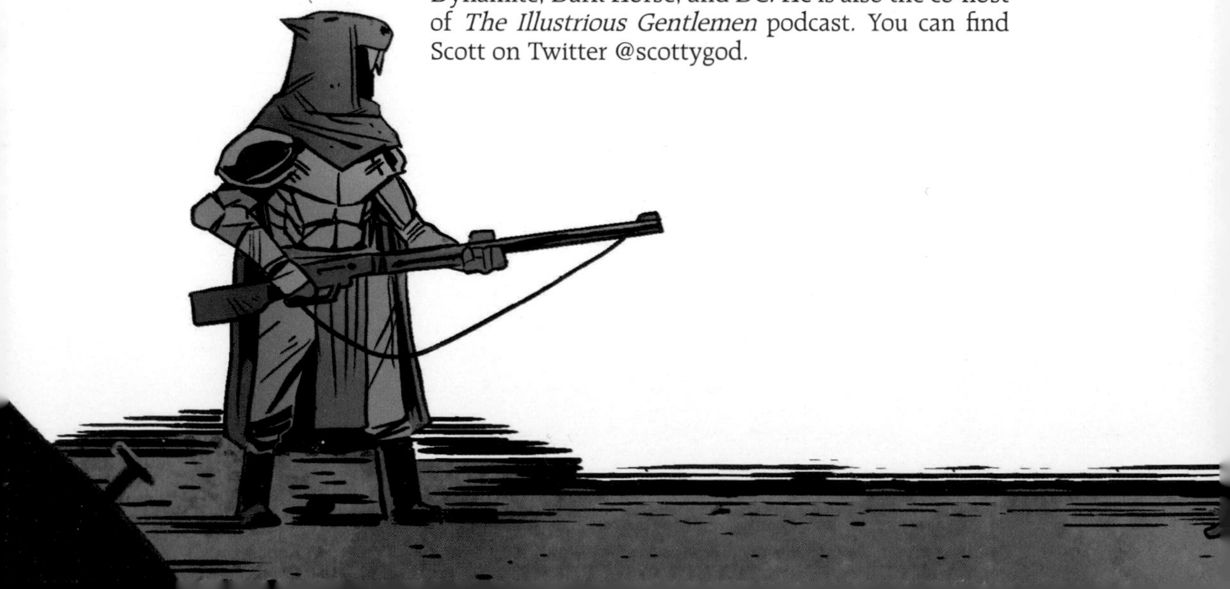